DANGEROUS HOMECOMING

When Catherine met Dominic Reston in Italy, their encounter seemed the stuff that dreams were made of. Dominic was free of the marriage that had blighted his life, and Catherine was far from the scandal that had shattered hers.

But now they were going home to England as an engaged couple, and every mile of moonlit sea their ship covered, Catherine felt herself coming closer to the whispers about her that would not die. There were the intrigues of her insidiously designing aunt, Lady Clarice Hubert, who would not rest until Catherine's exile from the privileged inner circle was made eternal. Then there were the temptations that Catherine was not sure she could resist. And, finally, there was the testing of her fiancé who may have vowed to love and honor her, but who could not forget one betrayal—and would not forgive another. . . .

THE CAPTIVATED COUNTESS

SIGNET Regency Romances You'll Enjoy

(0451)

- [ ] **THE BATTLING BLUESTOCKING** by Amanda Scott. (136608—$2.50)
- [ ] **RAVENWOOD'S LADY** by Amanda Scott. (128176—$2.25)
- [ ] **THE INDOMITABLE MISS HARRIS** by Amanda Scott. (125622—$2.25)
- [ ] **LADY HAWK'S FOLLY** by Amanda Scott. (133315—$2.50)
- [ ] **THE ARDENT LADY AMELIA** by Laura Matthews. (127706—$2.25)
- [ ] **LORD GREYWELL'S DILEMMA** by Laura Matthews. (143507—$2.50)
- [ ] **THE SANDALWOOD FAN** by Diana Brown. (130529—$2.50)
- [ ] **A DEBT OF HONOR** by Diana Brown. (114175—$2.25)
- [ ] **ST. MARTIN'S SUMMER** by Diana Brown. (143485—$2.50)
- [ ] **THE PRUDENT PARTNERSHIP** by Barbara Allister. (130545—$2.25)
- [ ] **THE MISCHIEVOUS MATCHMAKER** by Barbara Allister. (134788—$2.50)
- [ ] **YOUR OBEDIENT SERVANT** by Elsie Gage. (139135—$2.50)
- [ ] **THE LUCKLESS ELOPEMENT** by Dorothy Mack. (129695—$2.25)

Buy them at your local bookstore or use this convenient coupon for ordering.

NEW AMERICAN LIBRARY,
P.O. Box 999, Bergenfield, New Jersey 07621

Please send me the books I have checked above. I am enclosing $＿＿＿＿＿
(please add $1.00 to this order to cover postage and handling). Send check
or money order—no cash or C.O.D.'s. Prices and numbers are subject to change
without notice.

Name ＿＿＿＿＿＿＿＿＿＿＿＿＿＿＿＿＿＿＿＿＿＿＿＿＿＿＿＿＿＿＿＿＿

Address ＿＿＿＿＿＿＿＿＿＿＿＿＿＿＿＿＿＿＿＿＿＿＿＿＿＿＿＿＿＿＿

City ＿＿＿＿＿＿＿＿＿＿ State ＿＿＿＿＿＿ Zip Code ＿＿＿＿＿＿

Allow 4-6 weeks for delivery.
This offer is subject to withdrawal without notice.

The Captivated Countess

by Barbara Allister

A SIGNET BOOK

NEW AMERICAN LIBRARY

For Denise Marcil,
who pointed me in
the right direction

SIGNET, SIGNET CLASSIC, MENTOR, PLUME, MERIDIAN AND NAL BOOKS
are published by New American Library
1633 Broadway, New York, New York 10019

First Printing, April, 1986

1 2 3 4 5 6 7 8 9

PRINTED IN THE UNITED STATES OF AMERICA

1

"Look, *signore*. Just a bundle of rags. Let us be on our way." The small, dark man cast furtive glances toward the pile of rocks that lined the narrow road leading into the hills.

"A bundle of rags? I never saw rags with hair before," said a smooth, cold voice. Even the liquid Italian could not hide the steel in the voice of Dominic Reston, fourth Earl of Harwich. The guide, even though he had just met the man that morning, recognized the danger and was silent.

Swinging down from his horse, Harwich approached the drab brown figure beside the road, a concerned look on his face. "Graves," he called—in English this time, "bring your water flask." He knelt beside the still figure.

Carefully Harwich eased the woman over on her back, tenderly brushing the dust-covered reddish-brown hair from her forehead. He noted with dismay the large bruise already purpling the left side of her face and the large knot near her hairline. But when he put his long fingers on her throat, he felt a strong pulse. "She's alive," he told his groom quietly. Almost without realizing what he was doing, he brushed the dust from her pale face and traced a small white line on her chin.

The older man knelt beside his master, checking her before lifting the woman's head and shoulders carefully, settling her against his thigh. His well-trained eye noted the fine fabric of her torn habit and the whiteness of her skin.

"*Signore*, it grows late. We must be on our way," called the Italian, clearly nervous at the thought of explaining the delay to his master, the King of Naples. Joachim Murat had not gained the reputation of being one of Napoleon's best generals by being understanding about delays.

"*Basta!*" One word and the anger in those dark-blue eyes silenced the Italian. A shiver ran down his spine.

Harwich, seemingly unconcerned about his own mission or the condition of his elegant boots and buff-colored riding breeches, knelt beside his groom. "Hold her head up," he said, holding the flask to her lips.

As the cool water touched her lips, the woman sighed and then coughed. As she felt the cool moisture against her lips, the woman ran the tip of her tongue over them as if to prevent any drop from escaping.

Holding the flask to her lips again, Harwich smiled as she drank thirstily. Running a hand through his wind-rumpled brown hair, he smoothed it back from his forehead. He leaned forward anxiously, his eyes investigating his discovery. What was she doing on this deserted road? For the first time in weeks, Harwich was intrigued. After the weeks in Vienna listening to one discussion after another about whether to approach Murat and then his time at the court of Naples wooing the man so that he would accept the English offers, he had been bored.

He raised his brows as if to ask his groom for an opinion. "A lady, sir," Graves said quietly in his deep gravelly voice, his eyes indicating the rich fabric of her riding habit and the fine leather of her gloves and half-boots.

"I agree." Harwich admired her long lashes as they flickered against her pale cheeks.

For a few minutes Catherine Durrell had been trying to open her eyes but without much success. At first she had been afraid; they had tossed her away only to return. Then her brow creased. How odd those voices sounded. Suddenly she knew everything was a dream. They were speaking English.

Making a supreme effort, Catherine opened her eyes and stared into the midnight-blue ones in front of her. She *was* dreaming. Any moment she would awake and her maid would serve her chocolate and rolls.

Harwich watched fascinated as Catherine's amber-brown eyes widened. The golden core at their centers made them seem even larger than they were. They dominated her face.

Catherine moistened her lips with her tongue. "Dominic?" she said in such a soft whisper that, had they had not been listening so intently, they would have missed it. The word brought a frown to both men's faces. Graves looked at his master with a silent question, but Harwich shook his head. Seeing the frown, Catherine tried to pull herself up.

"No, miss," Graves ordered. "You sit here and tell us what happened."

"Graves?" She sank back against him and released her hold on consciousness. She never dreamed about Graves.

The men exchanged worried looks. Bending closer, Harwich inspected Catherine more closely. Had he seen her in Naples, he would have remembered that mahogany hair, the large eyes, and her rich curves. But even Murat had addressed him only by his title. And Graves—where had she seen him? Seen him and learned his name, he reminded himself. Another thought stunned him. She had been speaking English, an English as pure and clear as his own.

As he stared at her as if willing her to open her eyes and answer his questions, Harwich considered his choices.

"Shall we leave her, sir?" his groom asked in a voice carefully lowered.

"Too dangerous." Harwich threw a quick look over his shoulder at the guide, who was nervously pacing his horse up and down.

"Get that medicine case Edwards insisted I bring," the earl said quietly.

A few minutes later he stood above Catherine, watching as Graves coaxed her to drink the bitter liquid. Then he and his groom carefully lifted her to her feet. Her face, already pale, lost most of its color. Motioning Graves toward the horses, Harwich held Catherine close to his side, her head pillowed on his shoulder.

"*Signore*, the horses," the guide warned. "We must leave."

Ignoring the Italian, Harwich mounted his horse carefully while Graves held the swaying Catherine. "Hand her up to me," he said quietly. "How far to that fishing village?" he asked in Italian as he settled the now unconscious woman into a more comfortable position in front of him.

"An hour, perhaps. A little more if you take the back roads. But the others?" He gestured down the road where the sound of hoofbeats grew louder.

"My wife became ill on our way home. We sent our other groom ahead with the luggage to prepare the staff while we followed more slowly. Don't you remember?" Harwich's cold eyes dared the guide to dispute him.

"This way, *signore*," the guide reluctantly agreed.

Slowly they wound their way through the narrow roads, leaving the main road behind. As the guide had promised, they were soon at a small fishing village. "My master sent word to the innkeeper. You are expected. When the moon is completely gone, expect your contact. Is there any further way I can be of service?"

"Summon the innkeeper. And give your master my thanks." The earl threw the man a small bag of coins that he caught expertly, bowing obsequiously before calling out loudly for assistance.

"How is she, your lordship?" Graves asked anxiously. He dismounted, handing his mount to a waiting stablehand, to take the unconscious woman from his master.

"Restless. And heavy. She may come around soon." He turned to the waiting innkeeper. "Three rooms. And send a maid to my wife at once."

"But, but, *signore*, we are but a poor inn. I was told only to have a chamber ready. I have no more available." The innkeeper followed the tall nobleman into the dark, musty inn, complaining loudly.

"Enough!" Harwich turned to his groom. "Take my lady to her chamber at once, Graves. Stay with her until someone comes. I will deal with this gentleman." He looked at the small, round man who was still talking rapidly and smiled fiercely.

Even before Graves reached the top of the small flight of stairs, only one voice could be heard. The older man breathed a sigh of relief and saw the man ahead of him indicate a chamber. He carefully laid his burden on the bed. "Send a maid at once," he reminded the servant. Sinking down in the only chair in the room, he mopped his brow. Leave it to the earl to complicate their lives. Of course, there was no other choice, he reminded himself. They were not pharisees.

Before long, he joined his master in the common room below. "How is she?" asked Harwich.

"Still sleeping. I hope we didn't give her too much."

"Nonsense. I watched Nurse rub more than that on Marybeth's gums when she was teething." He looked at his groom, who was nodding in agreement, and smiled. "I believe you miss my daughter more than I do," Harwich said laughingly.

"Nonsense, sir. But she is a fine young lady, if a

trifle hotheaded." The older man cleared his throat meaningfully.

"No, I refuse to listen to another lecture, Graves. I know my duty and have been considering my problem."

Recognizing that additional discussion would do little good, Graves merely nodded. At least his master was willing to think about it. "How soon can we expect our boat, sir?"

"Not until much later."

"And the lady?"

"A problem we had better check on." Harwich led the way up the narrow stairs, bending slightly to keep from hitting his head on the overhang of the next floor.

"These Italians must all be short," muttered Graves as he followed his master's lead.

"Or the innkeeper grows wealthy on headache remedies."

"Ha! More likely on smuggling."

"Hush! After all, those smugglers are the ones that will help us on our way to England."

"Or kill us, more than likely. And then where will Lady Marybeth be. I knew no good could come of this trip. I tried to warn him," Graves complained so low that Harwich could only hear a mumble.

Harwich scratched on the door, which opened only seconds later. Waving the curtsying maid from the room, they entered. Harwich wrinkled his brow in disgust as he noted, even amid the gloom, the dirty furnishings and sour smell of the room. "Open the window, Graves."

The older man hurried to the shuttered windows and threw them wide. The sunlight did little to improve the appearance of the chamber, but the soft breeze off the bay made the air more breathable.

Harwich drew the chair close to the bed and sat down, his eyes on the still-unconscious figure. "Have the innkeeper send up some wine. His best." At the raised eyebrows on the older man, the earl laughed. "And three glasses. I wonder about food?" He paused. "Doubtful. But check out the kitchen if you wish."

Even though the chair was little more than a hard stool with a back, the earl sat quietly watching the sleeping figure. How many people called him by his given name? Other than his close family and friends, no one. And it seemed so natural to her. He flexed his shoulders to relieve his tight neck muscles and crossed to the window to look out over the bay. The afternoon sun highlighted the golden tints in his hair.

To the woman on the bed he was a tall, frightening figure, his broad shoulders blocking the sunlight. Her half-smothered gasp caused him to whirl around and stare at the bed. With the sunlight behind him, he loomed ominously over the helpless woman. But Catherine gained control of herself, revealing her fear only as she clenched and unclenched her hands. She closed her eyes briefly as if in prayer and opened them again.

In those few seconds Harwich had regained his seat and sat frowning at her. Her eyes once again grew large, their golden depths spreading.

"You're still here," Catherine exclaimed, wondering, her voice as soft as a summer breeze.

"Did you expect me to abandon you as those others did?" he asked coldly.

"Others?"

"The ones who threw you into the rocks beside the road when they saw us coming."

Catherine stared at him so fixedly that Harwich began to fear for her reason. He watched in amazement as she lifted her hand to her mouth and bit down on the soft pad of flesh under her thumb. "Ouch!" She looked at her hand and then at him in amazement.

"Do you understand me?" He stood over her,

holding her hands in one of his. He didn't intend anyone to harm her until he had his answers. He watched in amazement as a smile made the woman's face come alive. "Damn!" He turned to the door and shouted, "Graves, Graves, get up here!"

A few minutes later the older man was startled to see his master standing over the bed, a frown on his face. His hand wrapped around both of the woman's was tucked beneath her cheek, and she seemed asleep.

"Send someone for a doctor immediately. That rascal belowstairs probably has one on his payroll," Harwich said as he tried to ease his hand away.

"No." Startled, the men looked at Catherine, who was struggling to sit up against the pillows. "Send word to my father instead."

"It would help if we knew who you were," the earl said dryly.

Catherine's eyes grew even larger as she realized he meant what he said. She turned to look at Graves, who also seemed puzzled. "Dominic Nicholas Reston! And you said you never forget a face," she said half in anger.

His temper already frayed, Harwich snapped, "Have done with your games, my dear? What is your name?"

"Catherine Dominique Durrell," she said quietly. The excitement at seeing him drained from her, leaving her eyes dark and her skin pallid.

"Impossible!" Harwich said, his anger causing his dark-blue eyes to flash and his shoulders to tighten.

"A word with you, your lordship." Graves motioned him to the hall. "Those eyes, my lord. Can they be so common?"

"What, then? How did an Englishwoman of her birth come to be in Italy?"

The groom nodded, his face as puzzled as his master's. "Maybe we should send for her father."

"First, let us see what game Lady Golden Eyes is trying to play."

Harwich stopped for a moment outside the door and watched Catherine dash a tear away angrily. He smiled. His close friends would have known to be wary. "Catherine Dominique Durrell, it has been some time, hasn't it?"

"Almost fifteen years." Her voice was calm. "At your daughter's christening. She was a beautiful baby."

"And you were little older yourself."

"I was almost eleven."

"So old," Harwich mocked her.

"Ten years younger than you, my lord," she reminded him. Her voice softened. "I was sorry to hear of the death of your wife. I would have written, but Mama was dying . . ."

"Was that when you left the Grange?"

"Shortly thereafter. My aunt took charge of me." Catherine's voice took on a rougher note. "I lived with her until my Season. Since then, I've been with Papa."

"And when was that? I don't remember seeing you in London recently."

"No. I've lived in Italy for the last eight years."

"Eight years? Then how did you know . . ." He broke off what he was about to say quickly. Exchanging a look with Graves, he asked quietly, "And how came your father to be in Italy, especially now?"

"If you believe my father would allow any war to disrupt his plans, you are sadly mistaken, sir. Besides, he has been here for the last ten years and plans to live here permanently. I even have an Italian stepmother."

His brow raised, Harwich looked at Graves and smiled. "And her family?"

"She has only one brother, an archbishop. Until my father became a Catholic, he refused to have anything to do with his sister. It made Maria most unhappy." As if realizing that she had been the only one giving any information, she smiled and asked, "And how came you to be in Italy, sir?"

Harwich smiled coolly. "On business."

"Business?" she asked, confused. Then her eyes widened. "Business? And your questions? Oh. But you couldn't think, wouldn't think." The words seemed to hesitate on her lips. She looked from one to the other, anger lighting her eyes. "Send for Papa. He will tell you," she demanded, and raised her chin determinedly. A ray of sunlight lit her face, highlighting an uneven scar that ran across her chin.

Harwich's eyes widened. Suddenly his voice was kind. "Give Graves instructions. He'll send someone immediately with a note." He motioned his astonished groom closer to the bed, listening quietly as Catherine, once she had been told where they were, gave clear instructions.

"But what if he isn't there?" she asked in confusion.

"Why wouldn't he be?"

"My groom got away. He surely returned to the villa to tell my father what happened. They may be looking for me now."

Graves patted her hand reassuringly. "Someone will know how to find him. Just tell his lordship what happened while I arrange to send someone off." He glanced at his master questioningly and then quickly left the room.

"How did you come to be beside the road?" the earl asked quietly.

She took a sip of wine from the glass he held toward her. "I was out for a ride. My groom and I were surprised. Before we realized what was happening, the men, whoever they were, had separated us. They easily overtook me and pulled me from my horse." She paused and drew a shuddering breath. "The one who held me smelled so bad. And he said, he said . . ."

"Don't think about it now. You're safe." Harwich leaned over to pat her shoulder, surprising both of them. "You rest for a time while I see that Graves has everything under control. Is there anything you need?"

"Some hot water and the maid, if she can be spared."

The earl nodded, looked at her closely once more, and left the room.

Catherine stared at the closed door for a moment before settling back on her pillow. Dominic in Italy. Never, even in her dreams, had she imagined that. She shuddered as she remembered those other hands, the hot breath. Resolutely she closed her eyes, reminding herself that Dominic would never let anyone hurt her.

Harwich, for once, was not sure of himself. Finding Catherine in Italy was rather surprising. And though he had known her as a child, he knew the woman not at all.

Those eyes—serious, playful, devoted—had haunted him for years without his ever realizing it. He laughed ironically. Both of his last two mistresses had brownish-gold eyes that seemed to mock him. How disappointed they would have been if they could have seen the original, he laughed to himself as he entered the common room just in time to hear Graves finishing his instructions.

"Send hot water and a maid up to my lady," he commanded. "And more of your best wine here." As he stared into the golden depths of his glass, everything came back as though someone had opened a book, a childhood favorite that had been long forgotten. The first time he had seen that face, there hadn't been a scar. He had been home from school, bored with his childhood games and still too young for adult ones. That day as he rode into a small copse of trees, he had heard someone call out.

"Sir! Oh, sir!" The voice had been so soft and faraway that he had instinctively looked at the clearing in the trees. At first he had seen nothing. Puzzled, he looked higher. And there she had been, her dress ripped, her face smeared with dirt and tears. One arm was locked tightly around the tree trunk and the other held the most bedraggled kitten he had ever seen.

"What are you doing up there?" he had asked, guiding his horse under the limb to which she clung.

"Horace tried to run away. I catched him." She smiled through the dirt and tears, one of the most engaging smiles he had ever seen. "Will you help me down?" she asked plaintively.

As willing as he had been to help, the task had been far from simple. Horace liked the tree even if Catherine was ready to get down. By the time he had both Horace and Catherine in front of him on his horse, the little girl was bleeding from a deep scratch on her chin. Although neither he nor Catherine had paid the injury much attention, when he finally delivered Catherine to her mother and Nanny, the women had stared at him so accusingly that he made his escape quickly.

On his ride home, though, he had to smile. Those eyes and that smile. She must cause her nanny problems.

He was right. Before the week was out, the woman was having palpitations. Catherine had decided that he was home simply to amuse her. After the third time she had escaped from her nanny to find him, Dominic bowed to the inevitable. When he was home, several mornings a week he would ride over to the Durrell home to take Catherine for a ride. Those had been some of the best summers of his boyhood.

Catherine had been fond of fishing and exploring around the pond. He had to rescue her several times before he finally decided to teach her to swim, at least for her own safety. As he thought of that time, he realized she and his daughter had much in common. Both had delighted in scrapes that usually involved destroying his boots or requiring his shirt to cover their torn dresses. Catherine had been a fearless little mischief. "I wonder how she and Marybeth would get along?" he asked himself quietly, amusement lightening his features. As he thought of Catherine lying beside that road, he frowned. Why was she in Italy?

As the late-afternoon sun dropped lower, Harwich hid his impatience behind his usual mask of boredom. Occasionally the sound of hoofbeats would cause him to look up, questioning Graves, who had an unobstructed view of the yard, and then returning to his book when the hoofbeats continued down the road. Only when the last touches of sunlight hit the innyard and the innkeeper and his helpers were scurrying around placing the poorest quality of candles on the tables in the common room did Harwich put aside his book. "Did you find something suitable to break our fast?" he asked Graves quietly.

"Some fish—fresh from the bay, if the cook is to be believed—and some soup. It will be ready shortly."

"Have them serve us in Miss Durrell's room. And be certain they provide enough chairs. No, don't tell me you'll eat here. I won't take a chance on your being poisoned by the food I see served here. Besides, think of Edwards' face if he could see us." The earl clapped Graves on the shoulder and left chuckling.

The older man straightened his shoulders and laughed quietly. His master's valet put on such airs, always reminding the occupants of the servant's table how important he was to his master. Graves laughed to himself. How Edwards had resented being sent home with the luggage and other servants! As he crossed to the corridor to the kitchen,

Graves thought of the various comments he would drop belowstairs. After all, hadn't he been with the earl since the boy was declared old enough for his first hunter. The thought made him grin broadly. A few minutes later the servants the inn boasted hurried to do his bidding.

Upstairs the earl knocked softly and entered. Except for the soiled riding habit and the bruises already discoloring her face, Catherine seemed more lively, less subdued. "My father?" she asked quietly, her voice trembling.

"No word. Remember, if he were looking for you, he would have to be sent for. We'll have word of him before long." He crossed to the bed where she sat propped up against dingy pillows. "Graves has promised that he has ordered a meal that will be suitable. They are to serve it here shortly. Tell me more of your life here in Italy."

Artfully the earl led her through a discussion of the villa, near to her father's studies at Restina, and her impressions of Italy. "Don't you miss the company of English people?" he finally asked.

"Yes. Oh, yes. Of course, we used to visit both Naples and Sicily. Papa even met Admiral Nelson at the Count of Naples'. Maria, my stepmama, was not allowed to visit because"—her voice grew deeper and more pompous—" 'no womenfolk of mine will associate with "that" woman.' How she regretted the fact. Did you meet her?"

"Lady Hamilton?"

"Of course."

"I have not had the pleasure." He frowned down at her. "Our circles are not the same." His voice was as frosty as his eyes.

"Too good to associate with a mistress?" she asked him amusedly. "Why, I remember the last summer when you used to sneak off to the house in the village where Squire Willowby's mistress—"

"You never could mind your own business,"

Harwich thundered. "It's no wonder you're in such a predicament now. Let me tell you, Miss Durrell, when your father arrives . . ."

A scratching at the door just as he was taking a breath to continue caused him to whirl and throw the door open. "Your dinner, my lord," Graves said, confusion in every line on his face.

Waving the small group into the room, Harwich crossed to the window. Looking at the woman on the bed, he noticed the darkness of her eyes and the short angry breaths that drew attention to her full bosom, more visible now that she had removed the jacket of her riding habit and wore only a thin blouse. He stared fascinated for a moment or two until he realized that he was not the only one watching her. "Put your jacket on," he said in a carefully controlled voice.

Flushing, Catherine struggled into the torn garment, pulling it closed quickly. During the brief meal neither Catherine nor Harwich exchanged direct looks, although Graves watched with interest as they glanced at each other and looked away. Catherine, still queazy from the blows to her head, refused all but the soup. But Harwich made a hearty meal. Graves was supervising the removal of the table when several horses pounded to a stop outside the inn.

"Papa. It must be him," Catherine said, her voice wavering slightly. She sat up straighter.

Harwich and Graves exchanged worried looks. Too many men around and their smugglers would not appear. "Check on it, Graves," the earl said, stepping out into the dark hallway. "The stableboy did take my note?" Graves nodded. "Good. After a few words with Catherine's father, she can be on her way home."

"Are you certain she isn't here simply to detain us?"

"No, but the opposition would have had to move

more rapidly than usual to pull this off. I'll speak to Mr. Durrell. Perhaps he can explain." The two men walked down the stairs and into the common room.

The scene that greeted them looked like a scene from a comic opera. Two men—Mr. Durrell, by the cut of his garments, and the innkeeper—were both shouting in Italian at the top of their lungs. Seated in a corner obviously ignoring the whole scene sat a middle-aged woman in a traveling cloak who seemed to be guarding two valises.

"But I tell you I know nothing of your daughter. This *signore* will bear witness. Only his wife rests abovestairs," the innkeeper said loudly.

"Wife, is it?" Mr. Durrell, a large heavyset man, swung around to inspect the newcomers. He frowned as if worried by something. "There you are, sir. Are you the one who sent me the note by this man?" He gestured to the Italian he had seated on the bench in front of him.

"Yes."

"Then take me to Catherine at once. If you've harmed her . . ."

By the time the door to Catherine's chamber had closed behind the two men, the common room had split into three groups: Graves, the staff of the inn, and the people who had accompanied Durrell.

Upstairs the situation was not much better. Durrell had taken one look at his daughter and drawn his pistol from his pocket.

"No, Papa. He rescued me," Catherine called, watching in horror as the earl simply squared his shoulders and faced her father.

"What?" Her father looked from Catherine to Harwich in confusion.

"I believe my note explained," the earl said quietly. But his anger was evident.

"Your note. Yours was the second I received today."

"What was the first?"

"A ransom note for one million lire."

"Where would we get that amount of money?"

"From the site."

"The site?" The ransom note had aroused Harwich's suspicions again, but his anger had been replaced by confusion.

"Herculaneum . . ."

"Where?"

"Papa has been studying the ruins of an old Roman city for the last ten years," Catherine explained. "I help sometimes to catalog what has been found."

"What do ruins have to do with Catherine's kidnapping?" the earl asked, puzzled.

"They must have heard of the treasure," Mr. Durrell explained. "But at least they don't know exactly what it is." He turned to look at his daughter with sad but fond eyes. "There seems to be only one solution to keep you safe, Catherine."

"Yes, Papa?"

"You will return to England with the earl."

2

For a moment stunned silence filled the room. Then everyone began to speak at once.

"I won't go. I absolutely refuse," Catherine said firmly.

"Absurd. Totally out of the question," the earl said.

Mr. Durrell let them get out their first indignation and then said in a voice so quiet and calm the earl had to acknowledge his power, "When we talked only yesterday, Catherine, I warned you of your possible danger. But you would ride with only old Giuseppe on a horse you knew was no match for your own." He looked into her eyes as if to force her to acknowledge the truth of what he was saying.

"But, Papa, I felt caged. And what about you and Maria? I'll wait to return with you."

The earl opened his mouth to speak but closed it when Mr. Durrell continued his explanation.

"Maria never leaves the villa unless she is well-escorted. Also, her brother is aware of the situation. He has promised to throw his protection of the Church around her." He paused for a moment but continued before the others could say a word. "The administrator has notified the King of Naples. He has been very supportive in the past. As soon as he hears what we have found, I have no doubt that we will be adequately protected."

Murat, Harwich thought, carefully hiding his surprise. He wondered briefly what type of treasure they were discussing. But if the find were as exciting as Durrell claimed, Murat might find a way to eliminate them and keep it for himself. If the King of Naples could betray a man like Napoleon, who had raised him to that rank, what would he do to ordinary scholars? As the arguments ebbed around him, Harwich refused to be quiet any longer. He walked into the center of the room and said, "A woman travel unchaperoned with two men? Society will not stand for it. Nor will I. She'd be ruined." His voice was so cynical that Catherine was startled.

Mr. Durrell turned to face him. Although some inches shorter than the earl's six feet, he stood proudly, his eyes boring into the flashing blue ones in front of him. "After this afternoon's fiasco, her reputation is already in tatters." As the earl raised his eyebrows in disbelief, Durrell went on, "You surely don't believe the servants here will refuse to gossip with my men. I don't suppose you wish to explain that you were just trying to protect my daughter when you introduced her as your wife or decided to have a quiet supper in her chamber?" Durrell asked quietly, his anxiety carefully concealed.

"Papa, he was a perfect gentleman. Nothing happened."

"If this were London, would society believe that?" her father asked.

"But I don't want to go to London and Aunt Clarice. Please, Papa, let me stay here." Catherine looked at him pleadingly, her eyes large and wistful. It was a look that usually won her whatever she wanted.

"No, my mind is made up." Her father turned his back on his disgruntled daughter, whose eyes shot golden darts into his unprotected back. It was for the best.

The earl had ignored most of the last exchange. Even chaperoned as they had been by Graves, he knew he had violated the social customs of the day.

He was caught. He squared his shoulders and said, "Very well, sir, I will wed your daughter."

Catherine's eyes grew as golden as the Italian sunset. She seemed to glow for a moment, but before she could agree, her father said, "Good heavens, man! My Catherine a countess? She'd have no more notion of how to go on than would a peahen. Good heavens, sir. I've known your family too long to doubt your word. Just get her to England. Her aunt and my man of business will do the rest. No lack of money, you know." He chuckled. "Marry her."

Her dream in ruins, Catherine wanted to weep, to scream. But she had been too well trained. Her eyes snapped. But she was silent.

Used to being pursued by matchmaking mothers, the earl was stunned. "But, sir?"

"Nonsense. You are an honorable man. Your father saw to that. Catherine has said more times than I can count that she has no wish to marry. If that is her wish, I've no desire to force it on her."

The earl cast a quick look to the rich charms of the woman who had her hand over her aching eyes. Gesturing to the older man, Harwich led him outside into the hallway and closed the door behind him, leaving Catherine fuming inside.

"Maria's done her best since Catherine's arrived in Italy, but the girl's refused them all. Not saying I've given up hope for a grandson altogether. Maybe when she's back in England. Never did understand why she left in the first place. Would think my own sister could have kept her in line," the older man explained.

As they walked into the common room, the earl listened attentively; he had to, for Catherine's father was using a mixture of English and Italian that was hard to follow. As the older man paused for breath, Harwich asked, "Have you thought of the social consequences of what you are asking me to do? I must spend some time in Sicily . . ."

"Splendid. Bound to be some gentlewoman there who would rejoice at a free trip home. I'll give you a draft."

"But how will I explain her presence to Lord Bentiwick?"

"What would you have done if I hadn't arrived? Left her here?"

Never! Then the earl smiled cynically. "You never did arrive, did you?"

"You've got the drift. Her maid is in the corner over there," Mr. Durrell explained, pointing to an Englishwoman about thirty-five years old sitting primly on a chair, staring straight in front of her. "I'll speak to her and then say good-bye to Catherine." He looked at the earl's face searchingly. "Take care of her, my lord. A letter wouldn't come amiss." The earl nodded and held out his hand. The older man clasped it warmly.

In the small room upstairs Catherine, had her head not been pounding, would have been throwing a tantrum, her first since childhood. To come so close. And to be returned to England like a parcel of dirty linen. She had no doubt of the reaction of Aunt Clarice. Her last interview with the lady still gave her nightmares. To return to the scene of her last social disaster was more than she could bear.

When the door opened and her father entered, she threw herself in his arms, her eyes filled with tears. "Please, Papa, don't send me away," she begged. "I'll stay inside the villa. Please?"

"No, my dear. Everything is arranged. Besides, I have something you must do. Tell no one. In the . . ."

As Catherine listened her eyes grew wider. "Of course, Papa."

"Remember. Until you reach England no one is to know you have it. Not even the earl." Catherine nodded and then hugged her father tightly. "I've sent word that you are to spend whatever you like. And use the Grange. It will be yours someday. Might as

well get used to managing it." His voice was rough
with emotion. After giving her a hug and a kiss on her
cheek, he stepped back. "Be good. And don't give the
earl any trouble."

Catherine smiled sadly. Her father never wanted
to admit she was a grown woman. "Will you come to
England?"

"As soon as the discovery is made public and this
cursed war is over." He looked at her closely and
smiled. "You didn't think I would abandon you, did
you?" She smiled weakly and shook her head. "Come
and give me one last kiss. It wouldn't do to have me
here when your transport arrives."

Reluctantly Catherine gave him the kiss he asked
for, and stepped back, her head held proudly and her
eyes full of tears she refused to shed. "That's my
girl."

When her maid entered some time later, Catherine
thrust her chin in the air and wiped the tears from
her cheeks, expecting to see the earl. With Davis
there was no need for pride. Fresh tears streamed
down her cheeks.

As if totally unmoved by her mistress's tears, Davis
bustled about the room. "A disgrace. That's what it
is. Your last good riding habit destroyed. Well,
thanks be, that can be set right enough as soon as we
arrive in London. Now you slip out of that torn
mess." Before she had done more than slip her
mistress out of her jacket, the door opened quietly.

Brushing her tears from her cheeks once again,
Catherine turned her back on the earl. "I waited for a
response, but you didn't answer," he explained.

Davis crossed to stand in front of him, her arms on
her hips and her eyes flashing. "Well, you can return
to the hallway and wait until my mistress has
changed."

"Changed? Not until we reach Sicily. In fact, you
look too neat to be part of our plan." Before the maid

could stop him, he called, "Graves!" A few minutes later the maid, much to her chagrin, was thoroughly mussed and covered with dirt. "That's better. Here's what we must do." Seating Davis beside her mistress on the bed, he outlined the plan. "Just stay up here until we come for you. You might as well try to get some sleep, Catherine," he urged, noting how pale she seemed in the candlelight.

As tired as she was, the throbbing of her head kept Catherine from sleeping more than minutes at a time. Despite Davis' objections she refused to take the draft of laudanum the maid tried to urge on her. As she lay on the bed and watched the sky grow progressively darker, Catherine was filled with fear, a fear she was determined never to show. The events of that afternoon seemed but distant memories as she thought of her future. London and Aunt Clarice. She dozed fitfully and then awoke to find her body drenched with sweat.

"Davis?" Awakening with a start, the maid hurried to her mistress's side. "Is there any water?"

A few minutes later the sound they had been listening for happened.

"They're here," Graves said in a voice so soft that they had to strain to hear it. "Italian only, his lordship says. And it would be best to seem less than aware of what is happening. These are dangerous men. Be careful."

Hastily the women gathered their few belongings and slipped into the corridor. The guttering candle barely illuminated the narrow stairs. Catherine stumbled once and almost fell but refused help. "No. I'll be fine. You need your hands free," she told Graves. A quick look at her face told the groom she realized the extreme danger of their position. "Davis will help me if I need it." With the maid's nod of assurance, the groom continued down the stairs and into the common room.

Seconds later the earl was at their sides. "Let them see those bruises, Catherine," he whispered in her ear as she stood swaying beside him.

"Molto bella," one rough seaman exclaimed, only to be silence a second later. An enormous hand caught Catherine's chin and turned her face toward the light. As Davis indignantly moved her way forward, Harwich waved her to one side.

"It is as you say, *signore."* The thick Sicilian accent was almost impossible for Catherine to follow. When the sailor dropped his hand and turned away, Catherine almost fell. "Bring them along. Quickly now."

Sweeping her into his arms, Harwich followed the man as casually as though he were following the Prince Regent through Carlton House. Glancing at each other, the two servants lifted the bundles and hurried into the night. A short time later they watched the few lights along the coast disappear.

"Sleep if you can," Harwich suggested as he placed Catherine between two bales. "Try not to notice too much. We should be in Sicily before morning."

"Now, Miss Catherine?" Davis asked, holding out the draft Catherine had refused earlier. She thankfully swallowed the bitter liquid, moaning as her head hit the side of the bales. Dipping her scarf in the seawater so close at hand, Davis laid it carefully over her mistress's forehead. "A good night's rest and she'll be herself in the morning," the maid assured the two men as they watched in concern. Under her breath, she uttered a swift prayer that her prediction would come true.

Much to the surprise of everyone in the little party, Davis' prophecy was fairly accurate. By the time they landed at another village, Catherine was awake and, if not fully recovered, at least well enough to bear stocially the ride through the hills to Messina. In the bright Sicilian sunlight her bruises brought sighs of sympathy from the few people they passed. From her hairline almost to her chin, Catherine was a deep purplish black, much like the slices of liver that they had seen in one market along the way. Unfortunately for the men of the party these sighs were accompanied by frowns from the woman and winks from the men.

Finally Harwich had had as much as he could endure. "Blast it, Graves," he said angrily, "the next time I decide to rescue someone remind me of today. And hurry up that donkey cart. I would like to arrive this afternoon if possible." He glanced at the cart, the only available transportation that they could find for Catherine.

"Wasn't there another cart to be had?" he asked for the third time that morning.

"If you'll notice, your lordship, this cart is rather conservative," Graves answered less patiently than before.

"Whoever heard of painting the fall of Carthage on the sides of a donkey cart?"

"It seemed the correct choice at the time. The owner was delighted to explain that Messina was a leader with Rome in that fight. Perhaps you would have preferred the one depicting the earthquake of 1780, the one with the bodies lying realistically under the rubble?"

"No. I'm sorry, Graves." The earl glanced back toward the cart proceeding slowly up the hill. Despite her protests to the contrary, he didn't like Catherine's pallor. Even as a child she had not liked to give into her weaknesses, never admitting when something distressed her. Once she had fainted, but only after helping him free a rabbit from a particularly nasty trap.

"We'll stop at the next inn for something to drink," he called. "I'll ride ahead to make arrangements."

"Go faster. Stop here. Will the man never make up his mind?" his groom muttered, but not unhappily.

This confusion was not like his master. He glanced at the cart and smiled.

From the time she had awakened that morning, Catherine had been discovering characteristics of Harwich that she wasn't certain she approved of. The happy, easygoing boy of her childhood had become a domineering, stubborn man. He rode ahead on a comfortable horse while she was forced to jolt along in this cart. Her innate honesty forced her to admit, however, that the dull throbbing in her head would have been worse on horseback. Why did he have to keep looking at her that way? She knew what her face looked like. Davis had not been quick enough to hide the mirror at the inn. If she hadn't been so determined, she would have been in tears. She bit her lip in vexation.

Davis, seeing her struggle, patted her hand. "Not much longer, Miss Catherine. And to think this is but the first part of our journey to England," she said brightly.

England—and Aunt Clarice. The thoughts chased each other in Catherine's mind. Eight Seasons had succeeded her own. Perhaps all would be forgotten. She laughed silently at herself, knowing her aunt's memory and waspish tongue.

Maybe there was still a way. She could stay in Sicily. No, she had promised her father, and one thing Catherine did was keep her promises. She sighed, resigned but not happy about her fate.

By the time they reached Messina that afternoon she had decided that she never wanted to see Dominic Reston, fourth earl of Harwich, again as long as she lived. He was not only stubborn and dictorial but also too handsome for her peace of mind. Every time he looked at her with those marvelous eyes, she shivered.

Despite her dreams, Catherine was eminently practical. Even during her own Season she had recognized her infatuation for what it was. Because her aunt's circle of friends didn't aspire to his, she'd not seen him. Of course, there had been rumors aplenty. But even the matchmaking mamas had given up on him early on after his year of mourning. His high-fliers and habit of disappearing into the country for weeks on end were impossible to disregard.

Even then, though, she knew he had set the pattern for the man she hoped to marry. A good sense of humor, dark hair, flashing eyes, a handsome face, and a tall slim physique—once she had thought she had found them all.

Before she grew even more depressed, the cart stopped. "Are we there?" Davis almost shouted.

"According to your driver, Messina should be just over the next hill. Once there, Lord Bentiwick should be easy to find. Do you remember the plan?" Harwich asked.

Catherine reviewed it quickly in her mind and then recited, "I'm to seem unconscious—delirious, perhaps—until I've been taken to my room. I'll remain there until you send me word that everything is arranged." She paused and then plunged into speech again. "Dominic—I mean, your lordship—"

"Come now, Catherine, after the last two days there is no need to be so formal, at least in private." He laughed a little, his eyes twinkling.

Graves watched amazed at his usual formal master unbending even that much.

Catherine began again. "Dominic, how long must we stay here?"

"I have no idea. Until my consultation with Lord Bentiwick is finished and we find both a chaperone and a ship to take us home."

"I don't know if I shall be able to keep this up."

"Now, Miss Catherine, I will be with you," her maid tried to reassure her.

"But I won't be able to go outside. Dominic, you must arrange that I be allowed at least a walk in the gardens. I shall go mad otherwise."

Watching Catherine become more and more agitated, Harwich reached down and captured her hands. "Catherine, look at me," he commanded. Wanting to remove that look of panic in her eyes, he promised, "As soon as it is convenient I will see that you are allowed outside. Do you understand?"

"Yes." Her voice was very quiet. She refused to look at him again.

"What else, Catherine?" He watched as she considered the situation. "Let me hear your objections now rather than later."

Her words came pouring out of her in a rush. "Taormina? Can we possibly go there? I've been to Palermo with Papa, but before we returned . . . Well, you know what happened."

To her surprise her request did not get the unqualified no she had expected. "What's there? Am I supposed to know the place?"

"Papa said they had a particularly fine Greek theater. In fact, there are Greek and Roman ruins all over the island."

"More ruins? Catherine . . ."

"And you can see Mount Etna from there," she added hastily.

"Hmm."

"It's still active. Maybe we could see an eruption!" The last statement was hardly out of her mouth when she realized that she had taken one step too far. "Just seeing the town of Messina will be enough if that's what you think best, Dominic," she added hastily, her eyes anxious.

"The town of Messina? A moment ago we were speaking of a walk in the garden."

"But I may never have another opportunity like this. I certainly can't see Aunt Clarice allowing me to return to Sicily," Catherine tried to explain.

Graves, his face stiff from trying not to laugh, was trying frantically to catch her eye.

Finally Catherine looked at him and then at the earl, whose face was impassive. "Perhaps we should wait until later to discuss it," she suggested in her softest, most demure voice.

"Perhaps we should," Harwich agreed rather sardonically. As if dismissing the idea completely, his next words were brisk. "Davis, your story is clear?"

"Yes, your lordship."

"Graves?" The groom nodded. "Then Messina awaits."

3

Their stories carefully prepared, the small party entered the town of Messina. Catherine, her bruised face carefully hidden from view, lay on the straw. Davis sat by her side, a worried look on her face. Only the owner of the cart seemed interested in anything around him.

The two men galloped toward the first inn they saw, a large imposing structure that seemed to dwarf the street on which it lay.

"Rooms, *signore*?" an eager stablehand asked.

"A guide to the home of Lord Bentiwick, the English ambassador," the earl requested firmly.

"Ah, *signore*, how unfortunate. Only last week he was here. Now he is gone."

"Dead?" Graves asked sharply.

"Dead?" The stablehand laughed delightedly. "No, *signore*, removed to Palermo. Now, how many rooms shall I tell the master to prepare?"

"A guide only at the present," the earl reminded him firmly. "Or shall we proceed on our own?"

"No, no, honored sir. A moment and I, personally, will guide you." The man disappeared into the inn without giving either man a chance to answer.

"Quite the businessman." The earl laughed quietly.

"Perhaps the innkeeper's son."

"Or sleeping with the man's wife," said the earl cynically.

Before Graves had time to more than sputter, their guide had returned, his apron left behind.

"This way, *signoris.*" He gestured down the narrow street.

"Slowly and carefully," the earl said quietly, gesturing to the cart that had only then stopped nearby.

To their guide's displeasure, no sooner was the earl introduced than an entourage of servants appeared to whisk the party into the large villa. Shrugging his shoulders philosophically, the man pocketed his reward and chattered volubly to the owner of the donkey cart, also returning home wealthier.

Whisking the company inside the imposing marble structure, Lord Bentiwick's secretary, Thomas Abbot, greeted them effusively. "Such a surprise, your lordship. I know his excellency will be delighted to hear of your arrival. A messenger will leave today." He looked around in confusion as Graves placed Catherine on a low bench near the stairs, Davis following close behind. "Your wife, my lord? We had not heard the news."

His response to their story was even better than they had hoped. Only a few months out of college, this young cousin of Bentiwick's was all too eager to help and almost personally affronted that such a lovely lady had had to suffer such indignities. And when he saw her face clearly for the first time, he was aghast.

It took the earl's voice to remind him of his responsibilities. "Is there a room for the lady?"

"Of course, sir."

"And I think a doctor. Don't you agree?"

The young secretary swelled with pride and nodded. "I'll send to the garrison. I'm sure you would prefer that an English doctor attend her." Abbot looked at the earl like a puppy wanting some attention.

"I'm certain that will be fine. But first the room."

Flushing, the secretary hurriedly consulted the

majordomo, nodding as the man spoke. "Carry the lady to the blue room," Abbot directed a footman. "You have only to ring for whatever you need to make your mistress comfortable," he assured Davis as she followed her mistress up the stairs. He turned back to the earl. "If we could speak more in the library, sir? Your room will be ready momentarily."

While the earl and Abbot dispatched letters to the doctor and Lord Bentiwick, Catherine was tenderly deposited on a vast, intricately carved bed surrounded by airy creamy lace draperies. As her mistress absorbed in delight the murals that surrounded her, Davis took charge. "A bath for my mistress. Make certain there is plenty of hot water and many towels." The Italian servants dispersed, she began undressing her mistress. "I believe we must wash your hair, Miss Catherine."

The last statement was the only one Catherine heard. "My head already aches. And you know how long it takes to dry. Please, let us leave it until later," she said quietly.

Looking at the purple shadows under her mistress's eyes, Davis agreed reluctantly. Catherine sighed and made herself comfortable on the soft bed. "These clothes most probably need to be burned, miss. I didn't want to mention it earlier, but I'm certain that inn was not as clean as it might have been."

Catherine laughed weakly. "I know. I was the one who spent hours lying on that dirty bed."

"Just my point. I didn't want to mention it at the time, but I'm certain I noticed."

"Davis, if you let me lie in a bug-infested bed and you knew it," Catherine almost shouted.

"Where else was there for you to go? Besides, the boat and the straw this morning were almost as bad." Ignoring her mistress's gasp, the maid answered the scratching at the door. "Put it over there in front of the fire," she directed as the footman delivered one of the largest copper tubs she had ever seen. "My heavens, Miss Catherine. Have you ever seen a more elegant tub. It is almost as big as the fountain in the garden outside your window." She inspected it closely from all angles, her mouth growing tighter every moment. "Humph! Just what I would expect from Italians," she said repressively.

Finally, the tub filled to her satisfaction, a fire in the fireplace to prevent chills, and a screen in place for modesty, Davis called to her mistress, who for some minutes had been trying to convince herself that it was not ladylike to scratch. "Miss Catherine, we are ready for you." Before her mistress passed the screen, Davis whispered in her ear, "No need to look at the decorations on the outside, miss. They are nothing to concern yourself with."

Her curiosity piqued, Catherine walked slowly around the tub, her face breaking into a smile. The satyrs chasing nymphs were easy to identify, but was that Apollo chasing Daphne? "I do hope Dominic has something equally as amusing." Catherine laughed.

"Miss Catherine, you come here at once. No doubt this is a bachelor household, and no one knew the impropriety of sending this object in here." Even after eight years of Italian culture, the maid tended to disapprove. "Fortunately, we will soon be in England, where this would never happen," Davis sputtered.

In a few minutes Catherine was neck-deep in warm water. Sighing deeply, she stretched out, the back of her neck sinking beneath the surface. "Your hair is getting wet, Miss Catherine."

"I suppose we might as well wash it," her mistress replied, her aches disappearing in the warmth of the water. "Ah, this feels heavenly."

By the time Catherine was sitting in front of the fire having her hair dried, the earl was enjoying the Roman bath that a previous ambassador had restored, surrounding it with murals of the temples as well as classical statues. The warm spring water kept the pool at a constant temperature. Harwich ignored Graves' mutter. "Indecent. No human being needs this much water to wash himself. Must save the servants time, though, not having to heat the water."

By the time Harwich was dressed, a footman had brought him a message. "The doctor is here, Graves. I'll see him before he sees Catherine," he called to his groom.

A few minutes later he surveyed the doctor Abbot had found for Catherine. Although the man seemed clean and sober, the doctor gave the impression that the earl was in his debt for his even considering to see a civilian, especially a civilian discovered under such suspicious circumstances.

The more he talked, the colder the earl's eyes grew. But even they were not enough to warn the hapless physician. Finally the earl smiled and said in a crisp, cold tone, "Perhaps it would be best if Miss Durrell were to see an Italian physician."

Both Abbot and the doctor stared at him in surprise. "But, your lordship, I thought . . . Lord Bentiwick would insist . . ." Abbot stuttered, trying to determine what was wrong. "I can assure you that the doctor is one of the finest on the island."

At the slightly raised eyebrow of the nobleman in front of him, the doctor became indignant and then wary. Obviously the man had friends in high places, with Abbot stumbling over himself to make him happy. Hastily the physician began to make amends. "Naturally Abbot had not informed me how serious the injuries to the lady might be." He continued in spite of the astonished look on Abbot's face or the cynically amused one on the face of the earl. "I will be delighted to examine her immediately." He raised one brow as if to ask why they were still standing in the library.

"Has the lady been informed of the doctor's arrival?" the earl asked, still in that quietly cold voice.

"Yes, Lord Harwich."

"I will accompany you, sir." He turned and walked toward the door, ignoring the startled looks on their faces. "And the other matter, Abbot?"

"Immediately, sir." Watching them walk up the stairs, Abbot breathed a sigh of relief and gave the bellpull a yank. "A chaperone . . ."

As the earl had suspected, the doctor's recommendations were the same as his own: bed rest for a few days, light meals, laudanum if the throbbing grew too much to bear. For a few minutes all seemed to proceed exactly as the earl wished. "And now, sir, if you would leave Miss Durrell and her maid alone with me so that I can examine her to determine the number of leeches needed to reduce her bruises?" the doctor asked, clearly expecting Harwich would immediately leave the room.

To both men's surprise, Harwich had the doctor in the hall almost before he could finish the sentence. "See that she follows the doctor's orders, Davis. I'll see the doctor out." To a man used to calm, rational behavior, his own actions were astonishing. But when he had seen that man reaching a hand toward Catherine, he knew he had to stop him. Minutes later, the doctor was still shaking his head. If that were the way noblemen acted, he would stay with the army.

Both Harwich and Catherine had a great deal of time for reflection. Even though Abbot found a chaperone in a few hours—albeit a reluctant one— Catherine was too exhausted and, now that she could admit it without appearing a weakling, too ill to consider leaving her chamber. For two days she slept, awakening only when Davis insisted that she drink or eat something.

For Harwich, Lord Bentiwick's absence meant

that he had to wait. Unfortunately, waiting bo him. Graves, regretting the absence of a boxing parlor or his lordship's clubs, began to slip away to a taverna near the barracks where the English were garrisoned. There he found one solution to his master's problem. With the garrison at such low strength, the officers used the taverna for their gaming. That evening Harwich joined their ranks.

"Lord Harwich," the colonel greeted him warmly. With introductions over, Harwich took his place at the table. Even the card games he was encouraged to join seemed to have lost their luster. Lady Luck favored him, even though he rarely concentrated. And instead of his usual urbane behavior, he was fast gaining a reputation as an eccentric.

The information he learned seemed at odds with the ideas in Vienna. Those left in Messina seemed to resent the British attitude toward Murat. If they had had their way, Italy would have been in English hands. "But Wellington had more friends in Parliament," the colonel explained almost sadly.

"And with Sir John Stuart and most of the men reassigned to Gibraltar, there's little hope of taking it now."

His evenings spent gathering money and information, Harwich spent his days riding and swimming, an activity he found helpful in his growing frustration.

When Graves entered the bathing room where Harwich had been spending so much time, even he was showing signs of impatience with his master. "Your lordship! Your lordship," he called. He waited until Harwich climbed from the pool to continue. "Mrs. Wilson, Miss Catherine's companion," he began.

"I know who the woman is. I hired her."

"Yes, your lordship. Mrs. Wilson and Davis have decided that Miss Catherine may rest in the garden this afternoon."

"They did, did they? And no one thought to inform me of their plan?"

Graves took a deep breath and reminded himself that shaking the earl had done little good as a child and would do none at all now. "Miss Catherine wishes to know if you will join her for tea," he said calmly. "What may I tell her?"

"Yes, blast it. Now find me some clothes, and be quick about it." Watching the carefully held shoulders of the man he had known since he had been a boy, Harwich was certain he had offended Graves. He would have been enraged if he could have seen the man break into quiet laughter as soon as he was well away from the door. If everything continued as it was going, Graves anticipated some pleasant changes in their lives.

Upstairs, confusion also reigned. For the first time in several days, Catherine had taken a look in the mirror. As a result, she was refusing to go anywhere. "But his lordship has already accepted your invitation," Davis reminded her mistress.

"Tell him I have changed my mind."

Mrs. Wilson, a softly rounded widow in her early forties, said quietly, "A lady must never get the reputation for being capricious."

"Capricious? With my face looking like this?" Catherine asked despondently.

"Actually, miss, you look much better than you did the last time he saw you," Davis reminded her.

"I do?"

"I'm certain he has been worrying about you. Graves has been sent to the door many times to inquire after you." the maid said.

"He has?"

"Come, let me experiment with your curls, Miss Catherine. Perhaps by pulling it away from this side and toward the left."

"But I have nothing to wear," Catherine wailed.

Davis left the answer to that in Mrs. Wilson's

capable hands. A short time later Catherine stood
before them in a cream muslin sprigged in teal blue,
her pelisse repeating that color. Eager at last to
escape the confines of her suite, Catherine was
almost out of the door to the hallway before Davis
and Mrs. Wilson, conferring on the serious problem
of whether or not Catherine would need a shawl,
stopped her.

"Miss Catherine," her maid said repressively,
"remember who you are."

Sighing, Catherine waited while the other two
gathered their sewing and shawls. As Mrs. Wilson led
the way down the marble staircase and toward the
terrace, Catherine looked around her. When Graves
had carried her in, she had been too tired to notice
the Greek and Roman artifacts set into niches in the
halls and along the white marble stairway. If only
Papa could see this, she thought sadly.

Her sadness was only momentary as she was
escorted into the bright sunshine of the October
afternoon.

Someone had arranged a group of padded benches
near a fountain. There, amid the still flowering
bushes, waited Harwich, his broad shoulders
showing to advantage in a deep-blue coat that
matched his eyes. Seeing the small procession, he
bowed.

When he raised his head a few seconds later, he
gasped. "How, how nice . . ." he mumbled, his
shoulders shaking slightly.

"Don't mind my feelings, Lord Harwich. What
were you going to say?" Catherine said bitterly.

"Miss Catherine, I'm certain you wrong his lordship," said her chaperone quietly.

"No, I don't. Look at him. He can hardly control
himself." Catherine stared at him for a moment
before showing her natural ability to laugh at
herself. "I know what a quiz I look like. I can only

rejoice that Aunt Clarice isn't here to see it. I knew I should have stayed upstairs."

Getting himself under control, Harwich seated her carefully, choosing a seat beside her for himself. By keeping his eyes on Mrs. Wilson, he kept his shoulders still.

"Miss Durrell, it's good to see you so . . ." And he then looked away hastily.

Catherine squared her shoulders. "So colorful?" She rose, forcing him to stand also.

"Colorful." He took a deep breath and glanced at her rather critically before asking Mrs. Wilson, "Do you watercolor?"

"Watercolor?" The widow was totally confused, but Catherine was not. She sat down hastily.

"Dominic Nicholas Reston, if you suggest such a thing, I'll—I'll . . ." she whispered.

"Never speak to me as long as I live. At least that's what you promised as a child," he reminded her in a low voice as he reseated himself, smiling broadly.

"I don't remember having this happen as a child."

"Oh, but I do. Maybe not quite as visibly," he added, remembering the time she had been thrown from her horse. He was amazed at himself. None of his friends in London would recognize him. In fact, he hardly recognized himself. "That is a becoming dress. The pelisse adds just the right touch," he added.

"Matches this blue-green on my neck, don't you think?" Catherine asked sotto vocco, baiting him.

"Please, Catherine. I'm trying. Leave me a little dignity," he whispered as he tried to subdue his laughter again.

Fortunately for both of them, the tea tray arrived. "Will you pour, Mrs. Wilson?" the earl asked politely. For a few minutes polite conversation about the weather, the lovely surroundings were all that was to be heard.

As soon as he thought it polite to do so, he asked Mrs. Wilson's permission to take Catherine on a walk through the gardens. The widow agreed, thinking what an attractive pair they made, his dark-brown hair blending close to the mahogany one. She sighed romantically. Had she heard what they were saying she might not have been so hopeful.

"Blast, you do look a sight, Catherine. Shall I have the doctor back with his leeches?" Harwich asked, his voice revealing his concern.

"No. I shall be perfectly fine shortly. In fact, if I wear a veil, I'm certain no one would notice."

"In a few days, perhaps."

"A few days? But I thought you planned to leave for England as soon as possible?" Catherine asked.

"It will not be possible to leave before our host arrives," Harwich reminded her.

"Bentiwick?" Harwich nodded, his face a mask. "And he's at the court of Mary Caroline in Palermo?"

The earl nodded again. "Thomas Abbot assured me that Lord Bentiwick will return as soon as possible."

Catherine looked at him curiously but could read nothing from his face. As the silence lengthened, the earl began to speak, but Catherine interrupted. "Yes. I know Aunt Clarice would be mortified at my manners, but I wanted you to know that I will help however I can."

"Help in what?" Harwich made his voice deliberately curious.

"Play by your own rules, Dominic, if you like. Just remember what I've said." She smiled up at him so sweetly that he felt an urge to kiss her, an urge he quickly repressed.

"Since Mrs. Wilson knows only the official story, we must return to her," Harwich explained as he led up the path toward the house.

"How did you find her?"

"Mrs. Wilson?" Catherine nodded, eyes golden brown in the sunlight. "Actually Abbot found her."

Their quiet voices signaled their return to the women waiting.

For the next two days, the routine varied little. Catherine was forced to spend the afternoon in the garden. Her guardians even permitted her to dine downstairs.

By the end of the second day, Catherine almost pulled Harwich down the walk away from her chaperone. "Dominic, you must find me something to do before I go mad. Mrs. Wilson won't let me read because of my injury. I can't even get close to the library." She pulled him around the corner and faced him squarely. "How would you like it if all you were permitted to do were to lie in bed or sew. Sew! Even Maria and Aunt Clarice knew better than that."

"And how am I to accomplish this? Remember she knows nothing of our background but what we've told her," he said quietly while watching her carefully. Lord, but she was lovely with her eyes flashing and bosom heaving.

"When is Bentiwick to return?"

He shrugged and said, "Any day now. Abbot had a message only yesterday explaining that it was impossible to leave the court at this time, but that situation could change any day."

"We could follow him there." Catherine looked up at him hopefully.

"No, but I have done some investigating." He paused and smiled down at her. "On the trip here you asked to go sight-seeing. I think that can be arranged." He watched happily as a warm smile lit her lips and her eyes.

"Taormina?"

"Messina, first."

And see Messina they did. Carefully chaperoned by an indulgent Mrs. Wilson and Davis and driven by Graves, they explored the piazzas and rabbit-warren streets of Messina. The first morning they spent investigating the mosaics of Messina's cathedral, built, as Harwich was quick to inform them, by Roger I in the twelfth century. Later they visited Angelo Mortarsoli's Orion Fountain and Calamech's statue of Don John of Austria. Just when Catherine was growing tired of churches, Harwich surprised her.

"Tomorrow Mrs. Wilson and I have arranged to go to Taormina. It means a donkey cart again and all day in the sun," Harwich hastened to add.

"Taormina," she breathed excitedly. "Oh, Dominic."

In spite of the donkey cart, Catherine enjoyed her time in the town established by the Greeks in the fourth century B.C. Sitting on the rocks of the theater and watching the smoke plume above Mount Etna, she shivered to think of hearing the works Sophocles or Euripides for the first time.

By the time the party wound its way through the narrow streets of Messina again, Catherine was exhausted, great purple shadows once again under her eyes. But she was happy. The formal man she had seen that first day in Italy was only a mask for the same warm person Dominic had been as a young man. She smiled at him as the cart pulled up to the Bentiwick villa and he dismounted from his horse to help them inside.

But that relaxed happiness disappeared a few minutes later as Thomas Abbot met them in the entrance hall. Bowing formally, he said quietly, "Lord Bentiwick has returned and wishes to see you as soon as possible, Lord Harwich."

4

His eyes regretful, Harwich bowed to Catherine, his hopes for a pleasant evening disappearing. "Tell Lord Bentiwick I will join him as soon as I have changed," he said quietly. "And, Abbot, if possible the ladies will dine in their suite tonight."

As he took the glass of sherry from his host some time later, Harwich watched the man cautiously. Although they had attended the same schools, Bentiwick was some years older than the earl. As a career diplomat who made his home wherever he was sent, he was something of an unknown quantity.

The older man took his seat across from his guest and studied him carefully. Andover had made a good choice for a representative. It was only too bad the earl favored Murat. "Tell me, Lord Harwich, what did you think of the King of Naples?" Lord Bentiwick asked, his face carefully bland.

"He's interested in holding on to what he has won even if it means deserting Napoleon," answered Harwich coolly.

"And you think England should agree if he will support us?"

Harwich looked the older man straight in his eyes. "That decision is not one that I am qualified to make. My job is merely to see that his offer reaches the Foreign Office."

The older man stared at him harshly for a moment and then asked, "And what is this story I have heard about Miss Durrell?"

For a moment the earl was nonplussed at the

sudden shift in conversation. "I found her beside the roadside. I believe Abbot wrote you about it."

"How strange." They both were silent for a moment. "Do you plan to return her to Italy?" the older man asked.

"No. She and her chaperone are to return to England. My escorts to Sicily promised to take word to her father. A reply came only yesterday," the earl answered, his usual social mask in place and his voice as disinterested as he could make it.

"You are sure this is Miss Durrell?"

"Certainly," the earl answered coolly without explanation.

Lord Bentiwick rose and crossed to the small table where the sherry sat. His back to the earl, he asked, "Can your party be ready to leave tomorrow afternoon?"

Harwich bit back a retort and smiled urbanely. "Certainly, Lord Bentiwick."

"I will send a message to the captain to expect you and the others. Would you care for more?" the older man asked, holding up the decanter.

"Thank you, no. If you will excuse me, sir, I need to speak to Mrs. Wilson and the servants."

"Shall you be joining me later for dinner?"

"With pleasure, sir." Harwich executed a sketchy bow and climbed the stairs to his rooms. Almost before the door had closed behind him, he said, "Graves, tell Mrs. Wilson and Miss Durrell I must see them at once—on the terrace, I think. You and Davis meet us there, too."

A short time later the small party gathered around a fountain chosen for its distance from overlooking windows. "We leave tomorrow," the earl said bluntly. "Listen for a moment, and then we can talk. Make certain you have warm clothes. If you need more, see if you can buy them tomorrow. Graves, you will be in charge of provisions. Spend as freely as you like. Are there any questions?"

A babble of voices filled the air. Finally Harwich said quietly, "You first, Mrs. Wilson."

"What type of ship are we sailing on? Will there be room for my goods?"

"Assume there will be. If not, I'll arrange for them to be shipped as soon as possible."

"Why tomorrow, Dominic, Lord Harwich?" Catherine asked, hastily trying to cover her mistake.

"Our host's suggestion. Are there any other questions?" As the group began to dissolve, the earl asked softly, "If you could stay for a moment, Mrs. Wilson?" He smiled at her kindly as she turned without protest.

"I know you are reluctant to leave Sicily," he said in a low voice.

"Not precisely, Lord Harwich," the widow said anxiously.

"Remember that whatever you need will be provided. There is a small house in Tunbridge Wells that I inherited from an aunt. I shall request my man of business to arrange for you to live there."

"No, my lord, you must not."

"Another place, perhaps. You are leaving the island as a favor to me. Allow me to see that you do not lose by this action," he said decisively.

"Let us talk again in England," the widow suggested, determined to make her own way if possible. They walked back toward the house. "When do we board tomorrow?"

"You will know as soon as I learn that," the earl promised. "I asked Abbot to have your evening meal served in your suite. Do you object?" Thankful that she could avoid a formal dinner, the woman shook her head.

While Harwich prepared for an evening with his host, the women were concerned with more practical measures. "How soon will we need our heaviest clothes?" Catherine asked as she and Davis sorted the few pieces of clothing they had brought with them and those that the earl had ordered as soon as they arrived.

The usually calm Mrs. Wilson was wringing her hands. "If only there were someone else to go with you," she moaned. "When we came to Sicily I promised myself I would never again sail except in June."

"Why?" the other two women asked, their eyes large.

"Oh, I just know it will be a miserable trip."

For Mrs. Wilson the trip was as bad as she had predicted. Even in the bright warmth of the mild breezes off Sicily, the lady suffered *mal de mer*. Huddled below in her cabin, she refused to see anyone but Davis until Catherine insisted that her maid needed some free time. After that, Catherine spent at least an hour in the morning and an hour in the afternoon attending her. The rest of the time she spent on deck with the earl.

For the first few days both he and Graves had watched her closely as if they expected her to collapse. She bloomed instead. Her hair, held back only by a ribbon, was rarely covered by the hood both Davis and the earl insisted she wear. And her skin glowed with health.

For the earl and Catherine it was a time of rediscovery. The first morning as they stood along the rail, the sails full of wind above them, Catherine turned to Harwich and said quietly, "Dominic, I wish to thank you for—"

"Any gentleman who had found you on that road would have done the same, Catherine," he interrupted. He shifted nervously.

"I wasn't talking about that, although I do appreciate it," she assured him, a soft smile lighting her eyes.

"Then what?" He turned toward her, a puzzled look on his face.

"For allowing me to tag along after you when I was a child."

"Allow? I couldn't stop you," he said with laughter in his voice.

"Don't gammon me, sir," she said, her laughter sparkling in her voice.

"Catherine, you wrong me." Harwich placed a hand theatrically on his heart, the other across his brow.

"Dominic Nicholas Reston . . ."

"Now you sound like my father when he discovered some new prank of mine." He turned to look out over the waves once more.

"Let me finish, sir," she demanded, stamping her foot.

"Now I know you are truly Catherine Dominque Durrell. I'd have recognized that foot stamp anywhere," he said laughingly.

"You certainly heard it often enough." She turned from watching the soft white waves on the blue-green sea to face him. "That is what I was trying to say. Thank you for sharing your summers with me." Her eyes were as golden as Harwich had ever seen them. "You could have ignored me or been cruel, but you weren't. Even after you went to the university, you found time to see me during the holidays. You were my hero." She tucked her arm into his as they began to stroll the area of deck they had been requested to remain within.

"Your hero?" Harwich asked, his face flushing slightly.

"Maybe hero isn't the right word," Catherine said thoughtfully before flashing him a mischievous smile, "although you did rescue me more times than I can count."

"Whatever happened to Horace?" the earl asked, trying to shift the conversation to something less embarrassing.

"He disappeared one winter. But he left his copies

behind." Catherine inspected him carefully from his brown hair, his chocolate-brown coat, and buff inexpressibles to his shining Hessians. "No, hero isn't quite right. I know; you became my measuring stick."

"Your what?"

"My idea of what a gentleman should be."

"Catherine, let it be." He shifted nervously. "Tell me about your work with your father."

"No, Dominic. This is important. You showed me a true gentleman cares for others, has a sense of humor, and is willing to listen to others' ideas. I imagine you are a wonderful father," she added softly.

Her companion swallowed hard and smiled briefly. "Now I must thank you," he said quietly. "But my daughter probably would disagree with your description." A bleak look erased his smile.

"What's wrong? Is there anything I can do?" Catherine asked anxiously.

Almost immediately the look was gone. "It is nothing," he assured her. "Tell me about the work you have been doing with your father."

The young Catherine would have demanded that he tell her everything. Now she simply gave him a thoughtful look and said, "Papa has always been interested in history, especially the Romans. He took a first at the university in Latin," she explained. "When Mama died, he decided to indulge himself a little."

For the next half-hour Catherine explained the work that her father and the other scholars were trying to do. Although Dominic was more interested in modern history, he listened fascinated as Catherine related discovering wine bottles still sealed and brilliant mosaics depicting the legends of Rome. When the bell sounded to mark the hour, Catherine started. "Davis. She probably thinks I have forgotten her. You should have stopped my chattering long ago." She paused and put a hand on his arm. "Thank you again."

As Harwich watched Catherine disappear into the passageway, he thought of her excitement as she described cataloging relics from a civilization long dead. "If only Marybeth had such an interest," he muttered, forgetting the age difference between them.

During the next few days Harwich and Catherine spent most of their time together either walking the deck or, when the weather was too rough, playing cards or chess in the officers' mess. From the first moment Catherine had seen the table there, she was fascinated by it with its rail and indentations to prevent the dishes from moving in rough weather. The farther they sailed from Sicily, the more she realized their practicality.

One day when the captain had declared the deck off limits to the passengers, she and Harwich were playing chess. As the pieces slid off the board again, Catherine said, "Oh, poor Mrs. Wilson."

"Poor Davis and Catherine might be more to the point," Harwich said dryly. "Why the woman didn't tell me the reason she didn't want to return to England was because she became seasick is very, very . . ."

"Irritating?" Catherine supplied. "If she had told you—and I'm not certain it was her only reason—would you have left her in Sicily?"

"No. But I would have hired someone to take care of her so that you didn't have to."

"Dominic, I simply sit with her, put lavender water on her temples. Davis does the difficult work."

"Then I should have hired someone to help Davis. Blast it! Why can't women be honest and open?"

"That's a question of a very cynical man," Catherine replied lightly, trying to change his mood.

"Not cynical, experienced," Harwich said bitterly. "Just wait until you get to London and see the ladies smiling at one another and then, when backs are turned, ripping one another apart. Damnation, they make me ill!''

"Are you saying that the ladies in London are the only ones that put on false fronts? Look again, your lordship. How many of your gentlemen friends enter bets in the betting books at White's that they, simply to win a bet, will manage to involve some innocent in their wiles?'' Catherine's voice was icy, her face stormy.

"Not as many as the women who set out to sell themselves to the highest bidder—caveat emptor!'' Harwich snapped, his usually handsome face twisted in anger.

Before she thought, Catherine said cuttingly, "Do you speak from experience, Lord Harwich?''

The earl stood up, his head almost touching the low ceiling. He glared at her and said in a voice too calm, "That, Miss Durrell, is none of your business.'' His shoulders straight, he stalked from the room.

For a few moments Catherine could only sit there stunned at her own words. He would never forgive her. But she had to try. Gathering up her skirts, she hurried into the passageway, but he was gone. When she knocked on his cabin door, Graves answered.

"He has probably gone on deck, miss,'' the groom assured her. "The captain has given him freedom of the bridge.''

That information made her feel even more terrible. He had been sitting inside amusing her instead of going on deck. She squared her shoulders and entered Mrs. Wilson's cabin. She would see him later.

As the storm grew wilder, both Davis and Catherine had all they could do to keep Mrs. Wilson comfortable. Even had the cabin boy not brought word that there would be only cold supper in their cabins, she knew she would not have left Davis with the woman alone.

In the days that the storm lasted and the captain requested they stay in their cabins, Catherine had many opportunities for self-analysis. Even though her infatuation for him was a thing of the past, she respected Harwich. And she wanted him to respect her. Only an apology and a full explanation would do. Having made her decision, Catherine waited impatiently for a chance.

When she received word that she could once more go topside, she wrapped her cloak about her and hurried on deck. On a ship as small as theirs, Harwich would be easy to find. To her consternation, he seemed to have vanished. By the end of the day, her frustration and anxiety had made her desperate.

During dinner with the captain and other officers, she conversed politely, smiled at the right times, and plotted. Harwich, sitting opposite her, looked at her coolly once or twice and continued his conversation with the first mate, ignoring the slight uneasiness he felt.

As she usually did, Catherine said good night and left the men to their port and their cigars. Before heading to her cabin, Catherine knocked on the earl's door. When Graves answered, she smiled at him. "The earl will be playing cards until late. He asked me to tell you to go to your cabin. He won't need you tonight," she said in a calm voice.

His cabin was lit by only one candle when Harwich entered some time later. Even after the second bottle of brandy he had polished off, he was fairly steady on his feet. He stripped off his neckcloth and slung it on a chair. "Mustn't tell Edwards how we treat these, Graves," he mumbled, shrugging out of his coat. He reached down to pull off a boot, became dizzy, and slumped down in the chair.

"Graves, have to help with the boots tonight," he slurred, his eyes closing.

A dark figure slipped from the berth and picked up one foot. The first boot slipped off fairly easily. The second took more effort. One final tug, a push from Harwich, and Catherine and the boot landed on the other side of the cabin. As soon as his foot touched softness, Harwich's eyes popped open.

"I think I might have gotten if off without help, but you did save me some effort," Catherine said grudgingly as she picked herself up and dusted herself off.

"You're not supposed to be here," the earl said disapprovingly.

"And I wouldn't be now if you hadn't kept hiding from me."

"My fault again?"

"No. Mine." Catherine lit the lamp that hung above the small table and sat down on the deck in front of him. She looked at him closely, as if trying to determine whether he would be able to understand her. She squared her shoulders, took a deep breath, and began. "This won't work again. Blast! I hope you can understand."

"Ladies don't say blast," her observer told her calmly. "Aren't I angry at you?"

"Yes, and you have a right to be. Dominic, I apologize. I said it before I thought. I know I was wrong. Can you forgive me?" Big tears welled up in her eyes, making them glisten in the lamplight. Before she could blink them away, one slipped down her cheek. Fascinated, Harwich watched it, his eyes following its path to her chin and the small white scar.

"Should have been more careful," he said, his voice less slurred.

"I know. A friend shouldn't hurt a friend."

"Not you. Me. Shouldn't have let Horace hurt you."

Catherine stared at him and then smiled. "Stand up, sir." As though he were a boy again, he obeyed. "Now come this way." A wry smile on her face, Catherine led him to his berth, settled him in, and just barely resisted dropping a kiss on his rumpled brown hair as he drifted off to sleep.

Blowing out the candle and the lamp, she slipped down the passageway into her own cabin.

The next morning Harwich stretched lazily, trying to ignore the ache in his head. Looking at his shirtsleeves, he sat up cautiously. He was still in his clothes. His boots lay in the corner of the cabin opposite the chair. The picture of Catherine dusting herself off assaulted him. It had been a dream, he convinced himself. He rose cautiously and picked them up, staring incredulously at a wisp of reddish-brown hair caught in one buckle.

Startled, he sat down and stared at his evidence. Some time later Graves entered with a tray. "Good morning, sir," he began, and then stopped in amazement. "Are you ill, your lordship?"

"Ill? Graves, find me some fresh clothes." He began stripping. "Have you seen Miss Durrell this morning?"

"Yes, sir. She was just coming out of Mrs. Wilson's cabin when I passed."

"Good. Knock at her door and ask her to meet me on deck in thirty minutes."

Catherine had been expecting the summons. As she wrapped herself in her cloak, she rehearsed her speech once more. Fearing that her nerve would fail her, she hurried on deck to stand in a protected corner.

When Harwich arrived a short time later, he found her close by the passageway, her face somber and her bright eyes dark with worry.

"Catherine, why did you do it?" he asked.

She didn't pretend to misunderstand what he meant. "It was the only way I could think of to talk to you alone. I couldn't go on as we were."

"But if you'd been seen?"

"I wasn't. Dominic, I didn't mean what I said. Please believe me," she pleaded.

"It was as much my fault as it was yours. I had no right to attack poor Mrs. Wilson that way," he said somberly.

"Shall we agree to disagree, then?" she asked.

He took her arm as they strolled around the deck. For a few minutes all was silence. Catherine was about to rephrase her question when he answered. "No. Do you want to talk about it?"

"No. Yes." Catherine stopped and stood looking at the waves, her hands gripping the rails so tightly.

"I don't understand," the earl said quietly, watching as she shivered and then swung back to face him.

"All the time I was in Italy I was safe," she began. "No one knew what had happened. There was no one to laugh at me."

"Laugh at you?"

She nodded and continued. "Oh, Dominic, when I went to London after Mama died, I was such a child. And Aunt Clarice made certain I remained one. She shipped me off to a seminary in Bath as soon as Papa had left the country. And there I would have remained had he not written that he was coming to London to see me. How I wish she had left me there." Harwich looked at her surprised by the bitterness in her voice. "That Season she brought me out. This was what I had been trained for." She looked at him and smiled ruefully. "You even had your part in it."

"Me? How?"

"The man I was going to marry had to be just like you." She looked at him somberly. "Very few men measured up to my memories. But finally I found one. It was toward the end of the Season. Papa had once again written postponing his visit. For once I wasn't crushed by the news. I had met the man. He was everything I hoped for, dreamed about." For a few minutes she was silent, staring out to sea.

"What happened?" the earl asked gently, his face concerned.

"He was a 'friend' of my aunt's." Catherine paused once more and swallowed hard. "They had a bet—a diamond necklace against a matched pair of grays— that he could compromise me without marrying me. And he did." She smiled at the shocked look on his face. "Oh, don't worry. He only stole a few kisses. My aunt saw to that."

Catherine looked like an old woman hunched over the rail. "I suppose she thought if I married, Papa might cut off the generous allowance he made her." Her voice was sad. "When we were discovered in an anteroom at the ball, Aunt Clarice simply laughed. Saying that young girls should know better than to believe handsome soldiers, she laughed at my distress. With no family to help me, I became the laughingstock of London. That's when Davis and I came to Italy."

Ready to face his scorn, Catherine looked into his face and saw there a bleak anger. Before she could turn away, he had swept her into his warm embrace and whispered in her ear, "How could she? Oh, Catherine? Why didn't you come to me? I would have helped you."

His sympathy when she expected anger destroyed Catherine's reserve. The tears she had so successfully held back for so long gushed forth, soaking Harwich's shoulder. Almost as if he were comforting his daughter, he held Catherine closely, letting her cry.

Her sobs almost gone, Catherine leaned weakly against Harwich, her cheek pillowed on his chest, listening to the beat of his heart. It felt so right to have his arms around her, to feel his breath on her hair. Without realizing it, she took a step closer. She listened in amazement as his heartbeat increased.

Suddenly Harwich realized that he was no longer holding Catherine to comfort her. His arms were wrapped around her, molding her to him. Startled, he dropped his arms and took two steps back.

Watching her stiffen her shoulders, he tilted her chin, forcing her to look at him. Her sparkling eyes still filled with tears were confused. "And yet, you still trusted me," he said, smiling wryly. When a sailor winked as he walked by, Harwich brushed the last tears from her cheeks. "Perhaps we should continue this dicussion belowdecks," he suggested, drawing her hand through his arm.

5

As they walked down the narrow passageway to the officers' mess, Harwich stopped for a moment. "You said your aunt made the bet." Catherine nodded. The gloom of the narrow hallway was too dark for her to see his face clearly, but she knew he was frowning. "Is she the aunt with whom you are to stay?" he asked, his voice concerned.

"Yes." Catherine seemed calm, although she was shaking on the inside.

"I won't have it. You must stay with me," he said firmly, his hand at her back guiding her toward their destination. To their surprise the room they had so frequently had to themselves was not empty. After greeting the captain and the first and second mates, who were poring over charts, Harwich and Catherine walked back into the passageway. For a moment they looked at each other in confusion. Then Harwich took the lead once more.

He paused in the corridor outside their cabins, reluctant to let her go. Reviewing their recent history, he asked quietly, "Will our reputations be totally destroyed if we talk together in one of our cabins?"

"Alone?" Catherine's heart raced.

His suggestion startled Harwich as much as it did Catherine. For a man adept at avoiding society's displeasure or gossip, he had to admit he was acting peculiarly.

"You are right. It would never do," he said, not realizing how evident his disappointment was. They stood there for a moment just looking at each other.

"My cabin is across from Mrs. Wilson's," Catherine paused and then hurried on as if afraid of what she was saying, "and if we left both doors open somewhat . . ."

"Davis and Mrs. Wilson could serve as our chaperones." Harwich smiled down at her proudly.

A few minutes later, their chairs carefully arranged in front of the open door, they sat awkwardly, aware of Davis' watchful eye as she sat sewing while Mrs. Wilson slept.

"Catherine, my dear," Harwich began, still slightly unsure of himself, a situation none of his acquaintances would have believed. For some reason she couldn't explain, Catherine's heart was pounding. She was certain he could hear it clearly. He cleared his throat nervously. "Catherine, you cannot stay with that woman. I forbid it."

Her eyebrows rose, but her voice was quiet. "I have no choice. Yes, I know you meant what you said about staying with you. But how would we explain it?" She continued, refusing to give him a chance to speak, "Dominic, I'm older now and, I hope, wiser. Besides, I shall be in London only a short time. I plan to make my home at the Grange."

The Grange was close enough for him to keep an eye on her, he told himself firmly. Yet the thought of her aunt made him livid. He stood up and began pacing the narrow cabin. "Why didn't you tell your father? Then you wouldn't be in this situation. If I were to find out that this had happened to Marybeth, I would have called the man out," he said angrily. "Your father had a right to know!"

Catherine sat there quietly, watching him pace back and forth. "He was in Italy. By the time I reached him, there was nothing he could have done." Her calm voice was at odds with the nervousness she felt.

"Are you still in love with him?" Harwich asked suddenly, staring down at her.

"No," she said sadly. "Dreams don't last when the reality is so ugly."

"What will you do if you see him again?"

"Ignore him. But I doubt if I shall."

"Why?" Harwich took his seat in front of her again and took her hands in his.

"I don't plan to go into society," she said quietly, her eyes on his hands. They were so strong. "My little 'adventure' has probably become a moral lesson for all young ladies to beware of."

Harwich sat back in his chair, releasing her hands. "No, all they're teaching young ladies today is how to dress well, to smile prettily, and to marry for the sake of family. My own daughter hasn't a thought in her head but clothes and flirting." He slammed his hand against the table and then was slightly surprised when it stung. "All she is is a pretty widgeon instead of the sensible little girl I love."

"How old is she, Dominic?"

"Fifteen." His tone made it sound as though it were forty-five.

Catherine smiled and patted his hand in sympathy. "At fifteen, clothes and one's future husband are all important. It's part of the growing process," she assured him.

He shook his head, not at all satisfied with her reply. "If that were all. Catherine, before I left for Vienna she told me not to worry about the succession because I would have grandsons as soon as she married. Good grief, Catherine, where does she get these ideas?" He ran his hand through his dark hair. "She is already planning to make me a grandfather."

Catherine could only watch, stunned, as he resumed his pacing. "It is all Agnes' fault," he said angrily. "I'm not ready to be a grandfather."

"Who is Agnes?" Catherine asked cautiously.

"Agnes Throckmorton, a distant cousin. My family decided that Marybeth needed a woman's guidance in social matters. I was doing nothing to find her a stepmother, my aunt reminded me. Agnes seemed the best of the lot." He smiled bitterly.

Before Catherine could reply, Graves was at the door. "The captain wishes to see you at your convenience, your lordship," he said quietly. Harwich nodded and watched him leave.

Catherine, her eyes dark with concern, walked over to him. "I need to sit with Mrs. Wilson now," she said, easing her words with a smile. "You find out what the captain wants."

He nodded his agreement and turned to leave, slightly embarrassed by his own revelations. "Will you join me on deck later?" he asked somberly, standing just inside the door.

"Of course." Catherine watched until he had disappeared, her emotions still in turmoil. What had she done? Suddenly she was exhausted. The emotional highs and lows of their discussions had drained her. Resolutely, she crossed the passageway, pulling her cabin door closed behind her.

As Catherine slipped into her chaperone's cabin, Davis looked up from the sewing she had concentrated on since she heard Graves' message. The lamplight cast shadows on her mistress's pale skin, giving her a haunted look. "You need to go on deck, Miss Catherine," Davis tried to insist.

Catherine, however, refused to listen. "I've already been up this morning. It's your turn now. How is our patient this morning?"

"Better. She drank some tea before she went to sleep a short time ago." Davis asked again, "Let me stay with her. I need to finish this. I'll go on deck later."

Catherine shook her head, gathered Davis' cloak, and smiled faintly. "You are not to return for at least an hour or longer," she said firmly, ushering her maid to the door. "You need fresh air to get the color into your cheeks."

"Little good it's done for you," Davis muttered as she walked briskly up the passageway in search of Graves.

As Catherine closed the door, her chaperone awoke, moaning slightly. Hurrying to her side, Catherine asked softly, "What may I get for you?"

"Nothing," Mrs. Wilson said weakly. "I'm sorry to be such a burden to you. How will I ever face Lord Harwich again? I have let him down completely." Her voice was worried.

"You simply lie there and get better. Lord Harwich understands," Catherine assured her as she held out a damp cloth so that Mrs. Wilson could freshen her face. As soon as that had been completed, Catherine sat beside the berth, a cup of tea in her hands. One sip at a time she persuaded Mrs. Wilson to drink an entire cup. Smiling her encouragement, Catherine fluffed her pillow, helped her change her gown, and smoothed her bed.

"So kind," the older woman murmured as she drifted off to sleep once more.

It takes such a little effort to be kind to others. Catherine thought as she placed a damp cloth freshened with lavender water on Mrs. Wilson's forehead. She settled back in her chair, picking up the needlework she kept at hand. If everyone were as kind as Dominic . . . Dominic? How was she going to face him after her disclosure that morning? He had been so kind, but now that he had had a chance to think about it, she was certain he would be shocked. "How could I be so lost to modesty?" she asked quietly.

"What? Do you need me?" mumbled Mrs. Wilson in a daze.

"I'm sorry I disturbed you. Go back to sleep." Catherine soothed her.

A short time later Davis returned, her cheeks

bright from the wind and the crisp salt air. "Lord
Harwich is on deck and asks that you join him, Miss
Catherine," she said as she hung her cloak on a peg.
"Yo go along and leave Mrs. Wilson with me."

Slowly Catherine made her way to her cabin and
up to the deck. Her fears were confirmed when she
glimpsed Harwich's scowl.

Seeing her, he hurried to her side. "Catherine, the
most annoying news," he said angrily.

The heaviness Catherine felt lifted a little.
"News?"

"From my talk with the captain. Instead of sailing
straight to England, we must stop at Gibraltar."

"Why?"

"The man won't say. Come walk with me." He
slipped her arm under his and began to prowl the
deck.

"Wait. Your legs are longer than mine," she was
finally forced to say, almost breathless from trying
to keep up.

Abashed, the earl stopped. "I'm sorry. When I lose
my temper, I usually like to walk it off. I forget you
don't walk as fast as I do."

"Nor do I have as long legs," she reminded him and
then blushed at breaking another taboo. When his
expression changed to a smile, she started to breathe
again. "Dominic, why are you angry? At longest, it
will only delay our journey a few days."

"A few days too many." Before he said anything
else, he caught himself. He asked quietly, "How is
Mrs. Wilson?"

"Somewhat better. The stop in Gibraltar will be
just what she needs." Catherine looked up at the tall,
handsome man at her side and asked, "Dominic,
what were you doing in Italy?" As she watched his
eyebrows rise, she hastened to rephrase her
question. "No, that's not right. Why did you decide to
come to Italy?"

He didn't pretend to misunderstand this time. He

dropped her arm and turned toward the rail. He leaned over it, his shoulders hunched together. "I had to get away from the *ton*, from the constant hammering of my family."

"Your family?" As a child, Catherine had envied him his numerous cousins, uncles, and aunts.

"This last year they have been a trial to me, and I to them, I suppose," he added honestly. "This Season they almost drove me mad. I cannot count the number of times I have been asked to dine, to go to the opera or to a musicale, only to discover that one of my aunts or cousins had invited me only as an escort for a pretty, young thing making her first bow to society." His face wore the darkest frown Catherine had ever seen.

"You mean they have been trying to marry you off again?" Catherine asked, trying to hide her amusement at the thought of Dominic forced by his own good manners to be polite to a girl little older than his daughter.

"Yes, blast it." He turned to look at her. "I had to get away. Maybe I should be pleased that we're going to Gibraltar. At least it postpones another round of new faces," he said bitterly.

"Why is this happening now? Even during my Season, your name was mentioned as a disinterested eligible," Catherine asked curiously.

Neither of them considered the strangeness of their conversation. It was as though they were children again, being honest as only children usually are. Dominic ran his hand through his wind-rumpled hair and leaned back on the rail to face Catherine. His face was grave. "My heir, my cousin John, was wounded last winter. He's recovered somewhat, but the doctors feel his recovery will be extended. Even then, they cannot promise completely restored health. He doesn't want my responsibilities and his too. Therefore, he asked me to consider marrying again."

"What good would that do? He still would be your heir." No sooner were the words out of her mouth than Catherine wished she could recall them. Her face glowed like the sunset. She whirled around, her back toward him.

"Catherine, Catherine." He laughed. "Sometimes you seem no older than you were when you asked the squire why he kissed pretty girls so much. Aren't you going to talk to me again? Come, look at me." He swung her around, his hands clasping her waist. For a moment they stared into each other's eyes before awkwardly stepping back. After a moment, Harwich once more offered his arm and they began to stroll the deck again.

She cleared her throat and asked, her voice still trembling, "What happened? You said you only discussed the matter with your cousin?"

"Somehow, I'm not certain how, his mother found out and the entire family was after me to make certain of the succession."

"The succession. Yes. Did Marybeth hear any of this?"

"I don't know. Why would anyone—"

"If she spent any time with her cousins or aunts, I'm certain she must have heard something. Don't you see, Dominic? That's the reason for her concern over providing you with an heir."

"She can't . . . they couldn't . . ." he sputtered, anger in every line of his body.

"Your relatives probably did very little. I'm sure Marybeth made the decision on her own. Not many older women are going to discuss a subject like that openly before a young girl."

"You don't know my aunts or Agnes," he declared, still angry.

"Haven't you discussed the issue with Marybeth?"

"Catherine, since Agnes joined my household, I've hardly seen my daughter alone. I'm not going to discuss that subject when that woman is present."

"Dominic Nicholas Reston, I'm ashamed of you," Catherine said firmly but sadly.

"What?" He turned to stare at her. "How can this be my fault?"

"You're a man used to making decisions. Yet you've allowed some . . . some cousin, to tell you how to behave with your daughter. Didn't you ever wonder about what Marybeth thought was happening?" The more she thought of his daughter, the angrier Catherine became.

"Before Agnes came, we discussed the need for a woman to guide her," Harwich explained, slightly confused by the way the conversation was proceeding. "Marybeth thought it was a wonderful idea."

"And then you practically desert her." Catherine looked at him with reproach in her golden-brown eyes.

"Blast it, Catherine. I did no such thing. I saw her every day," Harwich tried to defend himself.

Catherine simply smiled sadly, remembering the day when her father's letter had arrived. As much as she cared for Maria now, she had felt so alone when the news of their marriage had arrived. She blinked away her tears and said angrily, "Then you should have discussed your remarriage with her."

"I will. I promise I will as soon as we get home," the earl said quietly, trying to wipe away the sorrow he saw in Catherine's eyes. As the winds rose and became cooler, they went below. Neither, however, could forget their discussion.

As Harwich changed his neckcloth, he couldn't forget how sad Catherine had looked. He remembered, too, the look on Marybeth's face when he told her he was leaving England for a time. She had clung to him so tightly, tears streaming down her face. His reaction to those tears made him cringe. She had looked so adult as she stepped back, trying to show that she could be brave. His letters to her from Vienna and Messina had been few, a line or two when he wrote his agent.

Before he had a chance to change his mind, he sat down at the table and began a letter to her. Without thinking of what he should say, he allowed his words to flow, telling his daughter about his love for her and his pride in the fact that she was his daughter. Even the question of the succession didn't seem as difficult to explain as he feared. Without reading it again, he sanded it and sealed it quickly. Franking it, he laid it on his desk ready to send to her when they arrived at Gibraltar. He sat back, stretched, and felt the glow of satisfaction.

Catherine, too, was thinking about their conversation that afternoon. But the more she thought, the more confused she became. Dominic had promised to marry again, but he had run away from his family's attempts to provide him with a wife. After she once more forced Davis into the open air, talked quietly with Mrs. Wilson, who managed to drink a cup of soup that Davis helped the cook prepare, and then returned to her cabin, Catherine's head ached. Giving up her struggle, she took a nap.

As she and Harwich walked on deck that evening, he poured out his news. "Telling her about my need to remarry wasn't as difficult as I thought it would be," he explained.

Catherine pulled the hood of her olive-green cape over her head, trying to prevent the soft sea wind from whipping her curls. She smiled at Harwich, encouraging him to go on as she fought to control her hair and the ties of her cloak.

"Here, let me," he said, laughing. He pulled her into a protected corner.

Turning her to face him, her back to the wind, he carefully tucked the last tendrils of her hair inside her hood, letting his hand softly caress her cheek.

Catherine, her eyes golden in the light of a lantern

that hung close by, looked at him nervously, afraid of her emotions. The lantern cast a glow about her head, highlighting her reddish-brown hair framed by dark material. Harwich tied her cloak, noting as he had earlier in the evening how lovely she looked in the simple golden muslin she was wearing. Almost without realizing what he was doing, he bent his head and kissed her softly, his hands resting lightly on her shoulders. Both kiss and embrace deepened as she responded. Her arms circled his neck while his pressed her closely against him. Her lips parted, following his lead. Pulling her even closer to him, he let his lips wander, nibbling her ear, breathing how sweet and warm she was. He kissed her again, his tongue taking liberties she had never dreamed of, his hands sliding up to cup her breasts. She started but then relaxed. His kisses drugged her and she unconsciously pressed her body to his.

Above them, the ship's bell signaled the change of watch. Startled, Catherine sprang back. She gasped, realizing what she had done. Her eyes wide and full of despair, she whirled and was down the passageway before the earl could stop her.

A few minutes later, he scratched at her door. "Catherine," he called. His voice only made her cry harder.

6

Until they reached Gibraltar late the next afternoon, Catherine stayed in her cabin or in Mrs. Wilson's, refusing to talk to Harwich or even to listen to the messages Graves tried to deliver. Both Davis and her chaperone ignored her eyes and unhappy face.

For Catherine, her actions with Harwich were simply proof of what her aunt had said: she was a loose woman who was unsuitable for society. When she thought of the way she had allowed him to kiss her and, worse than that, had kissed him back, she was appalled. Ladies did not behave like that.

When the ship dropped anchor, Catherine had decided to stay on board. For once, Mrs. Wilson absolutely refused. "The Earl of Harwich has arranged for rooms at one of the finest inns in Gibraltar, and we shall accept his invitation. Land, at last," Mrs. Wilson rejoiced. "And a bath in fresh water."

"Cream for our tea," Davis added. "And fresh bread."

"Come, Catherine. Davis has already packed a few things. The rest we'll leave on board." The thought of sleeping on land once more had given the older woman renewed strength.

As he and Graves handed the women into the carriage they had hired, Harwich tried to force Catherine to acknowledge him. Other than a quick thank-you, she kept her eyes lowered and stayed silent. The presence of others effectively prevented any discussion. But that state would not last long, Harwich promised himself. With the letter to Marybeth already sent and the thought of London looming before him, he was beginning to formulate a plan.

That evening, after hot baths, the ladies dined alone in the private parlor Harwich had reserved. While Mrs. Wilson contented herself with a clear soup and an omelet, Catherine, always willing to try something new, had paella. The combination of saffron rice, chicken, and seafood had interesting hints of spices she could not identify. "No, no more," she said quietly as the maid presented the pan once more for her pleasure. "Davis was right. That was extraordinary."

"I think you shocked the innkeeper when you asked for it," Mrs. Wilson laughed.

"Did you see his face? I wonder if it was to be his dinner?"

"If so, there is still enough left." Mrs. Wilson's face grew somber. "Miss Durrell, I apologize for my illness. It must have placed you in an embarrassing situation." Ignoring Catherine's protests, she continued, "If there is anything you wish me to know, please do not hesitate. After you and Davis cared for me, I feel I am in your debt." She hesitated, but not long enough for Catherine to speak. "I regret that you and Lord Harwich have had words. Please let me help."

Catherine's reply was just what her chaperone expected—a smiling refusal.

As Catherine slipped her sprigged muslin off her shoulders and prepared for bed, she blushed again as she thought of his warm lips and hands. Although she tried to be practical, to convince herself that she would forget him as soon as she returned to England, she knew she was only hiding the truth. She loved him—not with the infatuation of her childhood but with a love that made her blood sing and her mind reel. Her last thoughts as she drifted off to sleep were of him.

Her night in a comfortable bed did much to heal her spirits. As Davis laid out her clothes for the day, Catherine smiled and stretched, almost missing the message Harwich had sent. "What did you say?" she asked quietly.

"His lordship asked you to meet him for luncheon and seeing the sights. He will send for you as soon as he pays a call on the commander." Davis paused for a moment, holding up a dress. "Will this be suitable for today, Miss Catherine?"

Catherine glanced at the dress, a jade-green walking dress and pelisse her maid had completed on the voyage from Italy. "Certainly, Davis," she said, smiling her delight. "However did you manage this?" she asked as she ran her hand over the intricate ivory braid that bordered the cuffs and hem of her pelisse.

"I discovered it in Messina, Miss Catherine, when Lord Harwich sent me to purchase more clothes for us. And I have some elegant lace to trim a ball gown for you to wear in London," she explained, her face glowing with pride.

A few moments later a scratching sounded at the door and Mrs. Wilson entered. "How lovely you look this morning. What a clever choice. Although the sunshine is bright, the day is cool," she told Catherine. "Will you be warm enough?"

"I hope so." She smiled at her chaperone and asked, "Have you been to Gibraltar before?"

"We stopped here on our way to Sicily. It's an interesting place."

Catherine was startled by the sad look on the older woman's face. "Are you ill, Mrs. Wilson?" she asked, her voice concerned.

"No, no, my dear. I am much better," her chaperone assured her. "It's just—"

"What? May I help?"

"My husband was en route to Gibraltar with Sir John Stuart when he developed a fever and died."

"Oh, my dear, what memories this must bring back." Catherine was horrified to realize the strain the older woman must have been under. Davis, too, drew in a quick breath of sympathy.

"No, no, Miss Durrell. I am fine. In fact, now that we are here, Lord Harwich has promised to talk to the commander about my husband's personal effects," she said in a voice that although not happy was calm and quiet.

Catherine and Davis exchanged a quick look, each determining to do her best to keep the widow occupied. "Tell me what we can expect to see, since you know more about the place than we do," Catherine urged.

"I wasn't allowed off the ship. We only stopped to deliver some information from the Foreign Office," the older woman explained. Then her face lit up as she smiled. "But some of the officers' wives have told me that there is an interesting market where one can shop without spending vast sums."

"Shopping," Catherine said happily. "I wonder if Dominic has brought a present for Marybeth?"

"Dominic?"

"Lord Harwich," Catherine explained. "After our adventure, it seemed rather natural."

"And Marybeth is his wife?" Mrs. Wilson asked, trying not to let her worry show in her voice.

"His daughter," Catherine said, smiling. "And her father's darling, if his remarks about her are any measure of his affection."

"And Lady Harwich?" the older woman asked almost too casually, trying to remember if he had mentioned a wife when he had hired her.

Without realizing what she was revealing, Catherine replied, "She died shortly before my mother, about ten years ago. He had already spent more time back in London before I had my Season."

Mrs. Wilson looked at her charge thoughtfully
before saying firmly, "Well, we must be certain to
remind him that his daughter would enjoy a little
remembrance. Men sometimes forget what even the
smallest of gifts can mean."

A few minutes later Mrs. Wilson watched Davis pin
the last tendril of Catherine's hair into place and
settle on her curls her one bonnet, a plain straw
decorated to match her dress with jade and ivory
ribbons.

"We must not keep Lord Harwich waiting much
longer," she urged Catherine. "Graves said luncheon
would be ready shortly."

Picking up her reticule, Catherine followed Mrs.
Wilson from the room. At least Dominic was willing
to keep up appearances, she thought.

During the luncheon—a delicious fish poached in
wine with a salad of oranges and almonds for the
ladies and a heartier fare for Harwich—Catherine
smiled when she talked, which was seldom. But her
eyes refused to meet his. She allowed him to hand
her into the carriage he had ordered to show them
the sights, but she made certain the touch was light.
As they drove around the more-than-two-miles-
square rock, she sat in her corner of the seat, her
eyes firmly fixed on the narrow roads and buildings
that reflected the Moorish influence.

When they arrived at the castle, once a Moorish
palace but now used to house the commandant of the
fortress, Harwich's patience was at its end. When
Mrs. Wilson was stopped by an older officer, a friend
of her husband's, the earl took advantage of her
inattention to sweep Catherine into an alcove
looking over the garden.

"No, please don't turn away." He grabbed her arm
and held her lightly but firmly in place. In spite of all
his efforts, she still refused to look at him.
"Catherine, are you angry at me?" Harwich asked.

"What?" She lifted her head and looked at him in

surprise, the soft straw and ribbons making a lovely frame to her mahogany-colored hair, her eyes wide. "I know I shouldn't have taken advantage of you that way. Please say you'll forgive me."

"Forgive you? Dominic, I was afraid you would be appalled at my behavior," Catherine said, her voice breathy.

"These last two days? You've thought I was . . . ?" Before Harwich, stunned, could finish his thought, Mrs. Wilson and her escort had discovered them, the older woman's eyes narrowing as she looked about for the two servants, finding them standing under a window farther down the hallway.

"Are you ready to go, Miss Durrell?" Mrs. Wilson asked, her voice rather cool. She took the earl's arm, leaving the officer to escort Catherine. Stoically Harwich walked toward the carriage, a pleasant smile on his face and his shoulders even straighter than usual. "I understand you have a daughter?" Mrs. Wilson continued. "Perhaps our next stop should be at the market so that you may purchase her a little trinket."

Although Harwich agreed, his only thought was to get Catherine to himself once more. Why had he hired this busybody? he wondered impatiently as she continued to ask him questions about his daughter. Then the tiniest of smiles tilted the corners of his mouth. He had hired her to act just as she was doing.

As Catherine and Mrs. Wilson went from stall to stall, exclaiming over the beautiful leather goods and silk lace shawls, Harwich followed, managing at one stall to whisper in Catherine's ear, "Meet me in the parlor downstairs after Mrs. Wilson retires to rest."

Her nod gave him hope, and he turned his attention to the shawl she was holding. "Is this too old for Marybeth?" Catherine asked, displaying a white silk shawl.

"How old is she?" Mrs. Wilson asked.

"Fifteen," the two voices answered almost as one.

Her eyes going briefly from Harwich's amused face to Catherine's embarrassed one, Mrs. Wilson revealed nothing of the doubt that troubled her. "Somewhat, perhaps. But there are occasions when she dines with you?" she asked, her eyes boring into Harwich's face.

"Yes."

"She could wear it then. Or she could put it away for her coming-out." The older woman turned to Catherine. "Did you notice that exquisite lace over there? I believe I must have some if it isn't too dear. It is just the thing for afternoon gowns, don't you think?"

Until the market closed for siesta, Mrs. Wilson was exactly where custom dictated she should be, between Catherine and Harwich. Their shopping finished, they returned to the inn, where a sailor was waiting. "We sail on the evening tide," Harwich explained to the women, who had gone ahead to the parlor. Mrs. Wilson, who had regained most of her color on her day on shore, paled.

"The captain asks that we be on board by seven. I recommend we all get some rest before an early supper."

At the thought of food, Mrs. Wilson's face turned a pale shade of green. Shepherding Catherine before her, she hurried to her room, too disturbed at the thought of going back to sea to catch Harwich's unspoken question and Catherine's answer.

A few minutes later, Catherine slipped into the parlor once more, her face slightly worried. "If Mrs. Wilson looks for me . . ." she said unhappily.

"We'll decide what to say when it happens," Harwich reassured her, taking her hand. "We have to talk." He seated her in the room's only comfortable chair and pulled a stool over so that he could face her.

For a minute neither knew what to say. As their silence grew, Harwich leaned forward, his eyes fixed on the tip of Catherine's tongue as it moistened her lips. Pulling himself back, he broke the silence.

"Thank you for your help this afternoon."

"I hope your daughter likes her gift," Catherine said formally, wondering at Harwich's manner. He was clenching and unclenching his right hand, and he kept swallowing.

Rising from his seat, Harwich began pacing, trying to put his feelings into words. As he walked around the room, he watched Catherine, her eyes growing dark and wary. As the tension mounted again, he made one last circuit and then returned to sit in front of her.

Taking her hand, he said in a single breath, "Blast it, Catherine. We're friends. Marry me."

She blinked and then blinked again. "What?"

"Marry me. We've been getting along well these last few weeks, and we have known each other for years."

"Not really. Until last month you hadn't thought of me in years." Catherine looked at him straight in the eyes. "Tell me the truth, Dominic."

He ran a finger beneath the neckcloth, which now felt like it was choking him. "It is true. I hadn't thought of you in years," he admitted, shifting nervously on his stool.

"And if you hadn't been forced into it by my father, I wouldn't be with you today."

"But that's not the issue," he protested, standing up and pulling her up in front of him. "During the weeks we've spent together, we have been able to talk to each other much as we did as children. Wouldn't life be easier if we had someone to talk to, someone who understood us?" he said, resisting the temptation to pull her into his arms and kiss her until she agreed.

Her heart pounding so hard she was afraid that Harwich would hear, Catherine pulled her hands free and crossed the room, hoping to be able to think more clearly there. Unconsciously she rolled the hem of her pelisse in her fingers. "Marriage isn't just talk, Dominic," she said. Although she didn't realize it, her eyes were wistful.

"So marriage isn't just talk," he said teasingly, running his fingers down her cheek. "Tell me about marriage."

"Stop making fun of me," she said angrily, hurt because he seemed to be making a mockery of her dreams. "Why are you offering to marry me when you ran from a Season of lovelies? I suppose you feel obligated to after our evening." She turned her back, staring into the embers in the smoldering fireplace.

"If I didn't feel obligated in Italy, why should that change now simply because of a few kisses?" He smiled at her warmly as she swung around indignantly. "That's all they were, Catherine—kisses." His eyes took on a definite hungry look. "As kisses go, they were rather spectacular," he admitted, smiling down at her. His blue eyes refused to let her drop hers.

Taking a deep breath that made Harwich's heart beat faster, Catherine asked, "Why?"

"Why were the kisses spectacular?" he asked, laughing.

"No, why should we marry?"

Harwich guided her back to her chair once more. "Are you looking forward to living with your Aunt Clarice?"

"Not, but . . ." she began, once more rolling and unrolling the edge of her pelisse.

"I don't relish being the focus of every matchmaking mother's scheme. Besides, most of those girls are almost as young as my daughter. What should I say, 'Look, Marybeth, I've married someone you can play with?' "

"Be fair, Dominic. There's a vast gulf between fifteen and eighteen."

"Only in the eyes of society. Catherine, I took that

route once. We were babies playing at being adults. Within three years I had a daughter and a wife who lived only for pleasure. Are you going to condemn me to that again?" he asked bitterly.

"But you're older now," she tried to reason with him. "You'd know better how to go on."

"If my bride were that young, she would drive me insane." He held her hands tightly, leaning forward. His eyes pleaded with her. "I need someone to talk to. I need you, Catherine."

Before she knew what was happening, he was in the chair and she was on his lap. As he covered her face with kisses, he whispered, "Marry me, Catherine. Rescue me from this boredom." He skillfully unbuttoned the first few buttons on her pelisse, leaving her neck bare for further exploration. She gasped as his lips created sensations she had never dreamed of.

Her arms wrapped around his neck, she cradled his head. Then she pulled back suddenly, surprising him. "You're not doing this out of pity, are you?" she asked in a prim voice.

"Pity?"

"Because I told you what happened during my Season?"

"Catherine, that was eight years ago. This is now. Feel!" He grabbed her hand and put it on his heart. "Feel that. That's what being close to you does to me." He watched with delight as her eyes turned an amber gold. Her face wore a look of surprised happiness. He reached out both hands and pulled her against him, her head nestling between his neck and shoulder. "Sometimes I can hardly breathe, my heart is beating so hard," he whispered in her ear. "Marry me?"

Her ability to reason was fast disappearing under his warm lips and stroking hands. Catherine made one last attempt. "What about your family? Won't they resent me?"

"Why?"

"Dominic, you must admit that in marrying me you'll be marrying beneath you."

"Beneath me. What a wonderful idea," he said suggestively and nibbled at her ear.

Catherine pushed him away. "Why is it so wonderful? I'd like to know, and so will they."

Realizing that she had misunderstood him, Harwich stood up, taking her with him. He swung her around so that her eyes were level with his. "They will be so happy to see me married that they won't object. Besides, you'll be a countess and outrank most of them. Give them one of those frosty looks of yours, and you'll do nicely," he assured her as he stood her on her feet. "Besides, we'll get right to work on the problem of the succession, won't we?" he said, smiling down at her.

This time Catherine couldn't miss his meaning. She considered his question seriously. If only he had told her he had loved her. He had been honest; he wanted someone to talk to, a son, and peace from his relatives. She drew a deep breath and looked up at him confused.

"Marry me, Catherine?" he asked again quietly, stepping back and dropping his hands.

So softly that he didn't hear the word but only saw it form on her lips, Catherine said, "Yes." She breathed a prayer that it was the right choice.

The next moment she was back in his arms, held close to him. Her arms curled around his shoulders while his pressed her even closer. For a time the world was forgotten.

Finally Dominic took a deep breath, stepped back, and smiled. "Now we shall visit the commandant," he said firmly.

"The commandant? Why?"

"To get the address of a clergyman who can marry us before we sail."

"Before we sail? No, I don't think that's a good idea at all," Catherine said sweetly, softening her rejection with a smile.

"Why not?" he demanded.

"Think of your family."

"As long as we are married, they should have no objections," he said callously.

"Even Marybeth?" His frown was replaced by a worried look. "Dominic, I remember how it felt when I learned of Papa's remarriage. I refuse to do that to anyone," she said firmly.

"But it would be so much simpler here," he tried to persuade her. But he was weakening. He knew he did not want Marybeth to feel left out.

"Dominic Nicholas Reston, you are talking about my stepdaughter. Being a stepmother will be difficult as it is without your making it impossible," she said, her arms on her hips and her eyes sparking golden fire.

Harwich pulled her into his arms again and kissed her sweetly pouted lips. "You were always able to wind me around your finger," he said slightly unhappily.

"Me? Wind you?"

Another kiss stopped her protest. "I yield, little termagant," he said, and kissed her again.

The door flew open to reveal a distraught Davis and a less-than-happy Mrs. Wilson. She took one look at the couple and squared her shoulders. "I fear I must leave your employ, Lord Harwich," she said coldly.

"You do? Why?"

As the older woman sputtered for a moment before regaining her composure, Catherine stepped out of his embrace. "Wish us happy, Mrs. Wilson. Lord Harwich has just asked me to marry him," Catherine said, her whole face breaking into a smile.

"Married?"

"Oh, Miss Catherine," Davis sighed. "My mistress a countess." She slipped from the room to find Graves.

"We plan to marry after we arrive in London," Catherine was explaining.

"I want to marry here, now," the earl added, hoping the older woman would agree.

"Without brides clothes or family? I'm certain he was just teasing you, Miss Durrell."

The thought of the coming sea voyage forgotten, Mrs. Wilson led Catherine from the room. As she walked out the door, Catherine turned slightly, reluctant to allow Harwich out of her sight. Smiling reassuringly, he followed her.

7

The voyage from Gibraltar to Plymouth that Harwich had looked forward to with so much pleasure was disappointing. Except for meals and a carefully timed walk about the deck each morning, afternoon, and evening, he was isolated from Catherine. Mrs. Wilson, except for one minor bout with *mal de mer*, was so busy insisting Catherine make lists about the wedding that she forgot how much she hated sea travel.

"That woman never stops talking," Harwich complained as he pulled Catherine into the protected corner where he had first kissed her.

When she could breathe again, Catherine said, "She's only trying to help."

"But she hardly allows you out of her sight. Engaged couples are usually allowed more freedom," he protested, pulling her into his embrace again.

"Isn't that why you hired her?" Catherine laughed at him. Her lips were slightly open and the tip of her tongue moistened them.

"It would be better if you did avoid that in public," he said, his eyes bright.

"What?"

"Running your tongue over your lips."

"Why?"

"It makes me want to kiss you breathless," he explained, putting words to action. "Mmm. Thank God we'll be in Plymouth tomorrow," he said fiercely.

"Why?"

"Then no one can separate us."

"Dominic, remember you must talk to Marybeth before we can marry."

"I will." He kissed her eyes shut. "When I wrote, I told her to have Agnes bring her to Plymouth and wait for me."

"So she will arrive hoping to have her father to herself, and you'll present me," Catherine said, a snap to her eyes and voice.

"No, she won't." Harwich tried to soothe her. "I told her about you in my letter."

"How many letters have you sent her recently?"

"Only one. After you explained what she might think, I wrote her before we reached Gibraltar and saw it off the day we arrived," he said, untying the olive-green cloak so that he could kiss her neck. Finally he realized that Catherine, usually so responsive, was stiff. He looked at her closely, surprised by the anger and hurt he saw on her face.

"And just what did you tell her?" she asked, her fear causing her throat to close so that she had to force the words out.

"That I had met someone I had known before she was born and that I didn't think she would have to worry about the succession anymore."

"What? Dominic, do you realize what you said? Any reputation I had left will be in tatters. They will be counting the months on their fingers." Catherine was almost in tears. In fact, she was blinking rapidly to keep them from spilling down her cheeks.

Harwich turned her face up to his. He ran his finger under her eyes, wiping her tears. "Catherine, I did not use those words. Grant me some delicacy, my dear." He leaned down and kissed her lips softly. "She will love you; wait and see," he promised.

Although Catherine had reservations, his kisses made her forget about them temporarily. By the time the day had ended, Harwich had persuaded her that he was right.

The next day came all too quickly. As the ship sailed into port and the shoreline grew closer, Catherine had shredded one handkerchief and had begun to unravel one of the gold ribbons that adorned her olive-green traveling dress. Her straw bonnet, this time embellished with gold ribbons and a feather, did little to hide her face. She had been talking to herself all day. Unfortunately her words of wisdom had just frightened her more.

"I will not be afraid, I will not be afraid," she whispered to herself. Her hands gripped the rails, her knuckles growing white. Beside her, Harwich felt her tension and tucked her arm beneath his, drawing her close to his side. The chilly early-November wind whipped her skirts and cloak about her. The closer they grew to the docks, the more nervous she grew.

Suddenly the docks in front of them, already bustling with sailors and chandlers, looked ready to overflow as three carriages took their places at the end of the wharf. "Ours, wouldn't you say, Graves?" asked Harwich, pride evident in every word.

"At least the grays, your lordship. That team of chestnuts looks like your cousin's," the groom added, his eyes narrowed.

"My cousin's?" the earl said thoughtfully. He cursed himself for the words when he felt Catherine stiffen beside him. "He probably escorted Marybeth and Agnes to Dover," he tried to reassure her.

The thought of meeting his daughter and her chaperone had already been making her tense. At the thought of meeting more of his family, Catherine grew queasy. Her face, already losing its glow, became pallid. She pulled at Harwich's sleeve to get his attention. "You go and meet them alone," she suggested, "Mrs. Wilson, Davis, and I will follow after you have had time to talk to Marybeth."

"Nonsense, my dear. I want her to meet you immediately. Then I'll get special license and we'll be

married before evening. Graves, I'll need a change of
clothes as soon as we reach . . ." He paused and
laughed as he realized he had no idea where they
would be staying.

Graves nodded and turned back to watching the
docks. He took a deep breath as he got a better look
at one of the carriages, a large lumbering thing
several years out of date. His eyes narrowed specu-
latively.

Catherine winced to hear Dominic's request for a
change of clothes. She glanced down at the drab olive
of her dress and cloak, becoming though she knew
them to be. After weeks of putting fashion out of her
mind because of her limited selection, she wished
she had something new. Even though it was
November, perhaps Davis could freshen the sprigged
muslin in time for the wedding.

As the sailors dropped the anchor and lowered the
ladders and two small boats, Catherine stood as if in
a trance. Then she turned to look at Harwich.
"Dominic, maybe we—"

"Look, Catherine. That is my cousin John. Marybeth must be in the carriage," he said almost as if he
were a boy contemplating a great treat. A sailor
appeared beside them. "Only a few minutes until we
are home," the earl said quietly, guiding Catherine
and Mrs. Wilson to the ladder above the boat. "If I go
first to help below, can you manage?" he asked,
remembering Mrs. Wilson's fear of small boats.

A few minutes later the entire party was on its way
to shore, only one incident marring an otherwise
routine change. "I'm glad I was the one standing by
the ladder when you came down," Harwich whispered in Catherine's ear. Her face, already red,
turned almost crimson. "And those charms are all
mine." Remembering how his hand had stroked her
ankles as he hastily gathered her billowing skirt
about her legs, Catherine blushed again.

A tall, thin man, his face showing lines of recent

pain, waited patiently as the ladies were helped to the dock. As Harwich finally set foot on the dock, he started forward. "John, are you all right? Why do you put such strains on your health? Edwards and the grooms would have managed without you," Harwich asked.

His cousin looked at him curiously, his face unnaturally grave. "You have really set the cat among the pigeons now, old man," he said quietly as his cousin clapped him on the shoulder.

"What do you mean? Come along, John. I have someone I want you to meet." Harwich lead his cousin toward Catherine.

"That's just what I mean, Dominic. First you dash off, no one knows where, and then you write your daughter that you are bringing someone home with you," his cousin said as quietly as he could. "Have you no better sense?"

Before he could continue, Harwich stopped. "Catherine, this is my cousin John, the Honorable John Babbington. You may remember him. He visited me in Reston. John, this is Miss Catherine Durrell, soon to be the Countess of Harwich, and her chaperone, Mrs. Wilson." He smiled at Catherine and drew her close to him.

His eyes narrowed slightly, John Babbington bowed formally. He said, "I wish you happiness, Miss Durrell. And you too, cousin. Pleased to make your acquaintance, Mrs. Wilson." He stood up and looked at Catherine more closely. "Did Dominic say we had met before? Surely I would remember."

"My home is the Grange. When Dominic was home during the summer, he allowed me to follow him about," Catherine explained.

"Allowed? That's not the way I remember it," Harwich said, laughing.

His cousin looked at her closely, focusing on her eyes that now twinkled with merriment.

"Good heavens, you're the tagalong!"

"Guilty as charged, sir." She smiled and made a small curtsy.

"Come along now. Mother will be wondering where you are," Babbington said quietly, thinking of the surprise in store for his mischief-making mother.

"Your mother? Did she escort Marybeth?"

"Not quite, Dominic. The family decided that your daughter was too young to make the journey. Only Mother and I are here to greet you." He continued imperviously, "And before you say anything, you might thank me for seeing that you had your own carriage. Mother wanted us to travel all in one."

His dark-blue eyes almost black with anger, Harwich snapped. "My aunt has gone too far this time."

"Dominic, please," Catherine begged as he practically forced her to run to keep up with his long strides. Her stomach rolled uneasily. She finally stopped, forcing him to stop also. He turned to face her, his anger still evident. "Please," she begged, "don't act like this."

"How dare my aunt countermand my orders!"

"I'm certain she was only doing what she thought best," Catherine said, trying to convince herself as well as him.

"More than likely she just wanted to make certain she had some say in my life."

"Now, now, old man. That's my mother your speaking of," his cousin protested halfheartedly.

"And I would bet you a monkey to a pony that you tried to stop her when you found out her plans. Isn't that right, cousin?" Harwich asked, his brows arched sardonically.

Babbington simply looked at him silently.

Before Harwich could say another word, Catherine took her stand. So softly that Babbington could hear only an occasional word, Catherine said, "If you embarrass me, Dominic Reston, this marriage will never take place. Do you hear me?"

She stomped her foot for emphasis, her eyes sparkling with golden fire.

As Harwich took a deep breath, Mrs. Wilson, forgotten in the earl's fury, hurried toward them. "Is there some problem?" she asked anxiously, her eyes darting from one face to another.

"My aunt chose to meet us alone rather than bring my daughter," Harwich explained, the heat of his anger changing to ice. "We shall have to postpone the wedding until we reach London."

"Wedding? You were planning to be married today?" his cousin asked. He pulled down the sleeves of his blue superfine coat, gathered his greatcoat more closely about him, and nervously fingered a fob on his watch chain.

"Oh, how disappointing," Mrs. Wilson said. "Of course, Miss Durrell needs time to prepare more suitable wedding garments," she added thoughtfully. "How nice of your aunt to meet you."

The cousins exchanged rueful glances. Catherine, whose nervousness threatened to overwhelm her, smiled tightly. Harwich took a deep breath. He reminded himself that his aunt was a caring person, ruthlessly devoted to her family. "Let me present you to her. This way," he said pleasantly. His hand tightened over Catherine's. If his aunt tried to stop this marriage, he promised himself, she would soon find herself defeated. He said low enough so that only John and Catherine heard him, "Why didn't you persuade her to stay at the inn?" He nodded toward the large old-fashioned coach.

For the first time since sighting the ship, John Babbington laughed. "Convince my mother to change her mind? You've been gone too long, your lordship."

The affection between the two men was evident to Catherine as she walked quietly beside them. As Harwich asked questions about his daughter, Catherine wished she, too, had someone to share her problems with. The relaxed, caring man she knew on shipboard seemed to be slipping away.

When Babbington opened the door to the coach, Catherine gasped in surprise. The interior was decorated in poufs of lilac satin trimmed in white. The woman who sat in state there also wore purple, a rich dark-violet velvet trimmed with flouces of heavy lace. Her hat, a masterpiece of the milliner's art, made Catherine aware of how dowdy she must appear. Moving her cloak to make room for her guests, the lady inspected Catherine from the tip of her hat to her shoes peeping out from under the olive green of her dress.

As though dismissing her, she turned to her nephew. "So you have finally returned to your responsibilities, Harwich," she said coolly. The earl winced at the name and waited for her next volley. "Well, sir, do you intend to keep her name a secret?" She waved her hand toward Catherine. "Introduce me," she snapped imperiously.

Bowing slightly, Harwich helped Catherine and her chaperone into the coach. "Aunt Beatrice, may I present Miss Catherine Durrell and Mrs. George Wilson. Ladies, my aunt, Lady Ravenly." Before anyone had a chance to respond, Harwich took a deep breath and rushed on. "Miss Durrell has done me the honor of agreeing to be my wife."

The smile that was forming on Lady Ravenly's face froze into place. Her gray eyes seem to inspect Catherine even more carefully than before. "How"— she paused, and Harwich held his breath—"fortunate. Don't you agree, John? How nice to know that is one worry that has been removed from your shoulders." Her smile did not reach her eyes. Her fan snapped open as if she wished her nephew's knuckles were beneath it. "How convenient that my son thought to bring an extra carriage. John, you and Harwich arrange for the servants and luggage to follow in it. I will see Miss Durrell and her chaperone to the inn where we have been waiting for you."

In spite of Catherine's pleading eyes, Harwich obeyed. Before he left the carriage, he pressed her hand encouragingly and smiled.

While Harwich and Babbington organized the baggage and the rest of the party, Catherine was faced with a more formidable situation. After allowing her guests a few polite words of greeting, Lady Ravenly began her less-than-subtle inquisition. "You are quite a surprise, Miss Durrell. My nephew did not mention you before he left. You met on his travels?"

"No, Lady Ravenly," Catherine answered demurely. She was surprised at the resentment she felt toward Harwich. How like a man to leave when the situation became uncomfortable for him, she thought resentfully. Her anger was beneficial in one way, though: she was no longer as nervous. Her chaperone, on the other hand, was thoroughly intimidated by the viscountess. Mrs. Wilson sat facing them, her face carefully blank.

"Then, where?" Lady Ravenly asked bluntly.

"My father has an estate that borders Reston," Catherine explained softly. She had been beaten to her knees by the *ton* once before. This time she would not give in.

"By Reston? Borders it, you say?" Catherine nodded. "Any brothers or older sisters?"

"No."

The older woman smiled thoughtfully. "Knew the boy had more sense than he was given credit for." Catherine and Mrs. Wilson exchanged startled glances as the smile became a hearty laugh. "Yes, well." Lady Ravenly straightened her dress and hat and took another look at her passengers. "I don't suppose he warned you about his daughter?"

"Marybeth?" Catherine asked quietly. No wonder Harwich had said his family drove him mad.

"A rather outspoken young miss. Agnes, you do

know about Agnes?'' she interrupted herself to fire another question at her unwilling guest. Before she could continue, the coach stopped. ''The inn. Good. These old bones need more warmth than this carriage gives. Jenkins,'' she shouted.

A short time later Lady Ravenly, Mrs. Wilson, and Catherine stood before a roaring fire. ''Always travel with a steward, Miss Durrell,'' Lady Ravenly advised. ''It makes life so much more comfortable.'' Thinking of the way they had been escorted from the carriage and into this parlor, where tea was waiting, Catherine had to agree.

Putting her cup back on the tray, the older woman walked carefully around Catherine as though she were a statue on display. ''Hmm. Not too bad. Somewhat more rounded than usual. But she might work. Needs better dressing, more up-to-date. Don't you agree?'' she asked Mrs. Wilson. Catherine's chaperone gulped and nodded, moving out of the way as Lady Ravenly swept around Catherine for another look.

Catherine put her cup back on the tray with a sharp clatter. She crossed to the door and then returned without opening it. That woman was not going to make trouble for her or for Dominic. She forced a smile on her lips and said sweetly, ''Dominic has told me how thoughtful you have been, how you tried to help him.''

The older woman preened and smiled. ''The dear boy and my own darling son are like brothers. How could I do anything less?'' She took a seat on the small settee, motioning Catherine to sit beside her. ''I don't remember seeing you at any of the presentations recently. You were presented, weren't you?''

''To the queen. But it has been some years ago,'' Catherine assured her. How Aunt Clarice had hated that, she thought cynically, forced to take her place among the dowagers whose company she detested.

The door opened. Jenkins announced loudly, ''The Earl of Harwich and the Honorable John Babbington.''

"Give it up, Jenkins. My mother expects us," said Babbington crossly. "I never understand why you insist he travel with you, Mother. Tea, good. Do you want some, Dominic?"

Although Mrs. Wilson was giving the appearance of a lady who found nothing amiss in a butler announcing guests into a private parlor in an inn, Catherine was maintaining her composure with difficulty. When Harwich caught her eyes, the laughter in his was almost her undoing.

"Jenkins informed me," Babbington said dryly, "that your rooms will be ready shortly, ladies. He apologizes for the delay. Had he known of the number of people in the party, the arrangements would have gone faster." He picked up a cup of tea and sat close to the fire, a slight cough rocking his thin frame. Both Harwich and his mother looked at him anxiously. They exchanged a worried glance and then returned to their tea. As he listened to the rattle of teacups and polite conversation, Harwich thought of how the whole situation would have bored him only a few months before. He looked at Catherine and smiled.

As Babbington put his handkerchief into his pocket, he felt something crackle. "Dominic, here," he called as he tossed his cousin a packet.

"A letter from Marybeth," the earl said, a smile lighting his face. "I still cannot understand why you didn't bring her along."

"Let it go, Harwich," his cousin muttered, thinking of the scene the earl's letter had caused when Agnes had reported its contents.

While Catherine waited impatiently, her face a polite blank, Harwich read the single sheet hastily. When he looked up, his face showed nothing. His voice was the product of a thousand boring evenings. "You, Aunt Theodore, and Agnes must have been busy," he said softly. Only his eyes reflected the anger he felt.

"Now, Harwich. Your letter was very vague. Had we known how suitable Catherine was—"

"Suitable? You didn't stop to think before you sent my daughter into hysterics. I am the Earl of Reston and I know my duty to my family. What did you hope to accomplish by filling Marybeth's head with this, this nonsense?" He tapped the letter he held in his hand, knocking a second packet to the floor.

"What is wrong? What did they tell her?" Catherine asked anxiously, crossing to his side.

He pulled her within the circle of his arm and shoulder. "She was told I had married a foreigner. Don't try to play coy, Aunt Beatrice. Where did you get the idea?"

"Well, what could I expect?" she defended herself. "You've not been in England for several months. What were we to think? We had to think of the child."

"The child, yes," he said cynically. "I can imagine Aunt Theodora was interested in Marybeth. She forgets her name from one visit to another."

The room had grown quiet. The air was so tense that Catherine thought she could feel the hairs on her arms standing up straight. She edged closer to Harwich.

"Dominic, what does she say?" she asked softly.

For the first time since he had read his daughter's letter, Harwich was aware of everyone listening avidly. "I think you will agree that Miss Durrell and I deserve the right to discuss this in private." He yanked open the door. "Another parlor, Jenkins," he commanded.

"Nonsense," his aunt said in her usual brusque tones. "I'm certain Jenkins has the rooms ready by now. You stay here. This way, Mrs. Wilson. I do hope you find the room to your satisfaction. I usually travel with my own mattress as well as linens, but with Harwich's letter arriving so suddenly . . ."

Slipping the packet his cousin had dropped into Harwich's pocket, Babbington patted him on the shoulder. "Forgive us our theatrics, Miss Durrell," he said quietly. "When everything calms down, we are a rather likable group." He bowed and was gone.

Harwich shut the door and leaned back against it, his shoulders not as straight as usual. Catherine, her nerves already strung to the breaking point, sat on the settee, her eyes fixed on his face. Finally she could bear the silence no longer. "What did she say?" He sighed and crossed the room to sit beside her. "Don't do this to me, Dominic. What did she say?"

He picked up her hand, carefully lacing his fingers through hers. "It's nothing," he said quietly, wishing that he had kept his silence.

"Nothing? You caused that turmoil over nothing?" She stood up. Her eyes flashed down at him angrily. "It was bad enough that you abandoned me to your aunt without warning. But to use your daughter as an excuse for a family argument. You, you . . ." She turned to walk toward the door.

Before she had taken more than two steps, Harwich had her hand. He pulled her toward him until she was forced to take a seat on the settee again. "Catherine, it wasn't a ploy." He sighed. "She is afraid my remarriage means that I won't love her anymore."

Tears gathered in Catherine's eyes, turning them into amber pools. For once she did nothing to stop them from running down her cheeks, preferring instead to bury her face in his shoulder. "Oh, Dominic," she sobbed, "how alone she must feel. We must hurry to her."

"We will leave at first light," he promised. He pulled his handkerchief from his pocket to dry her tears. "As soon as she meets you, she will understand," he said quietly.

Catherine allowed him to blot her tears away. Her worries were not so swift to disappear. "Promise me that you will not expect her to accept me overnight," she said.

"Does that mean we must postpone our marriage again?"

"It might be best."

"Best? Best for whom?"

"For Marybeth," she reminded him. "At least give her some time to get to know me."

"That's what I want. To know you," he said quietly, kissing her quickly. Although she returned his kiss, he was aware of her hesitation. Standing up, he reached down and pulled her into his embrace.

"You dropped something," she murmured breathily a few minutes later. She pointed to an envelope on the floor behind him. Harwich bent down and picked it up, his eyes narrowed as though he expected the handwriting on the outside to reveal its contents.

"Open it," Catherine urged.

"After the last one, I'd rather not," he grumbled. He turned it over and frowned at the seal. He broke it open and stared at the short message inside. He started at it once more and ran his hand wearily through his hair.

"What's wrong?" Catherine asked dully.

"I must leave for London immediately."

"Marybeth? She's ill? She's run away?"

"No. Castlereagh wishes to see me immediately." He looked at her and smiled wryly. "Even if my aunt would permit it, Catherine, I cannot take you with me. I'll be traveling by horseback. Promise me you will stay with me and not your aunt?"

"Horseback? No. Promise me that you'll travel chaise part of the way—then you can rest." She smiled at him wanly.

"Until tomorrow, my dear," Harwich murmured and pulled her to him for one last kiss. Then he was gone. In the distance she heard him shouting instructions to Jenkins. Much later she sat up in bed startled. He had not promised. She settled back into the soft goosedown mattress, a smile barely lifting the corners of her mouth. But then, neither had she.

8

When his staff began their duties the next morning, Harwich was in London. As he waited impatiently while Edwards lay his neckcloths carefully beside him, he thought of the note from Castlereagh. "That will be fine, Edwards," he said curtly, picking up one of the starched linen cloths and whipping it around his neck.

"But, your lordship, you don't intend . . ." Edwards stopped as Harwich set a sapphire in place and picked up his hat and cane. "Very good, sir," he said quietly, pulling his face into his most disapproving expression.

The interview with Castlereagh was a difficult one. "What was Andover thinking of?" the foreign secretary raged.

"He understood that this was what you wanted," Harwich said calmly. He thought of all the objections he had made in Vienna and winced. "Our allies, humph! Talleyrand, I suppose." Castlereagh slammed his fists into his desk. "A year ago the man was encouraging Napoleon."

"A rather good indication of Napoleon's loss of power," Harwich reminded him. "As is this agreement." He crossed his legs, wondering for a moment what Edwards used to give his Hessians such a shine. Nothing Graves had tried had come close.

Castlereagh considered the document on the desk in front of him for a moment. Then he looked at Harwich, who was seemingly relaxed and comfortable. Only his hand fiddling with his fob revealed his dislike for the situation.

"It does seem to present some interesting possibilities. Does Murat have Napoleon's ear?"

"Not as he once did. The Russian campaign caused a decided rift there."

"As well as in other places. What kind of man is he?"

"Murat?" The older man nodded. "Ambitious, hardworking, and politically aware." He paused for a moment. "A rather good administrator, too, from what I was told."

"Did you make a firm commitment?"

Harwich looked at Castlereagh sharply. "I was merely the courier, and I told him so. Any commitments had to come from the Foreign Office."

Castlereagh got up, pulled the sleeves of his *corbeau*-colored coat down, and walked to a table containing a globe. He spun it carefully, stopping it with his fingers on Italy. "Bentiwick opposes this," he said quietly. Harwich sat there, his face carefully noncommittal. "He has thrown his support behind the Bourbons. Did you know this?"

"No, but it's no surprise. He was in Palermo when I arrived in Sicily and remained for some time." He looked at the foreign secretary and asked, "Have you received a recent report from him?"

The answer was the confirmation of all of Harwich's suspicions. The trip from Sicily had been rather lengthy. It had enabled him to renew his acquaintances with Catherine, however. His thoughts on her, he jumped when Castlereagh asked, "This Miss Durrell you brought back with you, can she be trusted?"

"I believe so. She is to be my wife, sir," he explained proudly.

"Your wife? Good God, man, have you taken leave of your senses. You've known her only a few weeks."

"More than a few weeks. Her father's estate and

mine march together. I have known her most of her life."

"Curious. You are certain she's genuine."

"Without a doubt." Harwich shifted uneasily in the chair, wishing the man at Jericho.

"Suppose I must wish you happy, then. When's the wedding?" the foreign secretary asked as he stood behind the highly polished surface of his desk and held out his hand.

"Soon." Harwich took the extended hand, made a sketchy bow, and left. If he had seen Castlereagh pick up a pen and write a note, he might have been less pleased to escape. "Have someone watch Miss Catherine Durrell," Castlereagh wrote. Sanding it, he sent it on his way.

Harwich walked quickly down the halls of the Foreign Office, nodding to his acquaintances but refusing to stop. With one difficult task out of the way, he was impatient to tackle the other.

A few minutes later he pulled his curricule to a stop in front of his home, a rather imposing structure on Berkeley Square built in the last century. Ignoring the facade, praised in most guidebooks of London for its elegant design, he hurried in, tossing his hat and cane to a waiting footman. "Where is my daughter, Thomas?" he asked his butler impatiently.

"In the schoolroom, your lordship. May I say how pleasant it is to have you at home."

"Thank you. Oh, Thomas"—Harwich turned at first landing—"prepare two suites. And have the housekeeper meet me in the countess's suite at"—he looked at his watch—"two o'clock."

"Well, well, well," Thomas muttered as he sent the footmen on various errands. Within the hour, the entire staff was aware that Lady Marybeth's letter had been correct.

In the schoolroom, Harwich was hardly in the door before he had an armful of laughing and crying daughter. He hugged her tightly.

"Papa," she cried as she hugged him in return.

"How is my little love?" he whispered quietly, laughing as she threw both arms around his waist as if she would never let him go.

"Now, Marybeth, that is no way for a young lady to behave," Agnes began.

Harwich glanced at his cousin and his daughter's governess. He frowned. "Come down to my study with me," he said, smiling at his daughter. When he noticed Agnes picking up her sewing to accompany them, he said firmly, "No, don't disturb yourself, cousin. I think my daughter and I deserve some time alone." Her face worried, Mrs. Throckmorton sat down again, an uneasy fluttering disturbing her stomach.

"Now tell me, poppet, just what you have been doing since I left," Harwich urged as they walked down the stairs, their arms around each other's waist. He stopped on a landing. "You must have grown an inch since I've been gone," he said in amazement, noting that the top of her head now reached the top button of his coat.

"Cousin Agnes has had to have all my skirts put down," Marybeth explained happily.

Sweeping her inside the study, Harwich closed the door behind him. As he listened to her relating events of the months he had been gone, he watched her in amazement. His dainty little girl was a woman, her blond hair tumbling in curls down her back. Her simple round gown hugged curves that he was certain had not been evident before he left. He looked at her carefully, amazed that this sparkling young lady with the laughing blue eyes was a part of him.

Her recital slowed as she noticed that he was not responding. "Papa?" Marybeth asked, her voice somber.

"Yes, little one?"

The familiar insult was too much. "I am not little," she said, her hands on her hips militantly.

"You are definitely shorter than I am," her father reminded her as he did every time the subject was introduced. He pulled her to him and kissed her lightly on her forehead to soothe her.

While he held her, he felt her shoulders stiffen. Her voice was almost a whisper when she asked, "Did you bring her with you, Papa?"

"Her?"

"Your wife?"

Harwich stepped back a step. He looked at her carefully. Raising her chin, he forced her to look at him. "Catherine will be here later today. But she isn't my wife." Marybeth's relief disappeared as he continued, "At least not yet."

"Are you going to send me away to school?" Marybeth asked fearfully, remembering her great-aunt's conversations. Her back was as straight as a ramrod, her chin held high.

"Do you want to go?" her father asked. He watched anxiously.

"I thought," she began, and cleared her throat nervously. "I thought you planned to send me away," she finished. The tears that were close to the surface spilled down her cheeks.

As though she were a small child, Harwich picked her up and sat down in a large comfortable leather chair, Marybeth across his lap.

"Who told you that?" he asked, controlling his anger with difficulty. He straightened her soft blue cloth dress over her legs and patted her shoulder comfortingly.

"No one," she whispered.

"Marybeth," he said quietly. His tone warned her to take care about what she said.

"I heard them talking. They said that your new wife wouldn't want me around, that you'd probably send me off to school or to the country. You wouldn't have time for me," she said hurriedly, sobbing a little.

Harwich stroked her curls, letting her lie against his shoulder while he thought of a way to soothe her fears. If only Catherine were here, he thought wearily.

When he had dried her tears, Harwich asked his daughter, "You know I love you, don't you?" He felt rather than saw her nod. "I would never willingly do anything to hurt you, baby."

She took a deep, quavering breath and her shoulders relaxed. "You're not going to let her send me away?" she asked, her voice still shaky.

"If I tried to do so, Catherine would undoubtedly send me to Coventry," he said, a laugh in his voice.

"Catherine? Is that her name? Does she speak English? Great-aunt Theodora said we'd probably have to speak Italian to her. My Italian isn't very good." Her words seemed to fall over one another. "I promised my governess I would try harder but—"

"Catherine will help you," he assured her. "But she speaks English. She is English. She only lived in Italy for a time," he hurriedly explained. He paused for a moment and shifted her weight to his other leg, stamping his foot slightly to restore its circulation. "Have you gotten heavier?" he asked, tickling her ribs.

"Let me go, Papa. No, don't." Laughing, Marybeth scrambled off his lap and hid behind the settee in front of the fire, a little girl once more.

"Come. Let's finish our talk," he said as he crossed the room.

Marybeth's face lost its happy glow, but she took her seat obediently beside him on a settee striped in silver and green.

"Do you remember when I was teaching you to swim?" he asked.

"Yes, Papa."

"I said I was going to teach you because little girls like to go exploring as much as little boys." She nodded, her eyes puzzled. "How did I know that?"

"You said you had a friend on the estate, and she kept falling in the pond."

"That's right. And Catherine was that little girl."

"She knew you when you were a baby?" Marybeth asked.

"No. Although she was at your christening."

"She was? Did she know my mama?" When he shook his head, Marybeth pouted a little. "Why was she there?"

"Her parents brought her. She was younger than you are today." He laughed softly. "I think she is as nervous about meeting you as you are about meeting her. Promise that you will greet her kindly this afternoon," he asked quietly.

Marybeth's face grew very calm. "This afternoon?" she asked, her voice surprisingly adult-like. She pulled away from him and stood up. "I'm glad you are home, Papa," she said, and bent to kiss him. "I'll be good."

As he watched his daughter walk out of the room, Harwich stretched and ran a hand over the back of his neck. What had he done wrong? he wondered. Glancing at the clock, he hurried to his appointment with the housekeeper.

Inspecting the suite that had been closed since his wife's death, he frowned. "Send the furniture to the attics," he said, certain that the white-and-gold furniture his first wife had favored would not please Catherine. He hesitated. He looked around thoughtfully for a moment and added, "Call Lady Marybeth. We'll let her see it first. It is time she had a suite of her own. If she would like this, she can choose her rooms, and you can install it there."

A few minutes later his daughter was once more at his side. "I used to play in here?" she asked, looking about her with a frown.

"Is there anything you want?" Harwich asked quietly. "I think it is time you moved out of the schoolroom and into a more adult setting." She threw her arms around him in excitement. "However, this does not mean your lessons are over, minx," he reminded her. "Let's see if there is anything here you would want." As the earl and his daughter seriously considered the furniture, the housekeeper and two footmen looked on approvingly.

Finally, Marybeth stopped, her brow wrinkled. "My mother chose this furniture?" she asked. Harwich nodded. "She really liked it?"

"She assured me she was delighted with it. It was all the crack."

Marybeth looked at him carefully under long lashes. Before she lost her nerve, she said, "I think I would rather choose my own furniture if you please."

"Take it away, men," Harwich said, smiling down at his daughter. She breathed a sigh of relief and looked around again, her eyes speculating on the silver blue of the walls.

As the footmen moved the furniture into the hallway, Harwich studied the walls, curtains, and floors closely. "Rugs, curtains, wallpaper—they all go."

"Everything?" the housekeeper gasped.

As Harwich nodded and took another look around, visualizing Catherine in the rooms, he felt a small tug at his sleeve. "Papa, may I have that?" Marybeth asked, pointing to a large rug in tones of blue and creams. He nodded. "May I have it in the schoolroom until my suite is finished?" She looked at him as if expecting him to disagree. When he merely smiled at her and nodded, she watched carefully as two footmen rolled it away. Dropping her father a curtsy, she hurried along behind, dreaming of her own suite. She could hardly wait to write Louisa.

The problem of the old furniture taken care of, Harwich looked around the room again. "Call in the painters immediately, Mrs. Thomas. A warm cream, I think. You know the color of cream you serve for tea, the thick kind," he said, stretching wearily. "I'm going to rest now. Call me as soon as Miss Durrell and Mrs. Wilson arrive."

With the new mistress expected shortly, the house-keeper squared her shoulders and marshaled her troops. Before the hour was out, an army of maids and footmen were polishing every surface in the house. In the pantry, Thomas readied the silver. And the painters had just finished covering the parquet floors with cloths.

All this activity did not disturb the earl. He slept peacefully for hours. He had just finished his bath when his cousin walked in.

"I told them I didn't need to be announced," Babbington explained. "After your message last night I wondered if you would survive." He sat in a chair and propped his feet on a low chest. "You don't plan to travel the world again anytime soon, do you?" he asked wearily.

"I'm safely in London. At least until Christmas," Harwich assured him, noting the pallor of his skin and the marks of pain beside his mouth. "I didn't intend for you to be involved in this, cousin." He poured Babbington a glass of brandy and watched as he downed it in one gulp. "Did Catherine come with you?"

"She's traveling with my mother. And, Dominic, my mother insists that she stay in Grosvenor Square until the wedding." He sighed tiredly.

Biting back a scathing comment, Dominic quickly donned his breeches and shirt. "Have you been home, sir?" he asked quietly. He exchanged a worried glance with Edwards.

"Ah, sir. You have forgotten." His cousin laughed weakly.

"Forgotten?"

"I am staying here at your request."

"Then I 'request' that you take yourself off to rest immediately."

"Have done, Dominic, I get enough cosseting from my mother and Cousin Agnes." He sighed heavily. "Besides," he added dryly, "I'm not certain I can stand thanks to that brandy of yours."

"That's never stopped us before, has it, Edwards?" Harwich mocked. Together he and his valet walked Babbington the short way down the hall, insisting that he allow them to put him on the bed.

"I will ring for Mr. Babbington's valet, sir. Together we make him comfortable," Edwards assured Harwich.

Left to his own devices, Harwich returned to his own room. He picked up a candle and opened the door to the adjoining suite. He stood looking around him for a moment before wandering back into his dressing room. When his valet returned a short time later, he was looking through his jewels. There on the dressing table lay a variety of stones. The rubies he had immediately discarded as he had amethysts and garnets. The sapphires were a possibility. He ran his hand over an emerald for a moment before turning to the diamond. Diamonds were too cold, he decided. That left only one choice. He smiled as he picked up the golden topaz pin and placed it carefully in the neckcloth. Catherine would be magnificent in topaz. He shrugged into the black evening coat Edwards held ready, frowning a trifle as the valet smoothed the silk over his shoulders to assure himself no crease marred its beauty.

He glanced at his watch and leisurely headed down the stairs to the small salon where his daughter and Cousin Agnes usually met him when he dined at home.

"Is she here yet, Papa?" Marybeth asked quietly as he entered the room and bowed to his cousin.

"No, poppet. She's traveling with your Great-aunt Beatrice." Marybeth's eyes widened slightly and then she nodded. "In fact, Aunt Beatrice has demanded that Catherine and her chaperone stay at Ravenly House until the wedding. You will have to wait until tomorrow to meet her." As Thomas announced dinner, Harwich held out both arms to the ladies. "Had I known our numbers would have been uneven, I would have invited Cousin Horace," he teased.

"Op, Papa, you wouldn't. Promise me you are only joking," Marybeth pleaded. "Last time he was here he dumped a syllabub all over my new dress."

"Marybeth, remember your manners," her chaperone reminded her sternly, frowning at the way she pulled her father's sleeve.

Harwich looked at the older woman silently before seating her. "Is that a new dress, poppet?" her father asked as he seated his daughter on his right. "That shade of . . . What color do you call it?"

"Apricot, Papa."

"Apricot makes you look good enough to eat," he said laughingly. Although his cousin kept giving him worried looks, Harwich conversed lightly with both of them, steering the conversation away from his approaching marriage.

At the first taste of the lightly seasoned clear soup that began the meal, he smiled. "My compliments to Jacques. This is the best food since I left Vienna."

"Vienna, Papa?"

He took a taste of the cutlet with mushroom fritters and nodded. "I wonder if I dare teach you to waltz? I'll have to ask Catherine."

"The waltz. No, Harwich. The waltz is not considered appropriate, especially for young ladies of Marybeth's age," his cousin protested.

"Isn't that the dance where the gentleman puts his hands on the lady's waist?" Marybeth asked in a hushed voice.

"Yes. And I can assure you that within a year it will be sweeping the ballrooms of England. We don't want my daughter to be behind in fashion, do we?"

Although Harwich waved away most of the second and third removes, only choosing a single slice of *boeuf en croute* and a slice of capon, he smiled and cut a large slice of cheese to accompany his apple tart. "Now I know I am home."

When dinner was completed, he rose and escorted the ladies from the room, bidding them good night as he slipped into the greatcoat a footman had waiting. "In the morning we'll visit Catherine together, poppet," he promised as he kissed her good night. The next minute he was in his coach, heading toward Ravenly House. He leaned back, satisfied that Catherine would approve of his actions.

As he watched his aunt, Mrs. Wilson, and Catherine being handed from the coach some time later, he noted his bride-to-be's angry gold eyes. Escorting them carefully into the small drawing room where he had been waiting, he continued to smile, not quite so happily, as he heard his aunt giving orders.

"To bed, Mrs. Wilson. No, I quite insist," Lady Ravenly said firmly as she escorted Catherine's chaperone to a waiting footman. "A bath, some tea, and a light meal, and I assure you will feel much better in the morning."

"Feel better?" Harwich asked Catherine quietly.

"Mrs. Wilson also suffers from travel sickness," she said, her teeth firmly clenched in a reassuring smile.

"Where is John?" his aunt asked in her strident tones. "I fully expected him to be here to greet us."

"I sent him to bed, Aunt. The last few days have exhausted him. No." He held up his hand as she began to look anxious. "He's worn to the bone. I promise you will see him tomorrow." He looked at Catherine and then at his aunt. "Why is Catherine staying with you when I have a perfectly good home in Berkeley Square?"

"And you can imagine what kind of talk there would be if I permitted that?" his aunt asked, raising her eyebrows.

"Talk? I plan to marry her tomorrow. When would there be time for talk?"

"Tomorrow. Nonsense. There would hardly be time to notify all the family." She walked back into her entry hall, its floor a spiraling pattern of black-and-white marble that ended before a magnificent staircase. "You may have ten minutes. After that, Jenkins will have someone show Catherine to her rooms. You, nephew, I will see no later than ten o'clock tomorrow morning." As they watched, she started up the staircase, a small but regal figure.

Harwich drew Catherine back into the drawing room, carefully shutting the door. "I apologize again for leaving you. Are you all right? Aunt Beatrice can be rather overpowering at times."

"Rather overpowering? Dominic, that woman knows nothing of tact. She even asked how often I . . ." Catherine caught herself before she finished her sentence. Her cheeks were hot and red.

"How often you what?"

Taking a deep breath, Catherine said quietly, "She is right. Tomorrow would not be a good day for our wedding." She blushed and looked at the floor as if wishing it would open and she could drop in.

Harwich looked at her and smiled slightly. "I think I understand," he said quietly. "A few days will enable you and Marybeth to get to know each other."

"How is she?"

"Frightened by the tales she overheard. She thought we would send her away. There may be more of a problem than I first thought," he admitted.

"What do you plan to do?"

"Introduce you and take you shopping."

"Shopping?"

"Your suite needs to be completely refurbished. And I think it is time Marybeth moved out of the schoolroom. I told her so today. If you like, tomorrow we can visit the furniture warehouses and let you both make your choices."

Catherine sighed and closed her eyes briefly. After weeks of traveling, she was ready to rest. She opened her eyes seconds later to see Harwich looking at her intently. "To bed with you, my dear," he said quietly. "I'll see you at ten." He kissed her softly.

"With Marybeth?" she asked before following Jenkins up the staircase.

"With Marybeth," he promised.

9

When Harwich walked into the large Egyptian salon the next morning with Marybeth on his arm, Catherine smiled at them hesitantly, wishing that she were more appropriately dressed. The jade and ivory dress that had seemed so smart on Gibraltar was undoubtedly out of style. In spite of the hostility she could read on Marybeth's face, a hostility that her father seemed unaware of, Catherine kept her smile.

The introductions over, they sat down, Catherine in a chair and Marybeth on the settee beside her father. With her best manners on display, Marybeth asked politely, "How does it feel to be at home once again?"

"At home?"

"In England." The young girl settled the soft periwinkle-blue merino more comfortably over her lap.

"Perhaps I should reserve judgment until I have settled," Catherine said quietly. "Did you remember to give your daughter her present, Dominic?" she asked, her eyes sparkling.

"Yes. As soon as Graves arrived with my baggage last night. I even woke her up," he said, smiling.

"Cousin Agnes said it was most improper, much too old for me," Marybeth reminded him, pouting a little.

"Even for evenings at home?" Catherine asked, remembering her chaperone's suggestion.

"At home." Marybeth savored the words. "Papa, what do you think?"

"If Catherine agrees," Harwich said cautiously.

When Lady Ravenly and Mrs. Wilson entered a few minutes later, there was an uneasy peace. After inspecting Catherine carefully, Lady Ravenly said loudly, "I absolutely refuse to have you traveling about London looking like that. Harwich, buy her some clothes. You should know the right places. You've been clothing your mistresses for years."

"Aunt Beatrice," he said in an icy voice, "remember that my daughter is present."

"Well, I'm certain this is not the first she has heard of the subject. Is it, girl?"

Marybeth sat speechless, her eyes widening. Her surface sophistication was fast disappearing.

"Lady Ravenly, I assure you that I will purchase my own clothes," Catherine said, her eyes flashing fire. "And whether Marybeth knows anything about the subject isn't the question. If she is to learn to behave in society, her elders must set good examples." She turned to her chaperone and smiled. "Are you ready to go?" Grateful for a chance to escape, Mrs. Wilson nodded and walked into the hall to don her cloak.

When Catherine and Marybeth followed, Harwich faced his aunt, anger in every line of his face. "If you were not my favorite cousin's mother, this would be the last time you would see me." Unable to resist the opportunity to strike back, he added, "By the way, your son will not be coming this morning. I called the doctor last night. It seems your little jaunt has set his complete recovery back some weeks." He turned to leave.

Lady Ravenly's cheeks turned as white as the lace on her cap, the circles of rouge standing out on her cheeks clearly. "Dominic, don't leave. Will he be all right?" she asked, tears streaking her face.

Already ashamed of his actions, he answered

quietly, "Yes, with rest. See for yourself. Thomas is expecting you."

"Dominic?"

"Yes?" He turned to face her.

"Will you allow Catherine to remain with me before the wedding?"

"Why?"

"These London gossips can destroy a reputation. Let me help. Even though there's bound to be talk, we can keep it to a minimum."

He closed his eyes wearily. "I'll speak to Catherine at luncheon today. Jacques planned something special."

When he joined the ladies, a nervous silence filled the hall. He took his hat and led the way to the door. "A visit to your man of affairs and then the jewelers, don't you agree, Catherine?"

"The jewelers? In this?" she protested, holding out a skirt she now knew was several widths too wide. "I think our second stop should be at a modiste's. Where do you purchase your clothes, Lady Marybeth?"

For a moment Marybeth forgot her resentment. Her heart swelled with pride to think that Catherine would consider her opinion. "A seamstress comes to the house. Cousin Agnes says I am too young yet to have a modiste. But my friend Louisa's sister is making her bow this Season. She says Madame Bertine is all the crack," Marybeth explained hurriedly.

"Madame Bertine. Do you know where her shop is located?"

"I know," Harwich said, and cleared his throat. He looked out the window uneasily. Stealing a look at Catherine a few minutes later, he was surprised to find her watching him, a faint smile on her face.

At the Inner Temple, he turned to Mrs. Wilson. "There is no need for the two of you to come with us unless you think you must. The coachman can drive you through the park or you could visit Madame Bertine's and begin your selections." A short time later they watched as the carriage began to move slowly through the traffic toward the modiste's fashionable shop.

"Your daughter is a lady, Dominic. Even after the shock of meeting me and the experience with your aunt, she behaved quite nicely. Maybe your cousin Agnes needs to take Lady Ravenly in hand," Catherine suggested as they climbed the steps.

"Catherine, Catherine." He laughed. "You are exactly what I have been needing." He held the door for her and asked anxiously, "Marybeth is not going to be a problem, is she? She was a little haughty this morning. But I'm certain as soon as the two of you have time together—"

"Don't rush her. Remember we all need time to adjust. Let us see if my father's man of affairs still recognizes me." She took his arm again and walked down the dim passageway toward the end of the building. "Have you ever wondered why men who are in charge of fortunes and estates have offices in such shabby buildings?"

"Perhaps these surroundings make their clients feel more secure. Or maybe they are afraid to go against tradition. This one?" Harwich asked. At her nod, he opened the door and escorted her in.

When they emerged some time later, the senior partner of the firm was their escort. "Do come again, Miss Durrell," he said quietly, handing her a draft to cover her immediate expenses.

"Immediate expense, ha! That draft would feed the royal household for a year. Not Prinny's, of course, just the king's and queen's," Harwich said as he handed her into a hackney cab. "Will you use my bank or has your father a banker here?"

At the bank their arrival was inconspicuous and their departure something of a royal progress.

"Where to now, your highness?" Harwich whispered in her ear.

"Madame Bertine's." Catherine settled back in the cab, rather pleased with the first part of her morning. After the scene with Lady Ravenly, she had been afraid she would duplicate the disasters of her Season.

At the modiste's they found Marybeth and Mrs. Wilson surrounded by fashion plates and ells of material. Nearby stood one of the assistants. As soon as she noticed the earl, the woman slipped into the back.

A few moments later, a small woman dressed in gray was at the earl's side. "Your lordship, what may we help you with today?" she asked in a less-than-perfect Parisian accent.

"All these ladies need new dresses."

"Me, Papa? I can have a dress from Madame Bertine?" Marybeth asked, her voice reverently hushed. When he smiled at her and nodded, she reached for the stack of fashion plates she had just discarded.

"My future wife and her chaperone need complete new wardrobes. Perhaps you have something made up at present?"

The modiste stood before each woman and then walked slowly around her. "*Oui*. A dress or two. I will take their measurements to be certain." She whisked all three ladies into small rooms, seamstresses with their tapes ready to assist them in disrobing and then to begin essential measurements.

Harwich settled into one of the small chairs, idly looking through the fashion plates and magazines Marybeth and Mrs. Wilson had been using. Before he had time to grow too bored, the ladies were back. Marybeth was so excited it was all she could do to walk instead of skipping.

"Shall I show you the finished dresses at this time?" Madame Bertine asked.

Pulling out his watch, Harwich frowned and shook his head. "No. We will return later this afternoon." Marybeth's face lost its happy smile. "We are promised now," he reminded her with a frown. "This afternoon, Madame, without fail." As he reached the door, he stopped and waved them toward the waiting carriage. Hurrying back inside, he had a word with the modiste.

Her face broke into a saucy smile. "Of course, your lordship," she promised, and slipped his gold into a hidden pocket.

By the time they reached Berkeley Square, Marybeth's disappointment was forgotten as she discussed with Mrs. Wilson the value of merino cloth for winter wear. Harwich, handing Catherine out of the carriage in front of his house, said, so quietly that she had to strain to hear, "I told the housekeeper you might want to tour the house. But with Madame Bertine expecting us . . ." He raised his eyebrow and nodded in his daughter's direction.

Catherine smiled up at him. She looked at the house in front of her. "I would need an afternoon at least if I were to see it properly," she agreed.

After Catherine met the senior servants and made an appointment with Mrs. Thomas to be shown the house, Harwich escorted her into the small salon where the others waited. The silence there was heavy with tension and four pairs of eyes fastened on Catherine, one pair rather fearfully. "Come, my dear," Harwich said formally. "I wish you to meet my cousin and my daughter's chaperone." As they greeted each other politely, each lady inspected the other carefully.

"And how is my cousin, Aunt Beatrice?" Harwich asked as though the scene that morning had not occurred.

"Resting comfortably. I do wish I could take him home with me. The doctor disapproved, though," Lady Ravenly said wistfully.

Remembering his cousin's remarks to the doctor, Harwich hid a smile. "You may visit him anytime you wish," he promised, knowing full well that the doctor had been told to allow her only a short visit once a day.

The other ladies were discussing their shopping. "And Papa said that I might have a dress from Madame Bertine. If only Louisa were in town so that I might tell her," Marybeth told her chaperone ecstatically.

"Nonsense, my dear. You are too young," Cousin Agnes said in her most repressive voice. Marybeth's happy smile disappeared.

Catherine, who had been listening quietly, looked quickly at Harwich. He nodded. "For such a special occasion, I believe my daughter needs a special dress," he said urbanely. His smile softened his words.

By the time the light meal was finished, a surface harmony once more reigned. "Madame Bertine awaits," the earl reminded them, and watched as Marybeth and Mrs. Wilson brightened.

"You do not have to accompany us, Dominic. I'm certain you will be bored," Catherine said as she let him drape her cloak about her.

"Nonsense. I plan to supervise," he assured her. Although she fully expected him to make his excuses and disappear to club after a time, Harwich took an avid interest in the proceedings.

Looking at the excitement on Marybeth's face, Catherine insisted that they choose her dresses first—an afternoon frock for the wedding, a new cloak and muff, and two dresses, one day and one evening, for the holidays. Choosing simple styles befitting her age, the three women draped one fabric after another around her before deciding. Her cloak, they decided, would be a honey-colored cloth trimmed in soft brown fur with matching muff and bonnet. For the wedding Marybeth chose a bright golden-yellow merino trimmed in brown braid with matching spencer. For the holidays they picked a soft pink kerseymere trimmed with ribbons of a slightly darker pink for evening and a warm blue plaid merino for afternoon. The last decision about the lady's clothing concluded, Madame nodded in satisfaction. The little one would undoubtedly set styles when she was introduced to society.

Catherine next turned her attention to Mrs. Wilson. In spite of the lady's protests, Harwich and Catherine ordered a selection of clothes in soft blues, blue-grays, lavenders, and mauves. The older woman remained adamant only on one subject: no fur on her cloak. With decisions about styles and ornamentation made, Mrs. Wilson was swept away by an assistant to try on the dresses Madame Bertine had set aside for her.

Madame then turned her attention to the third lady. Sweeping away the fabric she had displayed for the other two, she called for the richer, warm tones that the lady's reddish-brown hair, amber eyes, and soft peach complexion needed to enhance her properly. Catherine, who had worn the pastels demanded by her aunt during her Season, reveled in her choices. Harwich too made his decisions known. From habits to evening wear, he demanded that she have a selection of garments in her wardrobe. For riding, Catherine selected a moss-green worsted. Harwich added a chocolate brown and a teal blue.

"Do you wish to select the plates now, miss?" Madame Bertine asked, her calm exterior hiding her delight.

Catherine looked around her at the piles of material and shook her head. "Let me complete my selection of material first." She glanced toward Marybeth, who was sitting looking at the fashion plates. Although the girl would not have admitted it to anyone, Marybeth was tired, especially of sitting. Her head turned away and her hand over her mouth, she yawned. Mrs. Wilson, returning with two new costumes, smiled and then looked at Catherine, who was still surrounded by material. A slight nod in answer to her raised eyebrow urged the older woman to speak. "Lord Harwich, would you think it rude if I were to take a hackney to Lady Ravenly's? All this travel has exhausted me," Mrs. Wilson asked thankfully, allowing her exhaustion to show.

"A hackney? Nonsense, you shall have my carriage. It can return for us later," the earl said firmly.

He was surprised by his daughter a moment later. "Could Mrs. Wilson escort me home, Papa? I promised Cousin Agnes I would practice my new piece on the harp this afternoon."

Looking at her in amazement, the earl was ready to refuse when he saw Catherine nod her agreement. "Keeping one's promises is of paramount importance," Catherine said approvingly. Calling the footman, he had their packages carried out.

As he escorted them into the carriage, a small girl, obviously a seamstress, hurried after them. "Swatches for the ladies," she said, curtsying to them.

"Swatches?"

"So that we can find gloves and shoes to match, Papa," Marybeth explained, forgetting her father's experience.

"Of course." Her father handed her into the carriage, his laughter carefully hidden. "Thank you," he said quietly as he tucked the lap robe about Mrs. Wilson. She simply smiled.

Inside the shop Catherine and Madame Bertine were deep in conversation when Harwich returned. "I shall need an elegant day dress very shortly. Something appropriate for a wedding. A morning dress or two and an afternoon frock," Catherine said firmly.

"And some evening clothes. With the Little Season

almost upon us, you must be prepared," the earl insisted.

Madame nodded. Sighing, Catherine agreed.

After considerable deliberation Catherine chose a creamy kerseymere, its bodice, neckline, and hem ornamented with Brussels point lace, a pelisse in a slightly darker worsted trimmed in swansdown, and, ignoring Harwich's protests that she should wear a cottage bonnet of Brussels lace, a tippet and muff of matching swansdown.

The most important outfit chosen, Catherine quickly made her other selections: merinos in jade, deep blue, and a gold plaid for afternoon as well as muslins in gold, apricot, with matching pelisses for mornings. Harwich selected the material for the evening, his eye noting the pleasing effect of a bronze velvet, a rich terra-cotta figured satin, and turquoise satin against Catherine's hair and skin. "The bronze, first, Madame. Don't you agree?"

The fabrics chosen, they turned their attention to styles. Arguing good-naturedly, Catherine and Harwich inspected one fashion plate after another. The riding dresses they chose varied from one simply cut and trimmed with swansdown to a rather rakish design with military trimming. Although they agreed on the habits, Harwich protested the simplicity of the other dresses. Both Catherine and Madame Bertine insisted that her dresses be rather simple and straight, their bodices gored in the new fashion to display her figure to advantage—or so Madame persuaded him. Choosing simple ruchings and flounces as decoration for her dresses, Catherine allowed him to choose her pelisses, protesting only when he added a fourth cape to one. For evening she agreed on more elaboration, her dresses trimmed with overskirts of net, rouleaux, and leaves of satin and vandyked. In spite of Harwich's protests, neither she nor Madame Bertine would allow him to see the final design for the wedding. Leaving him alone in the outer salon, they hurried to a fitting room for their consultation. A short time later Catherine emerged; she cleared her throat to capture his attention.

Harwich looked up, stood up, and crossed to her side. He bowed slightly. "Ah, pretty miss, give me a token, a kiss, perhaps?" he whispered. His eyes were twinkling. "But do not tell my bride-to-be. You will recognize her by her green dress."

"Dominic, Madame Bertine will emerge in a moment. Do you like this?" Catherine asked.

He stepped back and inspected her, noting with pleasure the way salmon merino hugged her curves as though the dress had been made for her. The soft cream lace ruche and vandyked flounces added an illusion of more height. "Delightful," he said quietly, crossing to her side.

Madame Bertine bustled in, an assistant with her arms full close behind. "The pelisse and cloak," she announced, holding out the former for Catherine to slip on. The long, puffed sleeves trimmed with bands of swansdown fit over her hands. Madame checked their length and nodded. She adjusted the bodice slightly, settling the ruching and swansdown carefully before hooking the last hook in place. Finally she handed Catherine a new hat, a swansdown tippet that matched the pelisse. Satisfied that her patron was now the first stare of elegance, she smiled. The assistant carefully wrapped Catherine in a heavy teal-blue mantle lined in salmon velvet and trimmed in swansdown. The modiste took one last look and smiled again. Although not a beauty in the blond fashion so popular in the last Season, Miss Durrell had a certain elegance that would display her fashions well. "I will send word when you need to return for a fitting," she said quietly.

In the carriage Catherine leaned back against the gray silk. She said, "I had forgotten how I hated fittings."

Her weariness was evident to Harwich. He carefully tucked the fur lap robe about her. "A nice cup of tea. That's what you need," he suggested, looking at his watch.

Catherine brightened. Although Madame Bertine had offered wine and biscuits, Catherine had been determined to finish and had declined. "Yes," she agreed. He leaned forward to tell the coachman to go to Berkeley Square. "No, Dominic," she said quietly. "Grosvenor Square."

"My aunt's? She'll go on and on until you're exhausted. Besides, after this morning I thought you might not wish to stay there."

"Her support will do much to prevent gossip. She has a good heart in spite of her tendency to be blunt. Besides, I intend to retire as soon as we arrive."

"But we need to make plans," he protested.

"Tomorrow, please? I am to tour your home in the afternoon." She closed her eyes and yawned, turning her head away from him.

Seeing the faint shadows beneath her eyes, evident even in the growing twilight, Harwich agreed. He changed the orders and sat back. "What colors do you prefer for your suite?" he asked casually, picking up her hand between both of his, his fingers caressing her palm.

"Something light. Everything here seems so dark after Italy."

"Cream? White? Light blue?"

She was silent for a moment. "Cream." She let her eyes drift open and smiled at him. Her fingers tightened around his. "Something fresh and bright."

He sat back and pulled her closer to him, her head on his shoulder, the swansdown of her tippet tickling her cheek. All too soon the carriage stopped. "Tomorrow," he whispered as he escorted her inside. A few minutes later he took his seat again. He smiled quietly as he thought of Catherine's surprise when she saw her rooms. Tilting his hat over his forehead, he settled back, pleased with his world.

10

The refreshing morning of rest that Catherine had planned was rudely shattered with a scratching sound on the door shortly after she finished her tea. "Mrs. Hubert to see you, Miss Catherine," Davis announced as she carefully shut the door behind the upstairs maid. Catherine's face grew white as the sheets that were tucked around her. "Shall I send word that you are indisposed?"

Her mistress remained silent for a moment. Relaxing her fingers from the sheet she had been clutching, Catherine slid off the bed. "Have them tell her I am dressing. I will be with her shortly," she said, taking pride in the fact that her voice was steady.

As she sat before the mirror later, Catherine wished that Dominic were there. A short time later she rejected that idea. Chiding herself for her fear, she reminded herself that she was older and her aunt could do little to harm her. Davis combed through her hair, wrapping it in a high knot of curls on the back of her head, a few wisps of hair caressing her hairline.

"Do you wish me to accompany you, Miss Catherine?" Davis asked, stepping back to inspect her handiwork. Critically, she tweaked one curl into place. "If it is to look like the picture I saw yesterday, you will need to have a hairdresser cut the front. Your aunt may be surprised at you," she added, recognizing her mistress's nervousness.

Letting her maid ramble on, Catherine thought of the last time she had seen her aunt. It had been a triumph for the older woman and devastating for the younger. As Davis' chatter came slowly to a halt, Catherine stood before the mirror. The hair, though longer now, was the same. Her figure was fuller. Thanks to Madame Bertine, her frock was equal to any in *La Belle Assemblee*. The deep forest-green morning dress made the reddish tints in her hair seem brighter and her skin glow. The rich gold braid decorating the vandyked neckline, tunic, and hem gave her eyes a golden spark. Picking up her Kashmir shawl in a Norwich pattern, she arranged it precisely and squared her shoulders.

A short time later she walked into the small salon. "Miss Durrell," Jenkins announced loudly, and bowed slightly to her.

"Well, niece, I see you have done very well for yourself," a light voice said maliciously.

"Aunt," Catherine said quietly, taking her seat in a small chair opposite the settee on which her aunt was sitting.

"Don't call me that. You know I can't abide it." The woman looked around carefully and waved a small plump hand. "You have fallen soft, I see." Catherine merely stared at her, noting the overly rounded figure that seemed to overflow the bodice of her gown and the heavy cosmetics that tried to conceal the lines of dissipation. Her aunt's hair, once a soft golden brown, was now a brassy yellow.

"Well, haven't you anything to say for yourself?" her aunt demanded, rather shaken by the sight of the niece she had once declared impossibly homely.

"How is Uncle Hubert?" Catherine asked quietly, thinking of the quiet man who chose to live retired on his estate in Yorkshire.

Her aunt ignored her question. "How is it that I hear of your return when I visit my agent? You should have let me know as soon as you arrived in town."

"The trip was a sudden one." Catherine smiled as

she remembered Dominic's face when her father insisted that he bring her to London. "I planned to write when I was established."

"Established? Setting up your own household, are you? I would never have believed that your father would permit you to live alone. How did you come to know Lady Ravenly?" Clarice Hubert asked enviously. She glanced around the room, noting the Ming vases and jade and ivory that added color to the straw walls covered in Chinese figures.

Catherine settled back in her chair and smiled lightly. "Have you returned to town for the Little Season, Aunt?"

"Returned to town? Now I spend most of my time here. You know how dull it is in the provinces. Come, girl, what are your plans?"

"Aunt, how you flatter me. Girl, indeed," Catherine answered lightly, amazed by her own temerity. "I am not certain of my plans at this time." How fortunate she was not forced to lie, she thought. She had never been good at lying. She always began to stutter.

Jenkins opened the door. "Mrs. Wilson," he said loudly, the sound echoing around the small chamber.

"Catherine, were we supposed to visit Madame . . . Excuse me, I did not know you had a guest," the older woman said, backing out hastily.

"Do come in, Mrs. Wilson," Catherine said, the tiniest edge of relief evident in her voice. "Aunt Hubert, may I present Mrs. George Wilson, my chaperone. Mrs. Wilson, Mrs. Hubert."

"Your chaperone?"

"My father preferred that I not travel alone."

"It would have been scandalous," Mrs. Wilson said firmly.

"Are you still at the same address, Aunt?" Catherine asked quietly. Her aunt nodded. Catherine rose gracefully. "Then I shall write you later when I know more of my plans." She glanced at the clock

now striking the hour. "You must excuse me. I have
an appointment." She smiled once more and pulled
the bellpull. A few seconds later Jenkins appeared.
"Mrs. Hubert is just leaving," she said quietly, her
words very firm. As if in shock, her aunt rose, the
edges of her mouth tightening.

After the door closed silently behind her mother's
sister, Catherine sank back into her chair, her hands
shaking. She ran a hand over her face as though she
expected it to be dripping with perspiration.

"Your aunt? I suppose she must be very fond of
you," Mrs. Wilson said, smiling at her charge.

Had she seen Mrs. Hubert's face at that moment,
she would have retracted her words. The lady was
angry, her face almost purple with rage. "How dare
she dismiss me as if I were a servant," she said. Her
voice had lost its lightness. "That miss should have
remembered with whom she was dealing." Clarice
Hubert smiled unpleasantly.

Fortunately Catherine knew nothing of the scene.
Her nerves once more under control, Catherine
asked her chaperone, "Are you well enough to
accompany me to Reston House this afternoon?"

"Certainly. A good night's sleep does wonders."
The older woman paused. "Wouldn't you rather have
your aunt as a chaperone?"

"No!" Catherine's answer burst from her like a
shot from a cannon. She hastened to explain. "We do
not always agree. Also, Lord Harwich does not
approve of her."

"Well, I suppose you must respect his wishes. But
if you wish to change your mind, I will understand."

"Can you be ready shortly? Mrs. Thomas promised
to be ready to show me Reston House at one
o'clock."

That afternoon Catherine and Mrs. Wilson walked
through Reston House with the housekeeper. In spite
of Catherine's nervousness, she seemed in perfect

control of the situation. She discussed the linens and menus as though she had been dealing with them for years. Stopping to view the schoolroom, she smiled at Marybeth. For a moment the girl smiled tentatively, but a quick frown from her governess put her back to work. As they stepped back into the hall, Catherine asked, "Has Lady Marybeth made her choice of rooms? Lord Harwich told me that she was to move out of the schoolroom."

"Mrs. Throckmorton felt the decision should be postponed," the housekeeper said in a determinedly bland voice.

"She did?"

"Lady Marybeth was rather disappointed."

"When was this decision made?"

"At supper last evening," the housekeeper said quietly, only a tinge of disapproval coloring her voice. "Lord Harwich dined at his club."

"He did? Then Lord Harwich and I shall discuss this later," Catherine promised. After touring the house from the fourth-floor attic where the under-servants had their quarters to the kitchen and cold rooms below, Catherine sank into a comfortable chair in a small room she claimed for her own at first sight. Its windows looked out over a garden, rather bare at present but filled with roses in the spring and summer, or so Mrs. Thomas said. Its walls were covered in a striped silk in a light golden yellow. On its parquet floors was a beautiful rug in a mixture of gold, rust, and dark brown. The chairs and settee complimented the walls and rug with their needlepoint tapestries in earth tones and creams. Catherine smiled at her chaperone as she took a cup of tea from the tray the footman had placed on a low table in front of the settee.

"A very nicely organized house," said Mrs. Wilson. "I am certain that you will find everyone here cooperative."

"Almost everyone." Catherine rose and crossed to a window, her eyes dark with worry. Before she could explain, the door swung open.

"Here you are," the earl said, bowing slightly. "I'm sorry I was not here to greet you." He crossed to stand behind Catherine. "A message from the Foreign Office."

"Are you being sent away again?" Catherine asked softly, an anxious look shadowing her face.

"Away? No. My service for the government is over. Permanently, I hope." He caught sight of the tea tray. "Is the tea hot?"

"I'll ring for fresh." Catherine smiled and crossed the room.

With her chaperone present, their conversation was pleasantly ordinary as Catherine asked about his day. "Boring," Harwich said. "All those men do is talk. I did stop by my club and at St. George's, Hanover Square."

"St. George's?" Catherine asked.

"To arrange for the wedding. I have the special license right here." He patted his pocket.

Catherine sat down, her legs weak. Her heart hammered as if trying to break through her chest. "And?" she asked, her voice a whispy breath.

"The rector will marry us this Friday at two. That should give Madame Bertine time to finish your dress. I stopped by Fleet Street, too. The announcement will go out on Saturday in the *Morning Post*." He smiled at her. Taking his cup, he sat by Catherine on the settee.

Neither lady made a comment. Catherine simply stared at him. She had known the day was coming, but somehow she had managed to convince herself that they would wait until Marybeth was more familiar with her.

"Three days?" she asked after clearing her throat nervously. "I thought we agreed that Marybeth should have more of a chance to get to know me?"

He leaned back and fixed her with a midnight-blue stare. "Catherine Durrell, are you afraid of my daughter? Throw your heart over. We'll brush through just fine, you'll see." Glaring at him, Catherine waited, her eyes golden sparks. "Any changes you plan to make in the household? I'll set up household accounts for you. Remember it will be your home." Harwich shifted slightly in order to see her more clearly. "Come, now, there must be something," he said, teasing her.

"Nothing immediate. Mrs. Thomas and I agree that we shall continue as she has been for a time until I learn her routine." She stopped for a moment and looked toward Mrs. Wilson, who was trying hard to be inconspicuous. Before she lost her nerve, she plunged in. "Have you walked through the suites with Marybeth so that she can choose the one she wants?"

"She hasn't done so already?"

"I believe your cousin has some objections."

"Objections? That woman had better understand that my wishes are the ones that count in this household." He looked at Catherine and hastily added, "And yours, too, my dear." Making himself a mental note, he resolved to discuss the issue with his cousin in the morning. He smiled at his future wife and asked, "What are your plans for the evening, or did my aunt suggest anything?" His eyes caressed Catherine.

Startled by his sudden change in topic, Catherine said, "I, ah, we have not seen her. I left a message for her, but when she left the house this morning, I had a guest." Her words fell over one another in her confusion.

"A guest?"

Before Catherine could get the words out, Mrs. Wilson explained. "Her aunt. She seemed most charming."

"Did you contact her, Catherine?" he asked. His face was stormy.

"No," she said quietly. "She had word from Papa's agent. She uses him also."

"Good. You are not to see that woman alone again, Catherine. There will be times when we will extend her an invitation; she is family. She is also a member of a very fast set, according to the gossip of my club."

Despite her own agreement with the idea, Catherine bristled. She rose and crossed to the fire-place. Harwich smiled at the picture she made in the salmon outfit she had worn briefly the day before. His smiles quickly faded when he saw her face. "Catherine, you did not promise that woman you would stay with her, did you?"

"What?" she asked, a snap in her voice.

Glancing at the chaperone, who was regretting that she had mentioned anything about the visit, Harwich rose and crossed to stand behind Catherine, who was staring into the fire. He whispered in her ear, "What's wrong?"

As aware as he of her audience, Catherine turned around. Startled by his nearness, she stepped back hastily, hitting the fire irons. Only his quick thinking prevented her from falling into the burning coals. Her face was pasty white as Harwich carried her to the settee.

"Don't do that again. Promise me you will be more careful," he said in a shaken tone, his face worried.

"I won't," Catherine promised. Her voice was only a thread.

Mrs. Wilson held her hand over her racing heart and then fumbled in her reticule for her smelling salts. "Here. Let her sniff this," the older woman suggested, handing the vial to the earl.

He held it beneath Catherine's nose for a moment, nodding in satisfaction as he watched the color return to her face. Convinced that she would be all right, he crossed to a low table and poured himself a healthy tot of brandy from the decanter. He tossed it back and refilled his glass.

"Here. Have some of this," he suggested, holding the glass to Catherine's lips.

"No. Ugh. I hate that taste," Catherine complained as she swallowed.

"Then stop putting yourself in danger. I know that it will be difficult, but please try."

"I'll have you know that for years I have lived a perfectly normal, safe life."

"Are you saying that being kidnapped is normal?" he asked facetiously.

"That is not what I meant, and you know it." Catherine sat up and swung her legs off the settee, settling her skirts carefully around her ankles. Her indignation had done much to restore her equilibrium.

"This will be better for you," Mrs. Wilson said, handing her a cup of tea with cream and sugar, just the way she liked.

Glaring at Harwich, Catherine smiled at her chaperone and took the cup gratefully.

"I saw a handbill for the theater tonight. Would you like to go?" Harwich asked as though nothing intervened. "Not one of the best performances of the year, I am certain, but it should be amusing."

"A play? Will Lady Ravenly agree?" Mrs. Wilson asked.

"Undoubtedly. When I escort you home we shall see." Harwich sat down beside Catherine again. He leaned closer to her and whispered, "In a few days we will not have to ask permission." His soft breath on her ear made Catherine tingle just as she did when he feathered a kiss along her neck. Her heart raced wildly.

On Friday it was still racing. Her days had been so full that Catherine had little time to herself. Harwich had insisted that both she and Marybeth choose draperies and furniture before the wedding.

Although Marybeth had no trouble in selecting draperies and wallpaper, Catherine had been more selective. Her future stepdaughter had chosen pink silk paper for her walls with the silver-stripped satin for her furniture. Approving her choice, Catherine helped her select pink-and-silver figured draperies. They made a youthful frame for the girl, but she wanted something richer, deeper, more sophisticated.

Finally she made her choices. At the top of her walls she wanted a Greek key design in terra cotta, repeating the color in the satin draperies for the windows. For her bed, a huge but elegant rosewood frame whose columns dwindled to a thin fineness, she chose a combination of terra-cotta satin and cream lace. The rest of her furniture, in both her bedroom and her sitting room, matched the rosewood and were covered in cream satin that contained narrow stripes of terra cotta and forest green. Raiding the attics at Reston House one afternoon, she found pieces of dark jade that had been packed away when the fashions changed, as well as green-and-gold Sevres vases. For Marybeth she discovered a pair of figurines in the same pink as her room. Promising herself another inspection soon, Catherine glanced around the piled attic, its trunks full and its furniture neatly stacked and under dustcovers. She sighed and walked slowly down the stairs.

With Harwich demanding so much time, Catherine had to be firm about her appointments with Madame Bertine. Refusing his escort, Catherine chose to take Mrs. Wilson and Marybeth instead. When she arrived at Reston House one afternoon to call for her future stepdaughter, Catherine was surprised to find Mrs. Agnes Throckmorton waiting instead.

Always pleasant with the lady, Catherine smiled her greeting. "Is Lady Marybeth ready to go? The carriage is waiting," she asked quietly.

"I do not believe that Lady Marybeth needs to miss another lesson. She is rather flighty as it is."

Catherine felt chilled at the ice in her words. The incidents with the dresses and the rooms had obviously not been forgotten. Squaring her shoulders, she worked at keeping her smile. "How strange. Her father told me only an hour ago that he was delighted to have her go with me." She looked up the staircase. Hovering at the top, disappointment written in her face, stood Marybeth listening.

"Her father! Ha! What does he know?" Mrs. Throckmorton grumbled. "Who took care of his precious spoiled daughter when he was away? Now he tries to change behavior that it has taken me months to instill. Madame Bertine, indeed. It will be giving that little lady a false sense of her own importance."

Catherine took advantage of an opening as the older woman took a breath. "Lady Marybeth is important not only to her father but also to me," she said in clear, ringing tones.

"You will change your tune when you have to live in the same household."

"Stop," Catherine said, surprising herself with the firmness in her voice. She glanced up the staircase once more, hoping that Marybeth had not heard the woman's words. "I have her father's permission to take her with me. If you object, please discuss your objections with him." Catherine watched in amazement as Mrs. Throckmorton seemed to shrink before her eyes. Glancing around for Thomas and her footman, she noted gratefully that they had disappeared. But she had no doubt that they were within earshot. The story would be about both houses shortly. "Thomas," she called. He appeared a moment later. "Tell Lady Marybeth that I am waiting," she said quietly. "If you would care to accompany us, Mrs. Throckmorton?"

"No, thank you, miss." The refusal was as harsh as the earlier words had been. The older woman glared at Catherine and walked proudly up the stairs to her room.

The rest of the afternoon, although trying, was a delight. Marybeth had walked down the stairs gracefully and joined Catherine. Although both she and Mrs. Wilson noted the tear streaks on Lady Marybeth's face, neither had mentioned them. Keeping their conversation light, they exchanged glances and discussed their errand until Marybeth was in control once more.

Once in Madame Bertine's salon, each was whisked away to be poked with pins and stitched hastily into garments. Catherine, only a few steps away, was delighted when Marybeth called her in to look at each dress. Cautiously the girl considered each suggestion Catherine made, accepting most. She critically inspected each costume Catherine tried on, advising the use of braid instead of ribbons on one dress. Her face glowed with pride when Catherine gave instructions for the change.

Over at Grillon's later, all three ladies sighed tiredly. "If only looking fashionable were not so tiring," Catherine moaned.

"But if it were too simple, it would lose its excitement," Mrs. Wilson warned.

Marybeth simply laughed.

As Friday grew closer, Catherine began to show her nervousness. If Mrs. Wilson did not remind her, Catherine would roll the edge of the tablecloth across the table at breakfast. As she shopped for hats, shoes, and other accessories, her fingers worked nervously on her pelisse or her mantle. When Harwich slipped the beautiful topaz and diamond ring on her hand, he had to tell her to unclench her fist from the edge of her sleeve first. Marybeth began to keep a private list of the fabric that Catherine had creased. By the time Thursday evening was over, none of the ladies wanted to sit by her. Even Harwich noticed her habit when Catherine reached up to tuck the end of his neckcloth into his waistcoat. Before she had realized what she was doing, his careful work had been crushed.

"Catherine," her chaperone said more loudly than she intended. Dropping fabric, Catherine stood up and crossed the room to look out the window.

"Wait for me in the hallway, Marybeth," Harwich said quietly. "Ladies, and you too, John." He held the door open. Glancing back, both Marybeth and Lady Ravenly stifled a giggle. Catherine had the edge of the curtain in her hand. Harwich hurried to her side, taking her hands in his and turning her around. "Catherine." She didn't answer. "Catherine!" Startled, she looked up. "This habit of yours can be dangerous in public, golden eyes." He laughed.

"What?" She looked at him curiously.

"I would hate to have to challenge a man because you had untied his neckcloth."

Catherine blushed and hung her head. "I only do it when I am very unsure of myself," she explained, refusing to look at him.

"Then it's fortunate that this state of uncertainty will be over tomorrow." He looked down at her and smiled. Not trusting his own control, he hugged her and kissed the top of her bright curls. "Remember to have Davis pack for several days," he said quietly, and stepped back. He was breathing hard.

Her eyes wide and her throat choked, Catherine merely nodded.

"Don't be late," he said laughingly as he put his hand on the door. "I hate to wait." He slipped through the door and then turned and smiled.

Catherine's heart caught for a moment and then began to beat rapidly.

It was still pounding Friday afternoon as she waited in the vestibule of the church. With her father so far away, Babbington had been pressed into service not only as best man but also as Catherine's escort. Marybeth was her only attendant.

Taking a deep breath, Catherine nodded, and they started down the aisle in Marybeth's wake. Only Mrs. Wilson and Davis sat on Catherine's side of the church. Catherine had insisted on her maid's presence, needing someone who was all her own. Harwich's side, though not full, contained a wide variety of his relatives. "I promise you we have never eaten a bride yet, Catherine," Babbington had whispered as she hesitated at the sight. Remembering Agnes Throckmorton's hostile eyes, Catherine was not certain.

To Harwich standing in front of the banked candles, Catherine seemed to float down the aisle, her vibrant hair lighting the gloom of the cold November day. His heart was racing as he watched her come closer, the soft Brussels lace and kerseymere of her dress silent as she moved. Her fur tippet created a halo effect around her head. Although her hand was shaking on his cousin's arm, she seemed perfectly steady. For one moment he took his eyes off his bride to smile at his daughter, radiant in her bright yellow. Then Catherine was there. He reached for her hand and pulled her close to his side. He smiled at her, lost in wide golden eyes. Then he turned to face the altar.

11

By the time they reached the small estate outside London that Babbington had lent them, Catherine was almost overcome with nerves. Dismissing the footman, Harwich led her into the house, small compared to Reston. "May I present my best wishes, your lordship," the butler said in welcome. "Shall I show you to your rooms?" Catherine blushed furiously and then looked at the floor, hoping to hide her face. The butler kept his face impassive.

"Thank you," Harwich said quietly. Escorting Catherine up the stairs in the wake of the butler, Harwich felt her tense.

"If you need anything, please ring. Supper will be served whenever you wish," the butler said, his booming voice hushed slightly. He opened the door and waited for them to enter.

The suite, two bedrooms and a sitting room, was lovely, a fact Catherine realized only later. But the first thing she saw through the open sitting-room door was the bed. She stopped, half in the hallway and half in the room. Harwich gave her a slight shove, enough so the butler could close the door. "Edwards and Davis arrived earlier," he said quietly, his hand resting lightly on her stiff back. "Go. Change into something less formal," he suggested. She took two or three steps and stopped to look at him. He smiled and said, "Join me in the sitting room as soon as you change." His voice made shivers run up her spine.

The door to the sitting room safely closed,

Catherine sighed and sat in the chair beside the dressing table. Change, he had said. Spotting the bellpull, she headed across the room. Then she stopped. Dominic could enter the room whenever he wanted. Of course, he had done that in Italy. Even in London she was certain that if she had remained in her room longer than what he thought necessary, he would have appeared in her suite. No one had much success at telling him no. The thought of his entering her room while she was changing made her reach for the bellpull again.

Later Davis fastened the copper hooks on the back of the blue merino. In the firelight the copper lace around Catherine's neck was a reflection of the copper-brown curls that tumbled artlessly down her back. The maid secured the blue ribbons in her mistress's curls before handing her a rich paisley shawl that matched her dress. "Just as lovely as you looked earlier," Davis said, beaming with pride. Then a noise sounded outside the connecting door.

Before Davis could cross to the door, Harwich was inside. "I ordered supper served in the sitting room, Catherine. It just arrived." He had changed out of a blue superfine coat he had worn for the wedding. In its place was a loose jacket. In place of his starched neckcloth he wore a Byron handkerchief draped around his neck. Catherine caught her breath. "We'll ring later, Davis," he said quietly, and led Catherine into the next room.

Later, when Catherine tried to remember that evening, she was never sure of all the details. They had wine. She knew that. There was meat and cheese and laughter. At first she had been so nervous that her teeth had chattered. Dominic told her bluntly she was noisier than the crickets they had hidden in a box under squire's pew at the church.

He had chosen his subject well. Hidden behind the handsome man whose casual presence caused her heart to race and a strange heat to build was the boy who had cared for her. Of course, he had boxed her ears a few times.

"Do you remember when we went looking for those crickets?" she asked. Her eyes glinted with mischief.

"I am not likely to forget. If it hadn't been for the anticipation of the squire's face when those bugs began to sing during the sermon, I would have done more than box your ears when you ruined my new riding jacket. Dash it, Father was angry." He leaned back on the soft yellow settee and stretched, his arm casually draping across the back of the settee. He smiled at her. Suddenly she was nervous again. The edge of her shawl began to disappear as she rolled it nervously.

Giving her a moment to herself, Harwich crossed to the bellpull. "You may take the supper things," he said quietly to the footman who answered. "No, leave those." He rescued the last bottle of wine and the glasses. Returning to the settee, he poured them both a glass. "To good friends," he said, his voice rich with emotion. He lifted his glass to her.

"To friends," she answered, sipping hers more slowly. She looked at the rich garnet-red Venetian glasses in their hands, noting how the wine deepened their colors. "In some places people toss their empty glasses into the fireplace after a toast," Catherine said in her softest voice. She sat beside him quietly.

"Let's do it. I'll replace the glasses."

"No." They looked at each other as though they were children bent on mischief. "I dare you," she said firmly.

"I suggested it first," he reminded her. His eyes were a deep blue; they were laughing, and a spark of desire smoldered in their depths. "Are you ready?"

"No. They're too beautiful to destroy." Her fingers cupped protectively around the red goblet she held.

She raised it to her lips and drained it. She set it carefully on the table in front of them. Her tongue caught the last of the dark drops on her lips.

Slowly, carefully Harwich put his glass beside hers. He turned slightly, so slightly that Catherine was not certain why her heart began to pound. He leaned forward. His tongue touched the spot where the wine had been. For a moment she was as still as a sonata on paper. Then she sighed and leaned toward him.

Carefully, as if stalking a wild doe, Harwich circled her waist, pulling her across the slick satin and into his arms. Her eyes never left his. Their golden depths seemed to glow, to pulse in response to the beat of her heart. The pulse in her neck fascinated him. Lowering his head, he kissed it, working his way slowly up her neck and across her face. His lips were soft at first. Then the spark he had tried so hard to control blazed into an inferno.

Their kiss deepened. His tongue probed her lips, coaxing them open. Sighing, she slipped one hand behind his head and pulled him closer, her lips slightly parted. He pulled her even closer against him. Her feet left the floor and her head settled on his shoulder. Her kisses covered his face, his eyes. He slowly lifted his legs beside hers. His free arm began a slow, careful journey from her waist. Both were breathing hard. Their kisses grew deeper, his tongue making forays into her mouth that she answered. His hand cupping her hips, he pulled her even closer. His lips sought the creamy peach tops of her breasts as they peeped through the copper lace. She wiggled nervously. He returned to her mouth, his kisses begging that she respond.

Disappointed, she put both hands around his head, pulling it back to her breasts. The thin wool of her dress seemed too heavy for the heat of the room. Harwich discarded his jacket, awkwardly pulling first one and then the other arm free. Catherine slid a hand across his chest. A button, already slightly dislodged, gave way. Her hand touched his chest, her fingers wandering through the thick mat of hair. Her eyes wide, she watched as he shut his eyes and sighed. His pulse seemed to keep time with hers. Carefully she reached out a finger and laid it on his chest, experiencing the racing of his heart.

He groaned and pulled her hand away. His arms held her molded to his body. Hers circled him, discovering through the fine linen the rippling muscles of his back.

His control almost gone, he swung his feet under hers and pulled her on top of him, her eyes a few inches from his own. Gold fire locked with blue midnight. Their pulses slowed and their breath was almost normal when Catherine realized where she was. Startled, she tried to sit up, but Harwich refused to let her go. "You're my wife, golden eyes," he whispered. His breath on her cheek sent a shiver of passion through her.

Slowly, carefully, Harwich stood up, bringing her with him. She felt the muscles in his legs tense even through the merino of her dress. "Let Davis get you ready for bed," he said before he kissed her again. Her face, already flushed, burned. He stepped back and dropped his arms. For the first time that evening Catherine felt her old loneliness and fear. "Go on," he said again. He watched carefully as she crossed the room, impatient to have her once more at his side.

His change occupied only a few short minutes. However, Harwich was determined to remain in control, to teach Catherine patiently. He paced, his turns bringing him closer and closer to the connecting doors between the bedrooms.

In Catherine's bedroom, Davis hurried her mistress into a soft silk nightdress embroidered with roses and decorated with soft lace. She pulled the pins from Catherine's curls and seated her in front of the mirror to brush her hair. Only once did the maid speak. Catherine sat, her eyes looking deep into the mirror, seeking wisdom and answer to her feeling of being alone. Her hair fell in a reddish-brown curtain. Davis turned down the bed carefully, folding back both sides precisely.

"Haven't you forgotten my braid?" Catherine asked quietly.

"I thought, ah, doesn't Lord Harwich . . ." the maid mumbled.

"Lord Harwich?" Catherine echoed, her voice slightly puzzled. Then her eyes grew wide and her breath came in pants. A son, she had promised him a son. She crossed the room and climbed into the high bed. Her voice, only a thread, whispered, "That will be all, Davis. Thank you."

The click of the door behind the maid was the signal Harwich had been waiting for. He opened the door and closed it behind him. She was so beautiful in the light of the fire and the candles. He studied the picture she made in the bed, her red-brown hair falling in a rich rain over her shoulders, the white pillows piled high behind her. He took several deep breaths and then crossed to the bed. "Do you sleep on the right or the left?" he asked as casually as he could.

Catherine pulled the sheet under her chin more tightly. "The right or the left of what?" Her voice reflected her confusion.

"Of the bed." Harwich watched in fascination as the red appeared under the lace that barely covered her full breasts, up her neck, and to the roots of her hair. "Do you blush everywhere?" he asked curiously as he kicked his slippers off and laid his dressing gown across a chair.

Knowing she should close her eyes tightly, Catherine could not. She watched every move he made, the thin lawn nightshirt hiding little as her husband stood in front of the fire.

"Well, where do you sleep?"

"In the middle," she said, and then blushed again. Blushing at her age was so silly. She hadn't blushed in years before she met Dominic again.

He smiled and slid into bed beside her. "You forgot the candles," she whispered.

He looked at her carefully and then nodded. He slid out of bed, his nightshirt creeping up his thighs, and blew them out.

Returning to bed, he slowly, carefully, moved into place beside her once more. He moved closer to her and settled her against him, her head finding its natural niche on his shoulder. At first she was tense, almost rigid. He gave her an opportunity to grow accustomed to his touch. The unaccustomed wine, the comfort of his warm body beside hers, the rhythm of his heart beneath her cheek, lulled her to sleep.

Harwich felt her muscles relax, her breathing deepen as he fought for control. Feeling her soft regular breaths against his cheek, he groaned softly. She was asleep. Sighing, he kissed her lightly and waited, his hands softly stroking her side.

Catherine dreamed vast, fanciful dreams of exotic places, places warmed by a hot sun. She moaned and moved restlessly, seeking release from the heat. She pulled at her nightdress, its cool silk burning against her heated skin. It crept up, baring first her thighs and later her hips for her husband's restless hands. The heat grew. Gasping for breath, she moved to the side of the bed, sat up, and pulled her nightdress over her head as she had done during the hottest nights in Italy. Tossing it to the floor, she sank back on her pillows, her eyes still closed. She shivered slightly.

Harwich had discarded his nightshirt earlier. He watched the play of the soft shadows of fire on her pale skin, his breath catching in his throat. Her full breasts made his hands ache to hold them, his mouth hunger for their taste. As Catherine settled under the covers once more, he moved closer, his distance carefully calculated. "Are you awake, little cat?" he asked as he watched her stretch slightly.

She jumped. The covers fell back, revealing her breasts to the firelight and the cold. "Dominic?"

"Yes," he said, trying not to laugh at her confusion.

"Go away." She reached for the sheet to cover herself.

"Let me warm them," he said, his voice a husky whisper.

"Oh, Dom," she mumbled in a breathy voice. Her heart had begun to pound again. He pulled her closer to him, molding hip to hip. His control was slipping. She moved restlessly beneath him, the heat of her dreams starting a strange ache. Her arms wrapped around him, pulling him closer, detailing his rough hair on her sensitive breasts, learning the muscles of his back.

"Dom, you don't have any clothes on," she whispered in a puzzled voice. For some reason it did not frighten her.

"Neither do you, my cat." His mouth captured hers before she could make any protest. The kiss deepened. One of his hands crept lower, stroking her soft thighs. Catherine shifted restlessly.

Harwich carefully lowered himself slowly, halting for a moment as she adjusted to the feel of him. A swift thrust and he lay there for a moment. Then he began to move, slowly at first and then faster, even faster until he stiffened and collapsed in her arms.

Stunned, Catherine just lay there, her arms and legs still partially around him. As his breathing slowed, he pulled himself up on his elbows again and smiled down at her. "My cat," he said proudly, and kissed her.

As he drifted off to sleep a few minutes later, Catherine lay awake by his side. Held against him by the arm he had thrown around her waist, she shifted restlessly for a few minutes. The soft roughness of his legs intertwined with hers. His heartbeat, so loud and so steady, made her lullaby. She sighed and closed her eyes.

When she awoke early the next morning, the first thing she saw were his blue eyes. Harwich lay on his side facing her, his hair framed by the white pillow behind him. He smiled, a slow, easy sensual smile that hinted of passion. "Cat, my own golden cat," he whispered as he bent to kiss her.

It began as a soft delicate kiss, only the lightest touch of lips. Quickly it became more. Her lips opened and invited him in. Hands, lips, eyes, struggled to learn every inch of the lover. Catherine blushed furiously at his whispered words, but she pulled him closer to feather his face with kisses, to run her hands over the muscles of his back. "Dom," she repeated almost like a chant, her voice rising and falling with her excitement. Later, their passion spent, they lay, arms twined around each other.

Working with her father at Herculaneum, Catherine had seen statues and mosaics of men before. But the living colors of her husband's skin and hair fascinated her as did the muscles that rippled whenever he moved. After the bath that Harwich insisted she take and that did much to ease aches she had not been aware of, she dismissed Davis. Hearing the clatter of dishes in the sitting room, she waited until she heard the outside door click. Gathering her dressing gown around her— her husband had suggested that they dress comfortably—Catherine opened the door.

"So, you can still blush, lady wife," he said, laughing, drawing her closer. "Mmm. You smell so wonderful." He nuzzled her ear, nibbling on a lobe. Harwich pulled her even closer and kissed her deeply. Stepping back with effort, he led her to a small table where breakfast waited.

Some time later, as they lay intertwined on Harwich's bed, which he insisted they christen, Catherine looked at her husband, then snuggled close to him, giggling slightly as she felt her closeness affect him. Then her eyes widened thoughtfully. She broke into giggles of laughter.

Leaning down to run a finger over her soft lips, Harwich smiled. "Are you happy, little cat?"

"Yes, Dom. Oh, yes." She threw her arms around his neck and returned his kiss passionately. Her laughter, never far away, rocked her.

"Tell me what is going on that head of yours, Catherine Dominique Reston," he demanded, a wicked leer on his face.

She giggled harder. "Now I understand Papa," she said, her voice almost muffled by her laughter.

"Your father!"

"We found some pottery and I was suppose to clean it and catalog it. Papa came by to see how the work was progressing. He took one look at a vase I was cleaning and whisked me away."

"Why?" her husband asked, puzzled and slightly hurt that she would think of such a subject at that time.

"It was shaped like, like . . ." Even then Catherine could not force herself to say the words aloud. She leaned close and whispered them in his ear.

"Like what?" Both Harwich and Catherine looked down at that part of his anatomy.

"Catherine, tell me you are joking," he begged, his eyes blue as the evening sky.

"No. It looked just the way . . ." She leaned over him and whispered the rest of her comment so softly he almost missed it.

"You say the most exciting things," he said quietly, pulling her over him. He looked into her eyes and thought of her carefully cleaning the vase. He broke into laughter. "Oh, if I could only have seen your father's face." Both of them went into gales of laughter. "Those Romans must have had an interesting society," he said later when he could talk without laughing.

For the rest of their stay, Harwich and Catherine reveled in each other, learning and relearning habits, likes, and dislikes. To his delight Harwich discovered that the sensuousness promised by Catherine's eyes was matched by her actions. She trusted him completely and followed his lead willingly.

For Catherine marriage was a riot of sensations. Her husband taught her to know him and to know herself, helping her discover the feelings she had hidden for so long. After years of being an onlooker of life, she was living it.

12

When Harwich and Catherine returned to London, they plunged immediately into the social world. Although not as frightening as Catherine thought it might be, she longed for her quiet life, the reassurances of Harwich's private smiles.

From shopping for Christmas presents in the morning to balls in the evenings, Catherine found her days laid out in fashionable patterns. The first ball was the worst. Lady Ravenly had insisted that Catherine must be properly presented to the *ton*. Before they returned, Harwich's aunt had sent out cards for the family dinner and for the ball to follow in the ballroom at Reston House.

That evening Catherine sat in front of her dressing table. She waited for Davis to finish the elaborate confection of braids and curls her maid declared was the only suitable creation for such an important occasion. The tension that had been her constant companion during her Season had returned in full force. Lost in her worries, she did not notice when Harwich entered.

"Delightful," he said. Catherine jumped in surprise. "This is only a family dinner and a ball, not an execution," he reminded her. "And I promise to stay close by your side."

Knowing all too well the way his family and friends would demand his attention, Catherine forced a tight smile and nodded. Almost under her breath, she whispered, "I only wish my aunt were not to be among the guests."

Harwich frowned. Neither of them had been pleased to see that name on the guest list for the evening. "She has no power over you now."

Catherine nodded. But she knew her aunt's wicked tongue. She shifted nervously. "Don't you want to see what I've bought you?" Harwich asked, his finger tracing the line from her ear to her creamy shoulders. She started to turn around. He said, "Close your eyes and stay as you are."

A few minutes later she felt something cold on her neck. Her eyes snapped open. "Oh, Dom." Catherine's hand caressed the beautiful topaz and diamond necklace.

"I thought it would fill in that neckline," he explained hurriedly. He cleared his throat. As soon as he had discovered that she planned to wear the bronze velvet with its slip of figure hugging cream crepe, he had protested. "That neckline is too low. I won't allow it," he had said firmly, forgetting that he was the one who had chosen the design in the first place. Catherine's eyes had shot golden fire, the same gold reflected in the topazes. "I bought them when I bought your ring. There are earrings, bracelets, and something for your hair." He cleared his throat nervously, waiting for her approval.

Dismissing Davis with her eyes, Catherine swung around and stood up. She took two steps and put her arms around his neck. "I suppose Edwards will be upset if I ruin your neckcloth," she mused, a gleam of mischief evident in her eyes.

"Blast Edwards," Harwich said huskily as she pulled his head down to kiss him.

They stood together some time later, Marybeth resplendent in her elegant pink gown beside them. Catherine's nervousness was back. This time she was able to hide it better. Her long kid gloves hid her damp palms. As she smiled graciously to each of her husband's relatives, she wished she had married an orphan.

When her aunt appeared a short time later, Catherine changed her mind. Her mother should have been an orphan. "Well, niece, I suppose you thought it amusing to keep your plans to yourself," her aunt said pointedly, stopping the line.

"I think you should lay the blame at my feet," Harwich said softly. "Perhaps this would be better continued later." He smiled at the person behind her, fortunately his cousin John.

"Humph!" At the sound Marybeth looked at Catherine's aunt nervously.

Catherine felt a tug on her skirt. "Is that real hair?" Marybeth asked, her eyes wide. Harwich's eyes danced. But he frowned disapprovingly before turning to his cousin.

"Bad *ton* to ask those questions in public, brat," her cousin whispered as he bowed over her hand. Marybeth's cheeks flamed.

Frowning at him, Catherine patted her step-daughter's hand. "That's all right, my dear. He's the only one who heard." Like a mother protecting her brood, she dared anyone to contradict her. Marybeth sighed and smiled.

The dinner, though an ordeal, was not as difficult as Catherine had expected. Her dinner partners were excellent conversationalists. The food, exceeding even Jacques' usual standards, was excellent. The first remove featured a turtle soup. Tasting it, Catherine resolved to ask how the cook ensured that all his soups be served hot. Mentally complimenting Lady Ravenly, Catherine carefully noted the dishes Harwich chose. He had preferred the sole to the river eel in parsley sauce, had eaten both squab and duckling, and had asked for a second slice of baron of beef. During the sweet-and-savory course, he rejected the pastries, tarts, and gateau Saint-Honore for the Stilton cheese and other savories.

She smiled and gave the signal for the ladies to leave. As they entered the large drawing room, she smiled at Marybeth, who reluctantly crossed to her side. "Is it time?" the young girl asked wistfully, and looked at the tea tray longingly.

"I'll have Thomas send up a tray for you later," Catherine promised, remembering the midnight suppers her parents had shared with her. "Now say your good nights." Catherine's eyes followed the girl proudly as Marybeth made her curtsies.

Across the room other pairs of eyes narrowed. A mouth thinned. It forced a smile as Marybeth said good night. Sitting to one side, Catherine's aunt noted the other woman carefully. Later that evening she would find someone to make the introductions.

The receiving line at the ball lasted much longer than either Catherine or Harwich preferred. Finally freed, they glanced at each other. Harwich held out his arm and swept Catherine into a set that was forming. They made a striking couple, he in his black-and-white darkness and she in her bronze light. Raising eyebrows, they danced five dances together that evening, and Harwich chose carefully the partners he thought she should accept.

"Your aunt did a remarkable job, and so quickly," Catherine said, waving at trees that set in pots around the edge of the ballroom.

"Have you checked the conservatory lately?" he asked, a laugh close to the surface. She looked at him in surprise.

"Aunt Beatrice raids everyone's home for plants for balls during the winter. She says it saves money."

"How clever." When they joined his aunt a few minutes later, Catherine was so sincere in her praise that Lady Ravenly glowed.

"Call me Aunt Beatrice," the older woman said after patting Catherine's hand.

"Where's Aunt Theodora? I was certain she would be here to inspect my bride," Harwich asked, looking around the floor.

"A problem in Scotland. Something about the succession," his aunt explained.

"Does that mean that the Marconi who calls himself my cousin will find himself cut off again?"

"Again?" Catherine asked. After all the people she had met that evening, she was having difficulty keeping the relationships clear.

"If anything were to happen to John, he would be my heir." His next words were just for Catherine. "But I'm working on a solution to that." He watched delightedly as a soft pink crept up into her face.

"Now what did you say?" his aunt asked bluntly.

"No, I think that I'd better withdraw my question."

Her nephew bowed to her and winked. Opening her ivory fan, Catherine tried to cool her cheeks.

That night as Catherine stepped up into bed, she stretched and then settled back, not bothering to hide a yawn. A few minutes later Harwich followed her. "When your rooms are finished, I may have mine done," he said tiredly. His arm reached out and pulled her close against him. "I told you not to worry, didn't I?" He felt a slight nod.

"Thank you for being kind to Aunt Beatrice. I get angry at her sometimes, but she means well."

His voice was so low that Catherine could hardly hear him. As she listened, his breathing slowed and she realized he was asleep. Tired as she was, Catherine could not sleep. A scene from the supper room worried her. Her aunt and Agnes Throckmorton had been deep in conversation. Finally her exhaustion won. She too drifted off, lulled by the heartbeat under her head.

Over the next few days Catherine knew she had been right to worry. As she entered a room where Agnes and her friends were gathered for tea, conversation stopped. Having been the object of gossip before, Catherine recognized the signs. When Mrs. Drummond-Burrell cut her at a ball but spoke to Lady Ravenly, Catherine went to Harwich.

Caught up in his own business affairs and with the meetings he had been having with the Foreign Office, he listened only halfheartedly. "Catherine, I'm certain you are only imagining things. It's been eight years. Even the biggest gossip cannot keep a scandal alive that long." He paused and picked up another neckcloth. "Do you like the oriental or the mathematical best?" he asked.

"Either one." Catherine crossed to pull the curtain aside and look out the window at the bare garden below.

So silently Catherine did not hear him coming, Harwich crossed to her and took her in his arms. She jumped. "See how tense you are. You were this nervous before the first ball. When you grow more accustomed to the *ton*, I'm sure you will relax." He kissed her and then left the room.

"It's only nerves! Ha!" Catherine threw open the door that connected their bedrooms. It banged against the wall, causing her to jump again. Davis had said that all the room lacked were the draperies. The walls sparkled in their light, fresh paint. She noted with pleasure the froth of lace above the bed and the matching curtains at the windows. Even without the heavy satin the room was livable. She crossed to the bellpull.

"Ask Lady Marybeth to join me, Davis. And find a footman to help us move my things," Catherine said firmly, ignoring the look of reproach on her maid's face.

"Lady Marybeth has another engagement, your ladyship," Davis said a few minutes later.

"Her words or Mrs. Throckmorton's?"

"Hers."

Catherine turned away to hide the quick rush of tears. It was the second time in as many days that her stepdaughter had found an excuse to avoid her company. Blinking rapidly, she forced a smile on her face and said, "The things in the chest first and then from the clothes presses."

After the many trips Harwich had insisted she make to Madame Bertine, it took almost an hour to finish moving her clothes. For the rest of the morning, the two women sorted the garments carefully. "No, Miss Catherine—I mean, your ladyship—"

"Davis, Miss Catherine is fine," her mistress assured her.

"It wouldn't be proper," her maid said primly. "Lady Harwich, the clothes for evening go in this clothes press. It is taller and wider so that the gowns do not have to be pressed so often."

Meekly, Catherine followed her maid's instruction. Her shoes also had their own separate storage cabinet. It had eight drawers, each drawer containing space for several pairs of shoes. "These are all mine?" she asked, puzzled. She had gone to a shoemaker to be measured for half-boots, slippers, and sandals, but other than the original order she had not returned.

"Lord Harwich had Madame Bertine send a swatch of material to the shoemaker as soon as you order a new dress. If you need shoes to match, they are ready by the time the dress is ready," Davis said calmly, her face carefully expressionless.

Catherine sank down on a chaise covered in forest-green velvet. "Is there anything else I should know about my clothes?" she asked, her voice choked.

"You also receive gloves dyed to match in appropriate lengths or in York tan or white kid."

"And?"

"Matching undergarments," Davis said almost in a whisper.

"No hats?"

"Lord Harwich felt you would want to choose your own."

Catherine closed her eyes, overwhelmed. Her own voice was little more than a whisper as she asked, "Does he really expect me to wear all this?"

Prudently Davis remained silent, quietly folding her mistress's shawls into place.

A tall footman who had been helping them move the clothes returned with a small trunk. "This was behind his lordship's boots. Edwards said it must belong to her ladyship." The young man glanced at his mistress and then looked away quickly.

Davis closed the door behind him firmly and turned to look at the small rounded top trunk they had bought in Sicily. She had sent the rest of the trunks to the box room. She opened it as if she expected to find some horrible surprise. "It's the clothes you brought with you, Miss Catherine." The maid did not even notice her mistake. Slowly she unfolded each one, noting with dismay how out of style they were.

"If you think they are worth your time, you may have them," Catherine said. "I only want this." She lifted her olive-green cloak from the bottom and slipped it around her. With her eyes closed, she relived that night on the deck when Harwich had wrapped his arms around her and had kissed her.

"Your ladyship, look!" Davis held out a tightly sealed map case.

Catherine took it gingerly, almost as if her breath would cause it to fall apart. "Papa's treasure." The slightly cool, rough-textured metal case began to warm in her hand. "As soon as you finish here, see me," she said thoughtfully. The case still in her hand, she hurried into the earl's sitting room. "Edwards, find me paper and pen."

As she sanded and sealed the letter she had written, she sent for Davis, who was still putting clothes away. "Have this delivered today. Tell the footman to wait for an answer," Catherine told her maid. A short time later the footman left the house.

Hurrying down the street, he didn't notice the small man who watched him carefully before signaling a second man to step in his way, knocking him to the ground.

"Sorry, sir. There, now's that the thing." The man in the neat and clean farmer's smock helped the footman up and dusted him off. "Coo. Now, that's fancy outfit," he said admiringly. He took a quick look at the address on the letter he had stolen and then bent over as if picking it from the ground. "Must of dropped this, governor." The footman glared at him and then hurried on his way. A few minutes later the two watchers met briefly around the corner. "Addressed to some bloke at the Royal Society. Shall I get word to His Nibs?" the man in the smock asked.

"No. It will probably be an invitation to a ball or a letter about new furniture like all the others," the first man said.

"How long does he plan to have us watch her?" the man in the farmer's smock asked. The small man shrugged his shoulders, returning to his spot in the shrubbery at the center of the square.

Waiting impatiently for an answer, Catherine dressed for tea. She entered the golden room where she, Marybeth, and Mrs. Wilson usually met. Her hands shaking slightly, Catherine clasped them tightly together. Until the last few days, Marybeth, excited to have won her release from her governess, was waiting when Catherine arrived. But she wasn't here today. A few minutes later the door opened. Catherine looked up eagerly, her face slowly losing its hope as the older woman entered.

"I'm surprised you wish to have tea with me," she told her former chaperone bitterly.

"So you have heard the rumors Mrs. Throckmorton has been spreading." Mrs. Wilson smoothed the soft lavender worsted carefully around her.

"And you don't believe them?"

"My dear, after our weeks together I am certain that they are false."

"But they're not."

"You and Lord Harwich were having an affair?"

"What?" Catherine's face paled.

"Mrs. Throckmorton has said the only reason he married you is because your father forced him to sign a confession and promise to marry you." The older woman looked at her former charge as if trying to read the truth from her face.

Catherine had risen and begun pacing. The ribbons that were to hang down from the high waistline of the pomona-green dress were in her hands. "Mrs. Wilson, would you be willing to tell Lord Harwich what you just told me? I can assure you that this rumor is false."

"Certainly. Would you like me to talk to him now?"

"He's not at home."

"When he returns, you can arrange it. Now have some bohea." Mrs. Wilson leaned over to inspect the tea tray that the footman had just placed on the table in front of the settee.

In spite of Mrs. Wilson's valiant efforts, Catherine refused to be soothed. A hundred plans dashed through her mind, all of them guaranteed to win her society's approval. She paced nervously, destroying one ribbon after another almost systematically.

When a scratching sounded at the door, Catherine turned eagerly. It was a footman with a note. She looked at her aunt's cramped handwriting, and her stomach tightened alarmingly. Her aunt needed to see her tomorrow morning about a message from her father. Catherine read it again, but the message did not change. She looked up. The footman was still there. "Yes?"

"The messenger is waiting for a reply," he said.

A reply? Catherine looked at the note and crossed

to a small desk she had brought down from the attic.
She sat for a moment, gathering her thoughts. Then
she dashed off her reply, written in her best copper-
plate, and sealed it. She looked at the seal of the
Countess of Harwich for a moment and hoped it gave
her aunt heartburn. "Give this to him," she said. She
crossed to sit beside Mrs. Wilson again.

The evening was a long one. Knowing that
Harwich planned to visit the Daffy Club, Catherine
had refused all her invitations, choosing to finish her
Christmas list instead. Harwich, except for presents
for Marybeth and herself, had given her a list of
names and asked her to select appropriate gifts for
each person on it. Besides the customary vales, each
servant at Reston House and at Reston itself was to
have a present. Fortunately, the housekeeper had
been able to help with those for the underservants at
Reston House. Davis and Edwards helped with some.
But Catherine was still mulling over many of the
others.

By the time she retired, Catherine's head was
hurting. The footman she had sent off earlier had
returned only minutes before. The man her note had
addressed had been working and had only just
returned. His reply had been curt. He would visit her
to discuss the situation two days hence. Catherine
sat in her room listlessly while Davis released her
hair from the imprisonment of pins and then
massaged her scalp.

"You are too tense, your ladyship. Do you wish a
sleeping draft?" the maid asked, worried by the
tense muscles she felt beneath her hands. Her
mistress had not been this tense since the last days of
that disastrous Season. Then it had taken months for
her to recover fully. Moving her hands, Davis
massaged the back of Catherine's neck and then her
shoulders. Satisfied that her mistress's muscles
were not quite as tight as they had been, Davis

braided her hair loosely and slipped a crisp white silk nightdress on her.

Climbing into her new bed, which seemed strangely naked after the heavy velvets encasing the one in Harwich's suite, Catherine sighed and buried her face in the fresh pillows, their soft spicy scent redolent with roses, sandalwood, and a hint of cinnamon. She stretched once and fell into a light sleep.

That sleep was interrupted some time later when Harwich climbed into bed beside her. "Wondered where you were, little cat," he said, his voice slow and softly slurred. "Like this. Not so closed in." He pulled her close to him and kissed her deeply. The faint taste of wine on his lips made her remember her wedding night. She pressed closer and rubbed her hands over his bare chest. She leaned over and kissed him. Then she pulled back abruptly. He was asleep. Flouncing back to her side of the bed, she glared at him for a few minutes. Then the silence was broken by a soft snore. She glanced at him, not sure of what she had heard. Then he snored again. She nestled down beside him once more, wondering how she was going to get to sleep. She shivered slightly as her feet touched the cold sheets at the foot of the bed. As if recognizing her presence, he turned and flung his arm over her, imprisoning her partially under him. Warm and toasty, Catherine drifted off to sleep.

When she awoke the next morning, Catherine eased herself out of bed carefully, trying not to disturb him. By the time he awoke some time later, she had met with the housekeeper and dressed for the day. Instructing Edwards to prepare a restoring drink, she was working on her accounts when Harwich called, "Catherine?"

She ventured into the bedroom and almost laughed. Her big and strong husband was sitting in

the middle of her lacy bed, his head in his hands.
"Yes?"

"Where are we?" he asked, his voice not as strong
as usual.

"In my bedroom," she explained, trying hard not
to laugh.

"Then it wasn't a dream."

"What?"

He edged over to the side of the bed and swung his
feet off carefully. Using the steps he usually disdained, he cautiously stepped off to the floor.
"Remind me to send word to see if John survived
this," he mumbled, heading for her dressing room
and handy basin.

Her face impassive, Catherine kept her amusement to herself. When Harwich reappeared a few
minutes later in his dressing gown, he looked pale
but more like himself. Gratefully, he took the
restoring draft from his valet and followed Catherine
to the sitting room. He winced and his stomach
rolled alarmingly at the sight of the breakfast tray.

"What's in it?" he asked with effort, pointing to
the silver pot.

"Tea. Shall I pour you a cup?"

He nodded slowly and sat carefully down on the
settee. "How do they do it?" he mumbled.

"What?" Catherine was trying hard to keep her
face straight.

"How do people go through this every morning?
They must enjoy pain." He looked around for a clock,
suddenly remembering they had promised to ride
with Marybeth that morning.

"I sent word that you were indisposed. But you
should make time for her later today." Catherine's
face shadowed as she thought of the way Marybeth
had been reacting to her.

"I will as soon as I find that captain," he promised,
holding his cup out for a refill.

"What captain?"

"The one at the Daffy Club. He brought us a new beverage he had discovered when he was fighting in the colonies. Bourbon, I believe, he called it. I had only two glasses before supper. And I drank no more wine than usual, I am certain of that."

He rubbed his head and leaned back against the settee. His dark hair made a splash of color against the cream satin.

Catherine crossed to stand behind him. Much as Davis had done for her the evening before, she massaged the back of his neck and his shoulders. "Ahhh." His sighs of pleasure made her feel warm. She continued for a few minutes and then dropped a kiss on his head. "Don't go," he said, capturing her hand and pulling her around to sit beside him. He pulled her close and held her for a moment before kissing her. "Hmmm. You smell so fresh and clean. What are your plans for the day?"

Catherine sat up, her back straight and her feet primly planted on the floor. "I've agreed to have tea with my aunt." She looked at the storm clouds in his face and hurried on. "She received a letter from Papa, she says."

"Your father? That's strange."

"He did expect me to be staying with her," she reminded him.

"Not if he received my letter, he wouldn't." Harwich's face was thoughtful.

"What letter?" Catherine asked for the second time, her eyes flashing.

"The one I sent him from Gibraltar." He glanced at her face and explained quickly. "I simply told him that if I gained your consent, he would soon be my father-in-law. And I gave him my address."

Catherine moved back into the corner of the settee and simply looked at him. Usually in control of his emotions, Harwich shifted nervously under the golden-brown gaze. Then the soft smile he loved so well softened her features. He pulled her close again and kissed her eyes closed. He had just captured her mouth when they heard scratching at the door. "Come," Catherine called, setting her now rumpled skirts about her more primly. Her husband shut the door to the bedroom behind him carefully.

"The draperies for your bedroom are ready to be hung, your ladyship. Will it be convenient?" the housekeeper asked.

Her husband's muffled "Blast it!" made Catherine blush. "After luncheon would be better," she suggested quietly, her cheeks as pink as her stepdaughter's favorite dress.

"Very well." The housekeeper curtsied, her face rather stern as though in disapproval. She left the room, a smile curving her lips as she thought of relaying the earl's reaction to the prune-faced uppity maid who served Mrs. Throckmorton.

The door had scarcely closed behind her when Harwich opened the door and picked Catherine up. "Close the door behind us," he ordered quietly, nuzzling her neck.

"Dom, we can't. What will the servants think?"

"Whatever they want." He set her on her feet and twirled her around. "Good," he said, noting with satisfaction the hooks and eyes that closed her morning gown. "Buttons take too long." He punctuated each opening with a kiss that started Catherine trembling. Pulling her sleeves down, he freed her of her bodice and lifted her out of the skirt. He frowned at the sight of her stays. "I wish you wouldn't wear these," he grumbled as his fingers unlaced them.

"This from a man who complains when my evening frocks are too low?" Catherine asked, her eyes softly glowing. Free from the stays, her breasts tumbled free, filling his waiting hands. He pressed her back against him, letting her feel his desire. "Let's christen this bed properly," he whispered.

13

At luncheon that afternoon Catherine blushed as she met the earl's warm gaze. Even now she could hardly believe her reactions to him. Her eyes, still heavy with passion, smoldered. But mindful of her duties as hostess, she encouraged conversations.

Marybeth who now joined them for luncheon each day and dinner when they did not have guests, looked at her father, a strained smile on her face. "Are you feeling better, Papa?" she asked, glancing suspiciously at her stepmother.

Harwich caught the glance and changed his answer. "Ask me about it after luncheon, poppet," he said, waving away the wine he was offered. "Lemonade, please." Catherine's mouth twitched. Harwich glanced at her and then whispered to his daughter, "Daffy Club last night."

Marybeth looked thoughtful. She nodded, not quite understanding. "Where are we going today?" she asked. His note had only said they would be going out.

"Ah." He winked at her. "That's a secret. Too many ears here."

She giggled nervously, looking from one woman to another. Cousin Agnes was frowning. Marybeth's happiness evaporated, and she twisted restlessly in her chair.

"Young ladies do not wiggle," Mrs. Throckmorton snapped, her face disapproving. "Are you certain you can spare the time to take Marybeth out, Harwich? After being gone so long, I am certain you have much to catch up on. We had planned a walk around the square this afternoon."

"Feel free to continue with your plans," Harwich said. The older woman's face brightened. "However, my daughter and I have some errands we must finish." Catherine breathed a sigh of relief. Marybeth's smile made her feel warm all over. As Catherine glanced toward Mrs. Throckmorton, her stomach tightened nervously. The woman's look made her shiver. Mrs. Wilson, too, was uneasy. She glanced toward her host, but his attention was focused on his daughter.

As soon as luncheon was over, Mrs. Wilson sought Catherine out. "Does Lord Harwich need to talk to me this afternoon?" Catherine stopped sorting the invitations on her desk. "You have talked to him, haven't you?"

The younger woman flushed and turned back to the cards. "I really haven't had much time," she said softly.

"That woman means you no good. You must speak to him soon." Catherine nodded. Watching Catherine's hands reach for an edge to begin rolling, Mrs. Wilson changed the subject. "While I am out this afternoon, shall I visit Hookham's to see if there is a new book by the author of *Emma*?" Mrs. Wilson asked as if she had no other interests in the world except novels.

Grateful for her tact, Catherine agreed.

As Catherine prepared for tea with her aunt, she took great pains with her appearance. She rejected two dresses before accepting a third, a rich bittersweet vandyked about the neck and hem. Her pelisse, also in bittersweet, was decorated in bands of ermine about the sleeves, bodice, and hem. The mantle that completed the outfit was a dark brown lined with bittersweet velvet. Over the carefully placed curls, Davis settled a rakish brown hat, one side swooped up and the other down with a feather hugging the curve. As Catherine pulled on her gloves, Davis inspected her once more, standing back to make certain that the half-boots that her mistress wore did not alter the hemline. Satisfied, she stood back to let her mistress rise.

Her mistress, too, was satisfied. If not beautiful as she had dreamed of being as a young girl, she was fashionable and felt comfortable. Remembering the whites, soft pinks, and light blues she had worn then, she shuddered. "Do you want a cloak?" Davis asked quickly.

"No. With the robes inside the carriage I shall be fine." She picked up her reticule and left the room.

The ride, though not a long one, was enough time for her to remember the first time she had gone to live with her aunt. Still in half-mourning for her mother, she wore gray with black ribbons. Even she had to admit that she had looked less presentable than usual. But she had been so excited, so eager to please.

Her governess, a kind soul, had tried to calm her, but she had been unsuccessful. Forcibly restrained from hanging out the window, Catherine had absorbed each new sight eagerly, fearlessly.

She had been totally unprepared for the scene that had greeted her. Her aunt was entertaining guests for tea, a few fashionable matrons and several handsome gentlemen. "My niece? Show her in," a light voice had said.

Catherine had stood on the threshold a moment, surprised by the number of people. Seeing her aunt, she hurried to her and made her curtsy before bending to kiss the lightly powdered cheek her aunt had offered. She had waited, a sweet smile on her face, as her aunt made her inspection. "Your governess accompanied you?" she asked, one carefully drawn brow raised slightly.

"Yes." Catherine stepped back to allow her governess to come forward.

"Good. See my butler. He will send a footman to show you to your rooms." Embarrassed, Catherine and her governess made their curtsies and escaped, their eyes carefully not meeting. The butler had been waiting, his expression impassive. He signaled a footman who bowed and led them up the stairs.

As they reached the top of the stairs, Catherine saw on the floor below her reticule—one of her mother's actually—and had impulsively plunged down the stairs after it. Ignoring her governess, she hurried to pick it up. Then she heard her aunt.

"Dreadful isn't the word, my dear. I simply cannot understand how my sweet sister produced such a large hulking child. What I am to do with her I simply do not know."

Catherine had frozen for a moment. She picked up the reticule and dusted it carefully, holding it close to her heart. Slowly, ponderously, she made her way back up the stairs.

The carriage stopped, awakening her from unpleasant memories. When the door opened, Catherine was ready. She might not be the image of her mother, but Dominic appreciated her. She thought of their morning and smiled. The smile lasted through the formalities her aunt insisted on. As usual Clarice Hubert was not alone. "Catherine, Lady Harwich, this is the Conte di Perugia." The count bowed over her hand and added a few words in Italian. Automatically Catherine responded in the same language.

"Ah, we must not neglect this other, so beautiful lady," the count gushed. He smiled silkily at Catherine's aunt.

Catherine carefully took a seat across from him, her eyes cataloging every detail of his appearance from the black hair and soulful brown eyes to the skin tanned brown by the strong Italian sun. "I am surprised to see you here, Conte. I understand the

Prince of Rome had taken you prisoner." She watched carefully for his reaction. She wondered briefly why she did not trust him.

The count's agitation became apparent as he jumped to his feet and began to pace. "Falsehood. Absolute falsehood. Designed, dear lady, to cause despair among my people. Oh, that I could be home among them once more." He paused dramatically, waving his hands.

Rather amused by his theatrics, Catherine watched for a moment and then turned to face her aunt. "You said you had a message from my father," she said quietly.

"Yes. The count brought it. He came to me, naturally, because this is where your father thought you were staying."

"He did? How do you know my father, sir?"

"We met as I was waiting to leave Italy. Knowing I planned to come to England, he sent a message for you."

"May I have it, please?" Catherine held out her hand to take the letter.

"Ah, no, *signora*. He simply told me to remind you to care for the treasure." He looked at her carefully to see her reaction.

"The treasure?" Catherine frowned. Her father had warned her to tell no one, not even Harwich. Therefore, this man must be lying. But who was he truly? she wondered.

"The one he sent out of Naples with Harwich," her aunt explained casually. "The count has explained it all to me." Her eyes gleamed.

"Oh, Papa." Catherine laughed, trying to make the sound seem real. "He does enjoy his little games. Tell him when you write that his 'treasure' is now married, and he is a step-grand-father."

"What?" her aunt snapped, a frown marring the carefully applied cosmetics.

"Ah, *signora*, I do not comprehend?" the count said. His struggle with his pronunciation intrigued Catherine.

"I am my father's 'treasure,'" Catherine explained, settling back further in her chair in order to observe their faces more carefully in the light.

"You?" the count's face still was puzzled.

"A pet name, a name for someone who means something special to you," Catherine said patiently, hiding her nervousness and hoping there was enough truth so she did not turn red. She turned to her aunt. "Is this all you needed me for, Aunt Clarice?" The older woman nodded, still frowning. "Then I must be off." She stood up, forcing the count to stand also. "There are so many errands to run, for we leave for Reston soon. If I do not see you until after the holidays, Aunt, I wish you a Happy Christmas." Before either of them had time for more than a quick reply, she swept out of the room, pausing only briefly to allow the butler to wrap her mantle about her.

"Follow her," Clarice Hubert demanded.

The Conte di Perugia stared at her. He seemed taller, more powerful. "I shall, *signora.*" His voice was low and harsh. "But you will remember that I do not like to be told what to do, especially by a woman."

Clarice Hubert shivered slightly in spite of the warm fire and the shawls she wore. She nodded.

When the count emerged from the house a few minutes later, he was so intent on following Catherine that he failed to see the man who walked quickly beside the slow-moving coach. The man who reported to the Foreign Minister took careful note of the foreign-looking gentleman. The watcher, who had heard Catherine's orders to the footman, dawdled. He came close enough to the hackney the count had hailed to hear the Italian say in accented English, "Follow that coach." His eyes grew narrow and he swung up on the back, well hidden from the coachman.

For both the Conte di Perugia and the watcher, the afternoon seemed endless. As she struggled to unravel the count's reason for asking her about the treasure, Catherine visited one shop after another. After each stop, the footman would place a stack of boxes carefully in the boot. The last stop was at a jeweler's. After quite some time Catherine returned to her carriage, but the footman was not carrying any packages. The watcher made a note.

The count took more direct action. He swept into the shop. He said theatrically, as if it were the most important thing in the world to him, "Lady Harwich has lost a glove." He watched amused as the clerks scurried to find it. After a few minutes' search, the count clapped his hands, drawing their attention to himself. "When it is found, put it aside to be sent with the things Lady Harwich has ordered."

"Oh, but she—" began one of the newest clerks. The frown on the senior clerk's face made him stop quickly. "Yes, sir. Certainly, sir," the young man said hurriedly.

The count swept into the street. Inside, the clerk sighed in relief as he listened to the lecture about the necessity of respecting their client's wishes. Outside, the count cursed volubly when a small man ran into him, almost knocking him to the ground. The count brushed the man's helpful hands away and hurried to his lodging.

While Catherine was running her errands, the earl and his daughter were equally busy. Harwich smiled at his daughter, who looked more like a young lady and less of a girl each day. At first Marybeth's face was sullen. "What's wrong, poppet?" her father asked as soon as he had settled the fur lap robe over her. Its rich brown matched that on her new cloak.

"Nothing." She sat up straighter and aligned her feet precisely on the floor. She still wore a pout.

Refusing to be manipulated, Harwich leaned back into his corner without saying a word. His dark-blue eyes gazed steadily at her face.

Uncomfortable under her father's stare, Marybeth began to fidget. "Papa, don't stare at me. It makes me nervous."

"You won't tell me what's wrong. You don't want me to stare at you. Perhaps we should just go home."

"No, Papa." The next words were so low that he could hardly hear them. "I missed you this morning. I was looking forward to my ride."

"So was Catherine."

"Yet she got to spend all morning with you," his daughter said. Her jealousy was apparent even to him.

"Poppet, that was my fault, not Catherine's. I was unwise enough to drink too heavily last evening," he ruefully explained.

"Cousin Agnes says you would never have done something like that before you married Catherine," Marybeth said primly.

"And when has Cousin Agnes been such an authority on my behavior? I'm sorry, Marybeth. I hope it won't happen again." Harwich's tone told her that the subject was closed. "How many gifts do you have left to buy?"

"Ones for Louisa and Cousin Agnes."

After his own errand for part of Catherine's present, they plunged into Marybeth's favorite shopping place, the Pantheon Bazaar. Watching indulgently, Harwich followed Marybeth as she made numerous purchases, mostly for herself. By the time they returned home, Catherine was in her sitting room, the tea tray before her. "Tea. That's just the thing for these cold days." Harwich peered at the tray carefully.

"There are apple tarts." Catherine told him with a smile. As soon as she had learned how much he enjoyed them, she had made them a regular feature of the sweet courses. "Tea, Marybeth?"

Her mind still considering her wonderful finds, Marybeth smiled and nodded. "Papa, when are we going to Reston? I can hardly wait to tell Louisa about everything I've done."

"Remember. It is important that you not gloat," he reminded her. "If Catherine agrees and the Foreign Office will release me, I thought we might leave later this week. Have you any major engagements?"

Catherine reviewed her list of invitations and shook her head. "Many people have already removed their knockers from their doors. Most of the larger parties are over," she reminded him. "Will we remain at Reston until the Season begins?"

"I certainly wish we could. But with my mission still unresolved, I must be back soon after Christmas. If it hadn't been for Castlereagh, we'd be spending the holiday in London."

"Papa, we couldn't. Why, what would everyone think?" his daughter said. Her eyes were as round as her favorite sweetmeats.

"We are going, Marybeth. Lord Castlereagh decided to go home too." He turned to Catherine. "I'm certain you will want to visit the Grange."

"Yes." The one word carried a wealth of longing and homesickness.

"Will you give the orders for our removal or shall I?" he asked. "Have you invited Mrs. Wilson to accompany us?"

"I'll talk to Mrs. Thomas tomorrow. And Mrs. Wilson's already agreed to remain until after the new year. Dominic," she began, and then hesitated.

He sat casually, one neat booted leg thrown over the other, totally relaxed. He looked at her quizzically. She shook her head slightly as if to tell him she would finish the thought later.

"Papa, will the Prince Regent be at the ball tonight?" Marybeth asked.

"Rumor has it that he will be." Harwich put his cup on the tray and stretched lazily, draping one arm casually around Catherine. Marybeth instantly dropped her eyes, embarrassed by his breach in decorum. "Someone also mentioned that Beau Brummell will also attend." Harwich watched the expression on their faces change.

"They wouldn't, they couldn't have invited them both to the same ball," Catherine stammered.

"Prinny goes where he wants. So does George, for that matter," Harwich reminded her.

Marybeth crossed and stood beside her father, longing for the time when she could crawl into his lap and ask her questions. Harwich pulled a stool closer for her to sit on. "Papa." She paused.

He waited a minute and then asked, "What, poppet?"

"Why are they so angry with each other?"

Instead of giving her a quick answer, Harwich considered the question for a moment. Then he asked, "Remember when the groom lost your invitation to Louisa's birthday party?" She nodded, her face puzzled. "Why were your feelings hurt?"

"Because I thought my friend didn't like me anymore. I felt left out." Her face was very thoughtful.

"Was it giving up the party?"

"No. All I cared about was being with Louisa."

"Something like that happened between these two men. Only there's no groom to discover the invitation in his greatcoat and solve the problem."

"Brummell still refused to apologize?" Catherine asked, her distress evident in her face.

"He refuses no matter what anyone says."

"If it was the prince's fault, he should say he was sorry," Marybeth said firmly, lifting her chin belligerently.

"No one knows whose fault it was. Besides the Prince Regent is, is—"

"The prince," Catherine added. "And princes rarely see the need for an apology."

Marybeth stood up, her soft blue dress falling in graceful lines above her feet. She stood with arms crossed, thinking and tapping her foot. She looked so serious neither Harwich nor Catherine dared to interrupt her thoughts. The young girl crossed to the fireplace and then turned. "No matter if he is the prince or not, if he were wrong, he should apologize."

"I'm certain that you are right. You would if you were wrong. You are a very fair person," Catherine said, smiling at her.

Marybeth smiled back. Then the smile faded. Her father had said that it had been his fault that she had missed her ride. Remembering her attitude toward Catherine at lunch, Marybeth crossed to stand in front of her stepmother. Catherine held her breath. The girl said, "I was rude earlier. Please forgive me."

Catherine's smile was like a sunrise, all golden and glowing. She patted the settee beside her and said, "Certainly. Now tell me what you discovered." Although Marybeth was rather hesitant about taking her seat and seemed to pull away slightly, Catherine felt she had made some progress.

As she dressed for the ball that evening, Catherine wished for her stepmother's advice. She had been older, it was true, when she appeared on Maria's doorstep. But she had been so hostile. Thinking of Maria brought another problem to mind—her father's treasure. "Oh, Papa, why didn't you do this yourself?" she muttered as Davis soaped her back.

"Yes, your ladyship?"

Catherine waved her away and sank into the warm water, letting all her tensions flow away. She was almost asleep when the connecting door flew open.

"Catherine, are you ready?" Harwich asked,

striding into the room in the elegant black and white he favored for evening. She looked at him sleepily and blinked. "Davis should have had you ready by now." He picked up a towel and started to lift her out.

"Let me," she said, a sensuous smile playing about her lips. She stood up proudly and stepped out to stand on the rug before the fire. The firelight created exciting shadows on her skin. She wrapped the towel about her casually. "I had to have a bath. The air outside is so dirty."

"It's the coal dust," he explained absently, more interested in the soft curves she was patting dry than in the state of the air. Quick footsteps approached. He ran his hand over his hair, mussing the Brutus style Edwards had taken such pains with. "We are promised for the evening?" he asked. She nodded. "Have Davis tell me when you are ready." He escaped through the door only seconds before the maid appeared.

For once Davis did not have to remind her mistress to be still. As a result, it was only a short time before Catherine was dressed in a golden-yellow velvet gown with a crossed bodice that left most of her shoulders bare. Her braids and curls were swept to one side with an ostrich feather and diamond pins. She touched her lovely diamond pendant to make certain it was secure, and clasped diamond bracelets over her long white gloves. As Harwich entered her room again, his hair freshly coiffed, she smiled and held out her hand.

"You are certain this is a necessity?" he asked.

"The choice is yours. But our host is Lord Castlereagh."

Grimacing, he led the way out of the room. So softly that Davis did not hear it, he whispered, "But we will be home early."

They were. And Catherine had no regrets. From the moment she had met the prime minister she had felt as if she were on trial. He had quizzed her about her father and his work. The coolness in his manner had been apparent among the women also. It was a coolness that she had experienced before. As they lay together in bed that evening, Catherine gathered up her courage. "Dom, what am I going to do about Mrs. Throckmorton?"

"Who?" he asked sleepily, burying his head in his pillow and bringing her close to him once more.

"Cousin Agnes."

Harwich turned over and rubbed his eyes like a small boy. "What's wrong?"

"She doesn't like me," Catherine said. Then she winced. She had sounded like a spoiled child.

"She doesn't like many people."

"But she's turning Marybeth against me. And Mrs. Wilson says she has been spreading rumors." She rolled over on her side to see him better. "Will you talk to her?"

"Cousin Agnes?"

"No, to Mrs. Wilson. Please listen to her."

He yawned widely. Settling her on his shoulder, he promised, adding sleepily, "Hmm. Like you here beside me. So soft, so sweet." He turned his head and rubbed his cheek against her hair. For a moment Catherine held her breath, hoping for the words she longed to hear. As his breathing became soft and regular, she sighed and snuggled closer to him.

The next morning she poured her second cup of tea and smiled as he held out his cup for his third. He looked like a little boy, just awakened from a nap, his hair tousled like it had been after some of their adventures. "Let's go skating at Reston," she suggested, her eyes sparkling at the thought.

Harwich ran his hand through his hair, trying to smooth it. He let his gaze linger on her before he answered. The dressing gown she wore did little to hide her full charms. She bent forward to move the teapot so she had room to put her cup down, and the soft golden silk fell open, revealing her full breasts barely restrained by the deeply rounded neckline of her nightdress. "I don't remember this from last night," he said, catching the silk of her nightdress between a thumb and forefinger. He smiled wickedly.

She blushed. But the ease of conversation that they had developed made her say pertly, "Well, I was wearing it. You shouldn't have been so quick to throw it on the floor. Now, don't evade the original question. Will we be able to skate on the pond? Does Marybeth have skates?"

"Yes, and maybe," he said, deliberately being enigmatic.

"And what is that suppose to mean?"

He stretched again and put his cup down. "Yes, Marybeth has skates and maybe we'll be able to skate on the pond. It's still early and it may not be frozen."

"It will be." She smiled at him happily.

"What happened at your aunt's yesterday?" he asked, remembering her plans.

"Dom, it was very strange." He waited for her to continue. "There was no letter from Papa—only the Conte di Perugia. I didn't even know Papa knew him."

Harwich sat up straight, his attention riveted on her. "Are you certain he's genuine?"

"No. Oh, he's Italian. I'm almost certain of that. But I thought the count had been captured."

"And how did he just happen to visit your aunt?" Harwich asked. He stood up and crossed to stand behind her chair, his hands cupping her shoulders. "It seems too convenient somehow. I'll make some inquiries." Changing the subject abruptly, he asked, "What are your plans for the day?" He squeezed her shoulders and kissed her cheek casually.

"I'll speak to Mrs. Thomas about removing to the country. Then I have a meeting with a man from the

Royal Society, Thomas Thomson." She glanced at him curiously.

"Read his *Philosophical Transactions* last year. He seems to have a brilliant mind. Is he interested in your father's work?" Harwich pulled her out of the chair and hugged her before heading toward the door of his bedroom.

"I hope so. Will you be in for lunch?" He nodded. Catherine walked to the bellpull.

She finished her meeting with the housekeeper quickly. Mentally preparing herself for the disapproval she knew she would find, Catherine walked toward the schoolroom. Smiling her hellos, she explained why she had come. "Lord Harwich wishes us to be ready to leave for Reston by Thursday. Can you be packed?" She smiled as she noticed the self-satisfied look Marybeth gave her governess. "I will send a maid to help," Catherine promised. Catching sight of the clock on the mantle, she made her excuses and hurried to her bedroom to retrieve her map case. With a few minutes to spare, she entered her morning room. Taking a deep breath, she reviewed what she should say.

To her surprise her guest was not much older than she. After he was introduced, he glanced around the room as if expecting to see someone else. "Will you be seated, sir?" she asked quietly.

The gentleman, still slightly puzzled, sat in a chair across from her. He listened as she told her story, at first skeptically and later with interest.

"The discovery has not yet been made public?" Mr. Thomson asked. His voice radiated his excitement.

"It had not when I left Italy. Now?" Catherine shrugged her shoulders.

"You say you have proof?"

"Yes. Remember, sir, it must be handled with care. If my father's calculations are correct, it is almost eighteen hundred years old," Catherine said quietly, reaching for the map case. She broke the wax seal and lifted the top off. Slowly and carefully, she pulled the papyrus from the tube, hardly daring to breathe as she did so.

His voice hushed, Thomson watched her handle the delicate object. As soon as she had it free, he reached for it eagerly. His hands touched it delicately and unrolled the scroll a fraction of an inch to read the ancient Latin. He looked at Catherine, his face aglow with excitement. "And there are more of these? Many more?"

"My father and the others who discovered them call the place the Villa of Papyri. They believe most will be nothing but business records. Herculaneum was once a thriving city, you know."

"What a treasure," he said quietly, running a finger lightly, caressingly over the outside of the papyrus. "You know, of course, that this is not my field of expertise?" She nodded. "A colleague of mine at Oxford and another at Cambridge must have a look at it. We will be careful, I promise you." He slid the priceless document back into its case.

"You must be discreet. If it is possible to get cooperation without using them, don't mention my father or the place," Catherine urged.

"Papyri. A link to the ancient world," he said reverently. "You may rest assured that it will be handled with care. But it may be some time before we discover just what it says," he warned.

"We are leaving London for Reston very shortly. If you need me before the end of the month, you can reach me there."

Slipping the map case into his pocket, he bowed. Just as he was leaving, the door opened. "Thomas told me you needed to see me, Catherine," Agnes Throckmorton said in a petulant voice. She looked from Catherine to Mr. Thomson quizzically. "Already setting up a cicisbeo, Catherine?" she asked archly.

"Mr. Thomson is a member of the Royal Society,"

Catherine explained tightly. "He is interested in information about my father's work."

"Yes, your father." Mrs. Throckmorton's voice dripped with sarcasm. Mr. Thomson made his bow again and escaped quickly. As soon as he was gone, the elder woman turned to Catherine, "Well?"

"Harwich has decided we will leave for Reston on Thursday."

"Thursday? Why, I am certain I can never be ready. I have engagements I cannot cancel."

That suited Catherine perfectly. "Then you are welcome to remain in London. We will see you when we return."

Mrs. Throckmorton glared at Catherine and then smiled. "No. I will be ready."

Catherine shivered slightly and then quickly left the room.

14

With care and planning Mrs. Thomas dispatched the fourgons on Wednesday. By eight o'clock Thursday morning the rest of the household going to Reston were ready. Handing Marybeth into the carriage with her governess, Harwich promised her that she could share their carriage when they stopped for luncheon. Mrs. Throckmorton found herself in a carriage with Mrs. Wilson. "This time neither you nor Davis will have to care for her," Harwich had told Catherine the night before. A maid sat opposite them.

"Is this always the way you travel?" Catherine asked and settled into the lead coach.

"Why? Do you long for the donkey cart?" he asked, signaling the coachman to start. After the three carriages, there was the servants' coach and those for the baggage.

Catherine considered the question thoughtfully. "It was simpler then," she said, her voice wistful.

Harwich nodded and pulled her closer to him so that he could tuck the fur lap robe more closely about them. Her feet on top of the hot bricks, Catherine put her head on his shoulder and sighed. Turning to kiss her, Harwich tried to maneuver past her bonnet.

"Do you have to wear this now?" he asked persuasively, untying the bow Davis had arranged under Catherine's ear. Shaking her head, Catherine let him remove it and place it on the seat in front of them. "That's better," he said as he ran his finger lightly down her cheek. He leaned over and kissed her softly.

For Catherine, going to Reston was like going back to her childhood, to a time when she had no worries, no fears, to a time when she was confident, adventuresome. Even after their marriage, she and Harwich had been hedged in with social engagements, family obligations, and business. Even though these did not go away when they arrived at the estate, the pace was less hectic, more relaxed.

The first morning there set the pattern for the visit. Marybeth, escorted by Graves, rode off to visit her friend Louisa. And both Mrs. Throckmorton and Mrs. Wilson chose to spend the morning in bed. Harwich, already wearing his greatcoat, watched impatiently as Catherine walked lightly down the stairs, the long skirt of her dark-brown habit held carefully out of her way. The rich fur of her hat was repeated in the cloak Harwich spread carefully over her shoulders. "I thought you were in a hurry to see the Grange again," he said playfully into her ear.

She fixed him with a disdainful eye. "If someone had not . . ." she began sternly, her lecture dissolving at the look in his eyes. She hurried ahead of him, pausing beside the open door. "Well? Aren't you coming?" He laughed and followed her.

"Did you write to let them know you were coming?" he asked, throwing her into the saddle. Her horse, a frisky dark-brown mare, pranced a bit and settled down. Catherine kept a firm hand on the reins and reached to pat her neck. "I had our agent write when I saw him again. The tenants moved out at the end of October. They bought an estate nearby when our agent said he had no authority to sell the Grange."

"Will your father ever live here again? In England?" Harwich asked, his face serious.

"Not permanently. He loves Italy with a passion.

Nor would Maria find the climate agreeable," she
said, shivering slightly.

Harwich noticed and spurred his tall black
stallion. The mare followed him, her mane and tail
blowing behind her.

The Grange, much smaller than Reston, was ready.
The estate manager, Austin, was waiting when
Harwich lifted Catherine from the saddle. "Ah, it is
good to see you again, your ladyship." He bowed to
both of them. "You'll find things changed. Some
good, some bad." He led the way into the house.
"Most of the servants are new. Your father
pensioned off most of the old ones after your last
summer here."

The caretaker and his wife stood by as Catherine
and Harwich walked through the house. "It's dif-
ferent, not as I remembered it at all. It seems so dark
and gloomy," Catherine murmured, waving at the
dark wainscoting. "I remember it as a place of
laughter, of light."

"Are those your memories of the house, or the
people who lived here?" Harwich asked thoughtfully
as they entered the small salon.

Catherine paused as though struck by an arrow.
"The people. Of course, it was the people." She
turned and smiled at him, her eyes glistening with
her own fire. "Having you here with me makes
coming home easier," she whispered as she turned to
face him.

She was putting her arm around his neck when
Austin called, "Shall we have fires made up in
there?" She dropped her hand and smiled ruefully.

"Well, little cat?" Harwich asked, his eyes
twinkling.

"No, thank you. We'll be returning to the library
shortly," she called. She turned around again,
making a full circle, as if looking for some remnant
of her parents. Harwich stood still, waiting. Sighing
deeply, Catherine returned to his side, tucking her

arm into his. For a brief moment he put his arms around her and simply held her. "Thank you," she whispered after a while, and stepped back.

The meeting with the estate manager took the rest of the morning. Once or twice when Catherine seemed not to understand, Harwich explained. Finally, refusing luncheon, they called for their horses. As he walked outside with them, Austin asked, "When do you plan to inspect the lock room?"

"The lock room?" Harwich asked.

"My father's invention," Catherine said absently. "I thought he had taken everything away."

"Not the last time I saw it, Miss Catherine, your ladyship," the estate manager said. "It was during your Season. Your agent and I were sent to find some pearls and a diamond set for you to wear."

"That's right. They were my mother's. Do you have the keys?"

"Perhaps we should leave it until another time," Harwich suggested, seeing her shiver in the crisp air.

"You will need not only my key but that of your agent," Austin reminded her.

"That's right. It has a double lock. One key won't work without the other," Catherine explained to her husband. "I'll write London. Then we'll come back and inspect it."

"Perhaps we should invite Marybeth and Louisa. They enjoy an adventure now and again," Harwich said, smiling. Catherine shivered again. "Now it's time for home. Good day, Mr. Austin," he said as he helped Catherine mount.

The ride home over fields cold and ready for spring was a quiet one. Taking the shortcuts they had disdained earlier, they pounded across open fields, scattering the rabbits and field mice. As they crossed the last rise, they pulled their horses to a stop and looked down at their home. Its stone walls caught the sun and glinted golden. "Home," Harwich said

almost reverently. He held out his hand to Catherine
and smiled as she took it. "Our home."

When they arrived a few minutes later, they met
Marybeth and her friend. Harwich watched
impatiently as Graves helped the young ladies off
their horses. He cleared his throat and looked
pointedly at his daughter. Clearing her throat, Marybeth made the introductions in a cool voice. Her
father glared at her and would have followed her to
discuss her ill-mannered behavior, but Catherine
held on to his arm.

The atmosphere at luncheon was decidedly chilly.
During the soup, Mrs. Throckmorton complained
bitterly about traveling with Mrs. Wilson. The lady
in question had chosen to spend the day in bed. Then
she discussed the inconsideration of people who
forced her to cancel engagements simply on a whim.
Catherine and Harwich exchanged amused glances.
Although he was not pleased with his daughter's
attitude himself, when his cousin complained
because Marybeth had deserted her lessons, he interrupted her. "These are the holidays. With everyone
entertaining as they do, I have canceled lessons until
after the New Year. In fact, poppet, I believe your
governess plans to return home herself." He smiled
briefly.

"Why, who will take care of your daughter, be
responsible for her actions?" his cousin sputtered.

He stopped her with a cold glance. "I am responsible for her."

"And I," Catherine added quickly. The entrance of
the sweet course provided some distraction.

While Harwich met with his estate manager and
Catherine made plans for the evening entertainment
they planned to hold during the first week of the
New Year, Marybeth invited Louisa to her room.
After the dresses from Madame Bertine's had been
displayed properly, and Louisa, a blonder version of

Marybeth, had had an opportunity to try them on, they sat on the bed, their legs folded.

"Tell me everything," Louisa demanded. "It's so romantic."

"Romantic? Cousin Agnes says Papa was forced to marry her." The words popped out before Marybeth could stop them. She hurried on. "Promise me, Louisa, that you will never tell anyone what I just said. Word of an Englishwoman."

"Word of an Englishwoman," Louisa said solemnly. "Besides, your cousin doesn't know what she's talking about," she added a trifle smugly.

"What do you mean?"

"Well, you've seen them look at each other, haven't you?"

"Yes." Marybeth looked at her friend as if expecting more.

"Remember when my sister was in love with the squire's oldest son?" Louisa asked, her voice patient.

"Yes. But what does that have to do with Papa and Catherine?"

"She got all dreamy-eyed whenever he came around." Marybeth nodded her agreement. Louisa continued. "When your father enters the room, that's the way Catherine looks. And his eyes follow her around." Louisa sat back, her elbows propped on the pillows. "I hope that someday someone looks at me that way," she sighed and flopped back on the pillows.

Marybeth just sat there, her mind trying to fit Louisa's explanation with what she had seen. The problem being too difficult to solve immediately, she flopped beside her friend. "Is your sister engaged yet?" she asked.

Country life was pleasantly relaxed. As they had during their voyage from Sicily, Harwich and Catherine shared most of their days. In the mornings they went their separate ways—Harwich to oversee

his affairs and Catherine to visit the tenants, both at
Reston and at the Grange. The afternoons they spent
exploring—Reston, the Grange, and each other. At
least twice a week someone in the area hosted a
dinner, a dance, or a card party. In spite of Mrs.
Throckmorton's protests that these were provincial
and that if they went, only adults should go, everyone went.

The mornings were the times that Catherine
learned more about Marybeth. Instead of a haughty
young lady who cared only for attention, on the visits
she showed a sensitive side. At one farm at the
Grange where Catherine found a mother, ill herself,
caring for three sick children, Marybeth did not wait
to be told what to do. Quickly she picked up the baby
and changed it, holding it until Catherine could
change the linens in its crib. While the groom went
for the doctor and a neighbor's daughter to help out,
she sponged the other two children as Catherine
helped the mother. Even though the visit extended
longer than they had expected and it was an
afternoon she and Louisa planned to visit the village
to shop, Marybeth's only worry was that there was
no milk for the baby.

That afternoon two tired ladies climbed into their
coach. When the door closed, Catherine sank into
one corner and Marybeth into another. During the
drive home to Reston, Catherine sat up straight
when Marybeth asked hesitantly, "Is it true women
have babies when they sleep with men?"

Catherine gulped and squared her shoulders.
"Sometimes."

"Does that mean you and Papa will have a baby?"

"We hope so." Catherine kept her voice steady by
sheer will alone.

"Is it true that, that . . ." Her face red, Marybeth
couldn't get the words out. She leaned over and whispered in Catherine's ear. She sat back and looked at
Catherine questioningly.

"You saw it happening?"

"Louisa and I both did. We saw the puppies being born too. We sneaked into the stable." Although she sounded smug, Catherine could tell that Marybeth had some doubts.

"There are some similar events. But it's more, much more. When a person cares very much for another and has made a commitment to that person, every word or glance is important. Being close to him and having him close to you, sharing everything, is the most wonderful experience in the world." Catherine leaned back in her corner, a wistful smile on her face. "And when he touches me," she whispered, lost in her dreams.

Marybeth looked at the dreamy expression on her face and asked, "Are you thinking of Papa?"

Blushing, Catherine nodded. "Then you are in love with him. Louisa was right."

"Marybeth, were you worried about that?" Catherine asked, not certain where the discussion was leading.

"No. But Cousin Agnes lied," the girl said angrily.

Catherine looked at her sharply. "She did. And I know it. And she gets angry with me when I do something wrong. I do not lie." Marybeth had the light of battle in her eyes.

Gritting her teeth, Catherine tried to calm the storm. "Perhaps she made a mistake. None of us is perfect. Remember that the bible tells us to forgive people."

"She's not very nice to you. Are you going to forgive her?" Marybeth asked sharply.

The question was one Catherine had been trying to decide for herself. She sat up, her finger nervously rolling the edge of her cloak. "I'm going to try," she said quietly. "I'm going to try."

The problem stayed with her as the days before Christmas sped past. As she sat with her family in the Harwich pew at the gray stone church on Christmas Eve, Catherine sought guidance. The familiar carols filled her with love and hope. How she had missed them in Italy. Her husband's hand captured hers inside her muff as they listened to the words of Luke. Standing, her arm in his, at the end of the service, Catherine smiled at Marybeth. Her smile widened to include the others.

During the supper after church, Harwich kept glancing at Catherine. She was so alive, so vibrant in her dark-green dress trimmed in fur. He waited impatiently for their private celebration. Finally they were alone. The fire blazed like the emotion he was certain she could read in every line of his face. He held out his arms and she tumbled into them. Her hair smelled of bayberries and spices. He breathed deeply, as if he could absorb her essence.

Catherine was no longer thinking; she held him tightly, praying that nothing would ever part them. Her head found its natural resting place, and Harwich felt her hair brush his cheek. His arms tightened. He tilted her head back and sampled the sweetness of her lips, which parted beneath his.

Almost at the end of his control, he dropped his arms and stepped back. He led her to the chaise before the fire. "Wait here. I have something for you." He dashed toward his bedroom. Catherine, too, reached for the present she had hidden in a drawer in the small desk. "This is not your Christmas present," he said. She pouted. "At least not all of it. Happy Christmas, Catherine." He handed her a large basket tied with a bow.

"I have something for you also," she whispered, handing him a small box. "There are others for tomorrow. But this is for us." She looked at him and smiled. Carefully, almost as if they were afraid to rush, they opened their presents.

Catherine got the top off hers first and stared in amazement at a kitten, an identical twin to the one she had had as a child. "Horace," she said, stroking the sleeping kitten with a fingertip.

"Or Horatia. I couldn't be sure," he said almost as if in apology.

"Thank you." Catherine set the basket carefully on the floor and wrapped her arms around him. "Thank you. Thank you. Thank you," she said in between kisses. Finally, she pulled back. "Now finish opening yours."

Slowly, carefully, he opened the box. He pulled out a small donkey and a vividly painted cart. He looked at her, his eyes laughing. "How did you know?" he asked quietly as he held her close. He kissed her neck beneath her ear.

"Know what?"

"The fantasies I made up while I watched you sleeping in that blasted cart." Catherine looked into his smoldering eyes and smiled sensuously. "If you had looked at me like that then, we would still be in Sicily," he said huskily. "Come to bed."

As they opened their other presents the next morning, neither Harwich nor Catherine could keep their eyes off each other, their passion rumbling just below the surface.

The presents were numerous and tastefully chosen. Marybeth received clothes from Madame Bertine from her father and Catherine together, a pearl necklet from her father, and a locket with a diamond from Catherine. Surrounded by her books, handkerchiefs, and other trinkets, she found each new package more exciting than the last. The older ladies received their share of gifts also, from charming watches on chains to more dresses from Madame Bertine.

When Catherine opened her largest box, she laughed and asked, "Has Madame Bertine given up all her clients except us?" She pulled out a variety of muslin dresses in soft greens, deep blues, and yellow.

"For the Season," Harwich and Marybeth explained together. They laughed and urged her to open the next box. Slowly, reverently, Catherine ran her hand over the leather-bound volumes, autographed copies of Gibbon's *History of the Rise and Fall of the Roman Empire.*

"But how? He died—" Catherine sputtered.

"In 1794," Harwich interrupted. He smiled wickedly. "That's why it doesn't say, 'To Catherine, Countess of Harwich.'" Everyone laughed. Catherine smiled only for her husband, her eyes deep and golden. "Open the next," he ordered.

Catherine turned to her last box. It was long and flat. Throwing back the leather lid, she gasped. There, on white velvet, lay a cascading necklace of aquamarines and diamonds with matching hairclips, earrings, and bracelets.

"Let me," Harwich whispered, and clasped them around her neck. Catherine unhooked her spencer to let them lie next to her skin. "Beautiful. Absolutely beautiful," he breathed in her ear. Somehow she knew he didn't mean the necklace.

Marybeth was almost jumping with excitement. "Show us what you got, Papa," she demanded in spite of her cousin's best efforts. Harwich held out his hand proudly. On it gleamed, in rich gold and diamonds, an unusual stone. "What's that called?" Marybeth wanted to know.

"A tiger's eye." As Catherine had done earlier, Harwich smiled into his wife's eyes with intimate promise. "And thank you for my shirts, poppet." He bent and kissed his daughter.

"I'm getting better and better at sewing, Papa," she said proudly. "Even Cousin Agnes said so."

"Well, you can make my shirts whenever you wish," he promised.

The day was a pleasant one. As they gathered for tea later that afternoon, Harwich asked his wife, "Is Christmas like this in Italy?"

"No. Presents aren't exchanged until the feast of the Three Kings. This day is reserved for church and for family gatherings."

"No presents? I don't think I like that idea," Marybeth said pertly. She winked at her father. "But maybe we could celebrate again. Is it a long time away?"

"Greedy puss," her father said, and tweaked a curl. "One Christmas a year is enough for anyone."

Even Mrs. Throckmorton laughed when Marybeth asked, "Couldn't we have next year's early?"

Following local tradition, Reston was the host for Boxing Day visits. Catherine had prepared her staff well. When their visitors left, they were stuffed with cider, minced pies, and fruit cake. Bands of carolers in sleighs filled the cold air with music that made Catherine want to cry with pleasure.

"I don't want it to be over," she told Harwich that evening as they lay in bed.

"It isn't." He held up his hand in the candlelight to let his ring catch the light. "As long as you have your memories, little cat, it can never be over." He smiled at her, a smile that made her feel as if she were melting. "Let's make a few memories now," he suggested, looking deep into her eyes.

The next few days were very cold, and fog hugged the lanes and highways. The occasional coach that lumbered by reported that the fog in London was so thick no one could see more than a hand in front of his face. The farmers looked at one another dourly, predicting a long, hard winter.

After directing Austin to take his questions to the earl, Catherine turned her full attention to plans for the party. Their guest list was extensive and ranged from the squire's great-uncle to the smallest child permitted out in the cold. Not as formal as a ball, the evening included a dinner, both for adults and for the children. Marybeth was in alt as she planned her seating arrangements and made her place cards for her own dinner table. To Mrs. Throckmorton's continued protests, Catherine merely smiled and reminded her that these were tasks that Marybeth would be expected to do alone someday.

The adults who came for dinner would be joined by others later. Catherine provided dancing, card rooms, and for the gentlemen, a room to smoke. Marybeth approved the dancing for her guests and added lottery and other games.

As the acceptances poured in, both Catherine and the housekeeper grew worried. With the midnight supper, there might not be enough china and plate. With transportation as unreliable as it was, there was no way to send to London for more. Knowing she could use kitchen china if necessary, Catherine worried over the problem, hoping to find another way.

When they received the post after several days' delay, both Catherine and her housekeeper breathed easier as they learned that the roads were open so that they could get the supplies they needed. Sending the cook personally to the largest town near by, the housekeeper breathed a sigh of relief.

When they received the post after several days' delay, it brought another answer. "The key to the lock room," she called as she hurried to the entrance hallway and began giving orders. "Have someone tell Austin to meet us at the Grange in two hours. Next, send someone to the caretakers there, so that fires will be lit. And where's the earl?"

The butler listened impassively and nodded. "In the library, your ladyship."

"Dom, Dom, come with me to the Grange," she called as she almost burst into the room. She blushed in embarrassment as she saw not only his manager but the squire and his oldest son. "Excuse me," she said, and began to leave.

"Wait. Do you want to leave immediately?" Harwich asked, amused.

"No. I told them we would be there in two hours." Her face was still slightly flushed.

"I think we will be through by then. Don't you agree, gentlemen?" Smiling broadly, they nodded solemnly.

After Catherine left to find Marybeth, their faces grew more somber. "I don't like it. What would a spy be doing in our neighborhood?" the squire asked belligerently. "He's probably after you, Harwich. Traipsing off to foreign countries isn't natural." He paused and looked back at the door. "Isn't Lady Harwich's father still in Italy?"

"Yes." Harwich paused and looked at the spot where Catherine had stood. "I know she worries about him." He looked at the squire. "I certainly admit I may have drawn him here. But I need your help to find him," Harwich explained. "The tenants here and at the Grange say he's been around asking questions."

"What kind of questions?" the squire lowered his usual booming voice to a dull roar.

"Most people had a difficult time understanding him. He made them nervous because they thought he was French."

"We'll be having invasion rumors again," the squire boomed. "Took years for them to calm down last time." He ran his hand over his red hair liberally powdered with gray.

"Come, Father. With the news from the Continent no one would seriously believe that old invasion story," his son urged.

His father glared at him under thick red brows. "We'll be on the watch for him for certain. Word will go out to my tenants this very afternoon," the squire promised. "Italian, you say?" Anxious to spread the word among the tenants, they left shortly afterward.

Since snow had fallen recently, Harwich ordered the sleigh brought around. "May I ask what is so urgent that we *must* go to the Grange today?" he asked, his smile softening his words.

"China and plate," Catherine said, waiting for the reaction she was certain would follow. She wasn't wrong.

"What? You whisked me away from a meeting because of dishes?" he asked, startled.

"I won't ask my guests to eat off kitchen china, no matter what we find," Marybeth said stubbornly.

"And I can't be expected to serve midnight supper on it. Dominic, how did you allow your china and plate to fall into such disrepair?"

"Me? I thought the housekeeper took care of things like that," he protested.

Both of the ladies looked at him reproachfully. Then Marybeth explained in her most patronizing tones, "Cousin Agnes says that china and plate are two things one never leaves to servants. And wine, of course."

"Of course." Harwich could hardly keep his face straight. He looked at Catherine to share his laughter and found her nodding approvingly.

"When we return to London, I shall order some new china at once."

"Perhaps we can have our very own design," Marybeth suggested, her big blue eyes sparkling.

"Our own design? Is that possible?" Catherine looked at her husband. He nodded. "Well, that is certainly an idea we need to consider. What do you think about . . ."

Harwich listened to their discussion of china patterns and settled back. He looked from one to the other for a minute. A strange look crossed his face. Marybeth, her hands folded at the same angle as Catherine's, was mimicking his wife. Blinking once or twice to make sure he was not seeing things, he realized that even his daughter's bonnet had the same tilt as Catherine's. Mentally he began to tally the similarities.

As they sorted out china, two sets—one Spode and one Wedgwood—he noticed his daughter walked like Catherine and had even copied her wide-eyed smile. But she didn't seem to be mocking her. Deciding to talk to Catherine about it later, he willingly moved boxes to find the silver they were searching for, finally locating the silver cabinet under several boxes of broken china. Watching two hefty footmen strain as they lifted the box, Harwich wondered what else was there. "Be careful, poppet," he called as he watched his daughter pick up a ruby-red goblet. She flashed him a saucy smile and put it down carefully. "Catherine, is there more you need? If not, we need to be going. Both of you are turning blue." He made one last circuit of the rock-walled room. "Interesting. I wish I had his plans."

"Papa's?" Catherine asked, wiping the dust from her gloves on her skirt. She picked up her mother's jewelry case and handed it to the footman. Harwich nodded.

For the next two days Marybeth tried to encourage another visit to that treasure trove. Neither of the adults would listen. Even Louisa, usually the best of listeners, grew impatient. "I think you are making it up," she declared. Marybeth refused to say another word.

The major difficulties solved, plans for the party continued. The day before it occurred Harwich received a letter from London. The news, although upsetting, did not disturb him as much as the letter addressed to Catherine in the handwriting of a man. He walked slowly up the stairs toward her sitting room, the letter burning his hand all the way. Instead of waiting patiently, as he usually did, for her to share the news, he hovered above her. "Well?"

"Oh, Dom, Papa will be so proud!" She jumped up and hugged him tightly.

"Proud? Proud of what?" he demanded as he hugged her back.

"He's going to be nominated for the Royal Society because of his work at Herculaneum. Here, read the letter." She thrust it into his hands.

"What does he mean 'as soon as you arrive in London, we will discuss the disposition of this great treasure.' What treasure?" he demanded.

"The papyrus Papa had me bring to England. I promised I wouldn't tell anyone, Dom. Not until the Royal Society had a chance to look at it," she explained quietly, not liking the storm clouds in his face.

"You carried that, that—"

"Papyrus."

"Papyrus out of Italy, over Sicily, and then to England without telling me!"

"Papa made me promise. Would you want Marybeth to break a promise she had made to you?" Her eyes pleaded for understanding.

"Who did you tell about it?" he asked, his voice very stern.

"Only Mr. Thomson. I told you I was meeting with him," she said quietly.

"As soon as this party is over, we return to London." He paused and frowned. "Someone else must know. The servants report that Reston House was broken into this week."

His words made Catherine freeze. "Broken into?"

"Robbed. But nothing seems to be missing. I think I would like to investigate firsthand. Tell me more about this."

15

One morning after they had been back in London for almost two weeks, Marybeth burst into her father's study. Her eyes were flashing just as his did when he was very angry. "Papa, you must do something about that woman," she declared in tones that were clear and hard.

Harwich swung around and looked at her. The lists he had been studying fell to the desk. He stood up and led his daughter to a chair. "Now, Marybeth, tell me slowly what you mean."

"Ohhh, they make me so angry," she said as she pounded her fists on the arms of the chair. She got up and began to walk around the office, much as he did when he was angry. "I want to cry, Papa. They are so mean to her."

"Marybeth, sit down," he thundered. Startled, she dropped into the chair once more. "Now start at the beginning."

"Because it is warmer today, Catherine promised me we would go to Hookham's. Then Catherine's aunt came to call." Marybeth made a face that made her father want to laugh, but he controlled himself.

"She is Catherine's aunt, and we must be nice to her," he reminded her, wondering how such a nice person as Catherine could be related to someone as jealous as her aunt. "And?"

"Cousin Agnes was the only one besides me in the small salon when she arrived. So Thomas showed her in. Papa, those two women began whispering. Whispering! And Cousin Agnes told Louisa and me that we were ill-mannered when we did it." Harwich frowned but merely nodded. "Then Catherine came in." Marybeth mimicked their reactions. " 'You're looking well, niece. Still as slim as ever. Oh, well it prevents people from counting too obviously.' " She dropped to her usual voice. "Papa, what did she mean? Catherine blushed."

"She wanted to know if we were, ah, ah, planning to increase our family?" Harwich said, wishing that he had not promised himself never to leave one of Marybeth's questions unanswered.

"Increase our family? Mrs. Wilson is leaving soon." She stopped suddenly. "Family? Oh, Papa, a baby. Are we having a baby?"

Harwich ran his finger around his neckcloth and then sat back. "Not that I know of yet, poppet," he told her quietly, smiling at her reaction as well as his own.

"A baby would be wonderful," Marybeth said wistfully, forgetting the jealousy she had shown only a few weeks earlier.

"Is there any more, Marybeth?" he asked. Her eyes narrowed briefly. "Then tell me."

The story seemed to pour out. "Cousin Agnes and Mrs. Hubert told Catherine that she didn't respect her elders, that she needed to remember who she was, instead of putting on airs. For a woman whose name had once been connected with a scandal, she was acting too haughty."

Harwich stood up, his eyes blue fire. "Is Mrs. Hubert still here?" he asked coldly.

"Mrs. Wilson came in and I came in to get you. So I really don't know. They shouldn't talk to her that way." Marybeth was crying tears of rage.

"Run to your room, poppet, to prepare for your outing. I'll take care of this," he promised, the light of battle shining in his eyes. It was still there a few minutes later when he stood outside the door and listened for a moment to the conversation.

"The least you could do, Catherine, is tell your family about the treasure your father has found," her aunt said bitingly.

Harwich opened the door in time to hear Catherine ask, "Treasure? What treasure?"

"Whatever it is must be important. Everyone is talking about it." Clarice Hubert smiled at Mrs. Throckmorton, who nodded.

"Just who is this everybody you are quoting so freely?" Harwich asked as he walked into the room. He made a sketchy bow before taking his position behind Catherine's chair, his hands resting lightly on her shoulders. As he felt the tension in her, he frowned slightly.

"Well, you know how it is. Rumors can start anywhere." Mrs. Hubert tried to retreat. It was one thing to bait Catherine and quite another to deal with Harwich.

"You, Cousin Agnes?" he asked pointedly. The older woman merely shrugged. When she thought he wasn't watching, she glared at Catherine. The glare and the look on Mrs. Wilson's face reminded Harwich of his promise, long forgotten. He crossed to Catherine's chaperone and leaned down. "Will you wait for me in my study?" he asked quietly. Relieved to be escaping, she nodded.

Harwich crossed back to his position behind Catherine. As soon as Mrs. Wilson had left the room, he said firmly, "I believe it is time for you to leave also, Cousin Agnes." She opened her mouth to protest but took one look at his face and stopped. He held the door for her and shut it firmly behind her. Harwich looked at his wife. "Do you stay or go, Catherine?" he asked in clear, sharp tones.

"Stay." She lowered her eyes before the blaze in his and reached for the ribbon at her neckline. Harwich captured her hand and pulled her to her feet to stand beside him. She was shaking as he put his arms around her waist.

"Disgraceful," her aunt said in her most cutting tones.

"That's what I think also," Harwich said quietly, his anger still as strong as before. "Since you are here today, I know Catherine did not tell you of my wishes. You will never send for Catherine again. Nor will you be admitted to my house again. My wife"—his voice underlined the word—"has no need of relatives such as you."

The color beneath the cosmetics Mrs. Hubert wore was red. Her eyes blazed. "Told you, did she? Consider well, your lordship, just what damage one or two tongues can do." She watched gleefully as Catherine moved closer to Harwich.

"You remember, Mrs. Hubert, how close to the wind you've been moving." His eyes told her he knew the whole story—the gambling, the debts, the men. She blanched. "Perhaps a visit to a friend outside of London?" he suggested, one eyebrow raised. She glared at him and swept from the room.

"How did you know?" Catherine whispered, her body still shaking.

"Marybeth."

Catherine's cheeks blazed. "Oh, what must she think of me?" Her voice reflected the tears her eyes refused to spill.

"That she loves you." Catherine waited for him to finish the statement, but he simply held her until the shaking stopped. "She also told me that we should have a baby," he whispered as he held her close. Even through his coat he could feel her blush. He hugged her quickly and stepped back. "If this scene hasn't been too upsetting, I believe I know someone who wishes to visit Hookham's Library."

Catherine's soft thank-you kept him from remembering that one part of the problem still had to be solved. He saw his wife to the foot of the stairs and watched her climb them to her room. He turned and walked down the hall to his study.

"Is she all right?" Mrs. Wilson asked, and then lowered her eyes to her clasped hands.

As he assured her, Harwich considered his approaches. Finally deciding just to begin, he said, "Thank you for being there today."

"I think it made it worse for her," Mrs. Wilson said thoughtfully. "Had they attacked you or your daughter, she would have defended you with her last breath. But when she is the target . . ." Her voice dwindled to nothing.

"Catherine is rather vulnerable. But I plan to protect her. She won't have to worry about them again," he promised. "Before we leave for Reston, Catherine asked me to talk to you. I assume it was about this?" He paused.

"Not quite." Quickly she explained. His face looked like a picture of Zeus right before he hurled a thunderbolt. Mrs. Wilson slowly wound a bit of lace around her finger before she noticed what she was doing. Dropping it quickly, she clasped her hands tightly.

"Why didn't she tell me herself?"

"Would you have listened? Or would you have considered it just another of her fears?"

"Yes," he began. Then he shifted his feet nervously. "Maybe. Until she had been to a few balls after we married, Catherine was certain everyone was talking about her," he said defensively.

"And they were. Mrs. Throckmorton and her friends are terrible gossips with an entree to many households. You'd do well to pay more attention to your wife, your lordship." He flushed and stared at her. "Being thought to be in her pocket won't be as devastating as these rumors could be. Is there anything else you need to know?"

After she left, Harwich sat there thinking about what she had said. Restlessly he began to pace and then smiled. He stepped outside and gave his orders. "And tell her I will see her tomorrow at eleven in my study." He pulled his overcoat on and wrapped a muffler about his neck. Pulling his hat down as far as he could, he started out the door. "Tell the countess I've gone to my club," he told the footman.

His cousin was there, as Harwich had expected. Ordering a bird and a bottle, Harwich joined him.

Babbington listened carefully and then sat quietly for a few minutes. Finally he leaned forward and looked his cousin in the eyes. "It's not totally true. You shouldn't worry."

"I'm not. Do you think I give a tinker's damn what they think of me?"

"Yes." His cousin leaned his elbows on the tables. "If you didn't, you wouldn't be here."

Harwich nodded, shamefaced. "It's not really because of me." His cousin lifted an eyebrow. "All right, it's mostly for Catherine and partially for me. I don't want people to get the wrong idea about her."

Babbington slid back in his chair and slouched down. "No forced wedding?" His smile grew wider by the moment.

"Not unless Catherine is the one you're talking about. I had to be very persuasive. She didn't want to marry anyone," Harwich admitted ruefully. He slumped forward and looked at his cousin.

As they ate their capons and drank their wine, both men were silent. Finally Babbington said, "Forget it until you can talk to my mother, Dominic." The look on his cousin's face was comic. "Know she can be trouble, but in a social situation no one is more wise. No use rushing off, though, she'll be in early for the Season. Cousin Amelia is popping off her oldest daughter this year. How many years before it will be Marybeth's turn?"

"As many as I can make it," Harwich said, his voice rougher than usual.

Babbington laughed sympathetically and patted his shoulder.

Harwich spent the evening playing cards and

mulling over the advice he had been given. Leaving early, he tapped Babbington on the shoulder. "Walk out with me," he mouthed silently. Throwing in his cards, his cousin signaled for his coat. "I didn't plan to interrupt your game permanently," Harwich said.

"It's almost my bedtime or so the doctor says," his cousin explained. They stopped on the steps.

"I'll follow your advice," Harwich said quietly. "But damn me if I let Cousin Agnes loose on my household again." He walked down the steps to his waiting carriage.

"That's Graves," his cousin said as if he were seeing things. "How do you do it?"

"What?"

"Manage to have a carriage waiting for you when you walk down the steps?"

"Give you a ride, John?" his cousin asked, laughing. "It's really simple. Tell your groom a time and don't keep him waiting."

"What if you're playing deep? How can you leave then?"

"Finish the hand and call it quits. I don't lose as much money that way either," Harwich added.

The ride home was a quiet one for both of them. After bidding his cousin good night, Harwich leaned forward. "Just why are you driving tonight, Graves?"

"A message from the Foreign Office came late this afternoon. It wasn't marked 'Urgent,' but Thomas felt you should know before you went upstairs."

"The Foreign Office. Maybe Napoleon has surrendered before Murat expected." He stretched, the six capes of his greatcoat rippling as he did. "Good night, Graves." Heading up the stairs, his letter in his hand, Harwich turned it over and over, as if he could absorb its message. To his surprise, he was almost right. He had a meeting with Castlereagh at two the next afternoon.

Sometime later he entered Catherine's bedroom.

He stood looking down at her, his heart in his eyes. Crawling in beside her, he took her in his arms, and she moved closer.

"Dom?" she whispered, her eyes closed but her lips pursed.

"Dom. Go to sleep, little cat," he whispered, and kissed her softly. Obediently her breathing slowed and her sleep became deeper. Holding her, Harwich breathed a prayer of thanksgiving that he had been the one to rescue her. His arms tightened convulsively at the thought of Catherine in anyone else's hands. Secure with her in his arms, he drifted off to sleep.

Neither of his meetings the next day was pleasant. During the first he had to fight to keep himself from hitting a woman.

"I gave up my home to come and care for your spoiled daughter," his cousin had screamed when she discovered that he was sending her away.

"And that is the reason—the only reason, I might add—that I will provide your housing," he told her firmly. "You will have your cottage and a small allowance for food and upkeep. With your income from your husband, you should be able to manage."

Mrs. Throckmorton pulled herself up and glared at him. "That woman is the cause of this," she began.

"Stop. Do not say another word." Harwich bit off each word precisely. "Catherine knows nothing of this. This is between the two of us only." He stood and opened the door an inch or two. "I will notify you when my agent finds a suitable cottage."

"I have no say over where I will be living?"

"None. Unless, of course, you wish to support yourself." He smiled bitterly at her. "We will understand if you choose to have your meals upstairs until you leave."

Mrs. Throckmorton gulped and walked to the door, her mind already calculating how she could use the story in her hopes of destroying Catherine.

Had she been able to be at Harwich's meeting that afternoon, she would have rejoiced. The preliminaries over, Castlereagh explained. They were rejecting the treaty with Murat. Harwich nodded. He had known from the meeting with Bentiwick that there would be many difficulties. The next statement Castlereagh made made him stand up and lean across the desk, his eyes and body proclaiming his anger. "You did what?"

"I had your wife followed. Harwich, consider your story. Can you think of an easier way to plant a spy in our midst?"

"And what good would it have done? I'm a messenger, nothing more."

"But we didn't know she knew that." Castlereagh nodded. "I agree now we should have trusted your judgment. I'm only telling you because of a report you sent to Lord Denning at the Home Office. Yes, he sent word to me immediately." He looked at the man glowering at him and decided to plunge in. "The day she visited her aunt, my men saw him following her and decided he might be of interest to us." He looked at Harwich, who was wearing a stunned expression. "He seems very familiar with her aunt."

"Her aunt has peculiar friends," Harwich said harshly. "Every family had some dirty linen in it. She's Catherine's."

"What about the story about treasure?" Castlereagh asked, his eyes fixed on the earl's face.

"A papyrus Catherine's father sent to England with her. It's important enough to have him nominated for the Royal Society."

"So that's where Thomson comes in."

The blue fire in Harwich's eyes blazed higher. "While your men were watching her, they didn't happen to see who broke into Reston House?" Harwich asked.

"When?"

"While we were in the country."

Castlereagh settled back in his chair and shook his head. "When you left for the country, I canceled the watches. By then we knew she was innocent." The older man leaned forward over the desk. "Will you be making any more trips for England?"

"No." Harwich stood up and walked to the door. "But I do plan to speak out about the use of spies against English citizens." He shut the door on the foreign secretary's requests that he return. The idea of people spying on his wife made him angrier with each step. By the time he reached his curricule, he was almost running. Taking the reins from Graves, he whipped up the horses and sped around the corner.

"The streets are icy," Graves said quietly once or twice. Then he raised his voice to a dull roar. "The streets are icy, your lordship."

Gradually Harwich pulled the horses to a slow walk and transferred the reins to his groom, his anger still very close to the surface.

"Drive around for a time," Harwich said quietly. As they drove along the Embankment, Harwich signaled him to stop. They stared in amazement at the ice on the River Thames. "Still thin in the middle," Harwich said.

"Not frozen completely since Good Queen Bess's time," the groom added. "Must be something to see, though. People able to walk across the river as freely as a street."

Harwich sighed. "Let's go home." The first blaze of anger had turned to embers, still hot but banked.

Catherine did much to restore his spirits when he told her what Castlereagh had done. "I feel so important," she said, laughing at first, nervously. "You don't think they listened to our conversations, do you?" Her eyes were wide.

"They simply watched who visited you, whom you visited, and where you went. I saw the report myself.

I even know where you got this." He held out his hand proudly, the tiger eye gleaming.

"I'm glad they didn't tell you before Christmas. I wanted it to be a surprise."

"It was, my dear. It was. Come, Marybeth told me that she needed an audience for her harp. She told me she needed more poise." He wrapped his arm around her waist and led her to the music room.

As January drew to a close, Harwich received daily reports on the growth of the ice. The days were bitterly cold, so cold that Catherine insisted on fires burning all day and night in any room that was regularly occupied. The servants, used to huddling under thin blankets to keep warm, basked in the unexpected warmth. Finally the word flashed around the town. The Frost Fair was open. The Thames was frozen solid.

Despite Marybeth's pleas that they leave dinner unfinished and go immediately, Harwich refused. "I have a meeting with my agent early tomorrow. I should be through by luncheon. Shall we take our meal on the ice?"

Marybeth clasped her hands, already planning what she would wear. Catherine, too, was as excited as a child. Mrs. Throckmorton, who had joined them for dinner for the first time in days because she had grown tired of her own company, glared at him.

The next morning dawned clear and bright. The air, though very cold, was warmer than the day before. Harwich, slipping out of bed, leaned over to kiss Catherine. "Dress warmly, little cat," he reminded her, and laughed as she burrowed back beneath the goose-down coverlet.

When he walked downstairs after breakfast, the butler announced, "Mr. Smythe is here. As your study was very cold, I had him wait in the library."

"Thank you, Thomas." Harwich walked toward

the library and then turned around. "Have a closed carriage ready for Mr. Smythe in an hour. I think we'll take the sleigh, Countess and Lady Marybeth should enjoy it. Have Graves drive."

"Yes, sir." The butler stood as if at attention.

"And make certain any of the staff who wish to visit the fair have time to go." Harwich tossed the butler a bag of coins. "It may never happen again." Laughing softly at the surprised look on Thomas' face, Harwich entered the library. Upstairs a door opened wider.

With a client as astute as the earl, Mr. Smythe was ready with the facts and figures. Presenting Harwich with three cottages to choose from, he sat back, sipping his tea and waiting for the questions. And questions there were. Narrowing the choice to two, Harwich stood up and crossed to the window, noting the frost on the pane.

"The one in Salisbury is in best repair?" the earl asked suddenly, turning back to the fire. His agent nodded. The listener in the next room took a deep breath. "Buy it. What else do you have for me today?" Quickly they finished with all but one problem.

"And the house in St. John's Wood?" the agent asked.

Harwich watched the flames burn brighter and turned around quickly.

In the doorway stood Catherine, booted and gloved, her cloak on one arm. Her eyes were dark brown with pain and her face looked like she was in agony. She turned, slowly at first, and then picked up speed. Her heavy deep-blue cloth dress with its matching pelisse swung with her, making a bell shape. She pulled her cloak around her and plunged down the steps into the waiting coach. Harwich's cry, "Catherine. No!" faded into the distance behind her.

While Harwich shouted orders to his confused household, Catherine sat in the coach, the tears she refused to shed earlier running unchecked down her face. Her husband had a mistress. The thought seemed to hit her with new intensity each time it reappeared. A naive girl in her first Season might not know who lived at St. John's Wood, but she did. She brushed her tears away angrily and tried to think, to plan. But one thought ran through her mind: her husband had already taken a mistress. No matter that she had known his reputation from the start. The tight hold she had on her dream was slipping. Her tears fell harder until she slipped to the floor, her face buried in the fur robes. Her sobs hushed and she lay there in that state of relaxation that sometimes follows great grief. Suddenly she sat up. The carriage was still. She pulled herself up on the seat and raised the flap to speak to the driver. The scene before her eyes was astounding. They were on the Embankment. And there on the Thames was a fair with shops and rides.

"Where do you wish to go, your ladyship?" Graves asked quietly, signaling the footman to stay quiet. He had climbed onto the box of the carriage as soon as he had seen her appear, her face set.

His voice caused a new spate of tears to ooze from her eyes. "This will be fine, Graves," she whispered. For a few minutes everything was quiet. Catherine wiped her eyes and sat trying to think what she was to do.

"Let me get you a chair, your ladyship," Graves urged. He stood beside one of the windows on the Embankment side. "The fresh air might do you good."

Catherine dashed the last of her tears away and lifted the flap so she could see out. The cold air immediately cooled her hot cheeks. "What kind of chair are you talking about?" she asked, still trying to make sense of what she had just heard. Graves showed her one, a chair nailed to two wooden runners designed to be pushed by a skater.

"Let me hire a boy to watch the horse and I'll go with you," he suggested once more.

Her head aching from the unaccustomed tears, Catherine agreed. Before she changed her mind, Graves found a young man to stay with the horse and signaled the footman to return to Reston House to tell Thomas where she was.

The scene in the entranceway to Reston House was what the footman had always associated with Bedlam. The earl was in the library pacing, demanding that his horse be brought around and then canceling his order for fear Catherine might return. The hall was full of servants. Mrs. Thomas was wringing her hands while Davis moaned at the ingratitude of men. Edwards made the mistake of saying that he never thought her ladyship good enough for the earl and almost found himself mobbed.

While Mrs. Wilson tried to reason with Harwich, Mrs. Throckmorton sat smiling smugly. Marybeth sat huddled on a step near the bottom of the staircase. It was she who first saw the footman stumble in and called the earl.

"She's at the Frost Fair," the young man choked out, breathing hard. "Graves persuaded her that the fresh air would do her good."

"Does she know you came here?" the earl asked, his face revealing his surprise.

"Her ladyship didn't even know I was there," the man explained. "She was crying so hard at first." For a moment the earl felt a mass of hostile eyes on him. "She never even noticed when we stopped."

"Where is the coach?"

"Near Blackfriars Bridge. I can show you where we left it, your lordship."

"Thomas," the earl shouted, forgetting that the butler was nearby.

"Yes, your lordship?"

"Horses. Two of them. At once." The butler signaled and a footman was on his way to the stables. "Where's my coat?" Harwich shrugged into it quickly and ran down the front steps, the footman hardly able to keep up with him.

Marybeth looked after her father and then turned and ran upstairs, appearing a few minutes later in her heaviest cloak, pulling her gloves on.

Mrs. Wilson, having followed the earl out of the library, leaned tiredly against the newel post. "Where are you going?" she asked Marybeth as the girl ran down to look for Catherine. In spite of Mrs. Wilson's pleas, Marybeth was firm in her resolve.

Finally Mrs. Wilson tired of the argument. "Fetch me my cloak, my gloves, and my muffler," she said briskly. "If you are going, so am I. Do you wish to accompany us, Mrs. Throckmorton?" she asked, already knowing the answer.

Soon only Mrs. Throckmorton and the servants were left in the house.

16

After the turmoil of the last hour, the silence of Reston House was almost frightening. One by one the servants left the hall. Agnes Throckmorton smiled briefly and hurried into the library. "Take this and wait for an answer," she demanded a short time later. She sat down to plan their next moves.

Her answer was not long in coming. Less than fifteen minutes after the footman returned, she opened the outside door quietly and let them in. "They're all out. And the servants are belowstairs or in the housekeeper's room," she said, leading them up the stairs.

"Perfect," a smooth Italian voice answered. She beamed in pride. The third member of the party looked around cautiously.

"He's out chasing that precious niece of yours. Hurry!" The two women glared at each other for a moment and headed for the master suite. "This won't do any good. The Conte di Perugia has searched already," Mrs. Hubert complained, puffing a little as she tried to keep up.

"They probably had it at Reston," Mrs. Throckmorton reminded her.

"Well, you should have found it then."

Agnes Throckmorton threw open the door to Catherine's suite and then stopped. "With servants everywhere, there was little I could do. Remember, be as quiet as you can. There are people in the house now."

Cautiously the three entered the suite, checking

each corner, as if the servants were lying in wait. As the count approached the bed, he jumped back, cursing.

"What's the matter?" Mrs. Hubert asked.

"That animal," complained the man, holding his hand and nodding toward the kitten who stalked back and forth across Catherine's bed like a lion protecting its prey.

"It wouldn't be there. Look in that case on the dresser," Mrs. Throckmorton said in tones that made the man look at her sharply.

He opened the box she suggested and stared at the bracelets, necklaces, and earrings carefully fitted into precise slots. The count glanced over his shoulder. The other two were searching the clothes presses. Swiftly he slipped some of the larger pieces into one pocket. The smaller pieces, like the earrings and hair ornaments, he shoveled in the other. Caught by the beauty of the stones, he held one up to the light.

"How beautiful," a greedy voice whispered as a hand reached over his shoulder to take the aquamarine hairclips from him.

"Those aren't the treasure we were looking for," Agnes Throckmorton said, her voice a grating reminder of their errand. The two holding the jewelry exchanged glances, turned as if to return the pieces to the case, and pocketed them surreptitiously. "Here, help me with this," their third conspirator called. Reluctantly they crossed the room, glancing back at the case.

The turmoil belowstairs and the fact that many of the underservants had been released to attend the Frost Fair worked for the searchers. The fires burned brightly as they rifled Catherine's clothing. Their patience at an end, they began dumping drawers onto the floor where Horace pounced on the shoes, nightdresses, or cloaks as though they were toys designed only for him.

"Help me put it back," Mrs. Throckmorton demanded. She began throwing items into the presses.

"Why?" the count asked, raising his eyebrows as if to suggest she were deranged.

"So they won't know we were here." Her two confederates laughed loudly, so loudly that she turned to hush them.

"My dear," Catherine's aunt said smugly, "I prefer to leave a message that I was here."

Harwich's cousin turned red and then white. She gasped for breath. "Your name? They're certain to connect us. I'll have nothing to do with this anymore." She turned to scamper out of the room.

Before she had taken two steps, the Conte di Perugia had her by her arm. His large, strong hands held her tightly. He pulled her around to face him. "No one leaves without my permission," he hissed. Mrs. Hubert laughed merrily. "You, be silent." The words, uttered through his clenched teeth, made both the women shiver and look at him nervously. He smiled, a smile that caused shivers to run down the women's spines. Suddenly they heard voices in the hallway and the door opening. His eyes darted about the room, seeking a hiding place.

The door to the bedroom opened. The upstairs maid took one look at the room and began to scream, a high-pitched sound that was followed by the babble of voices and the sound of feet running down the hallway.

While the three conspirators searched Reston House, Harwich was looking for his countess. The carriage was where the footman had said it would be, but there was no sign of Catherine or Graves. "Graves said he would rent her ladyship a chair," the footman explained.

"How far does the ice go?" his master asked sharply. He looked out at the frozen river, which now resembled a busy street with food shops, taverns, and print shops. As Harwich looked out at the busy throng, he wondered how he would ever find her.

"Freezeland Street extends to London Bridge," his footman said. His face reflected the futility of Harwich's task.

"Stay with the carriage," the earl said quietly. "If they come back while I am gone, try to delay then. I'll return within the hour." He turned to go and then walked back. He flipped the man a coin. "For hot cider," he called. "Just keep the carriage in sight." He plunged into the crowd.

Blowing on his hands, the footman crossed the ice toward the closest stand selling hot drinks. His eyes widened as he saw the size of the coin the earl had given him.

When Mrs. Wilson and Marybeth drove along the Embankment some time later, there were coaches lining the bank. Marybeth, although disturbed by the scene between her father and Catherine, could hardly take her eyes from the exciting booths and swings that lay in front of her. Only when the sleigh turned around, heading away from the fair, did she look at the carriages parked along the Embankment. She had just turned to take one more look at the exciting fair when she saw their carriage. "There it is. Stop the sleigh!" Before Mrs. Wilson could restrain her, she dashed across the area and opened the door. The sleigh stopped nearby, and Mrs. Wilson hurried up.

"There's no one here," Marybeth said unhappily. The boy watching the horses could tell them little more than they already knew. They were just turning away, wondering the next step to take, when the footman, almost out of breath, hurried up.

Repeating what he had told the earl, the footman explained again. "His lordship told me to keep an eye on the carriage and try to keep her ladyship from leaving if I could," he said. Mrs. Wilson looked at

him as if she were going to say something. The
footman hurried on. "Then he told me to have something warm to drink." The older woman nodded her
acceptance.

"Both of them are out there?" Marybeth asked, her
eyes sweeping the expanse of ice and frolics. The
footman nodded. Marybeth looked at Mrs. Wilson for
a moment, a rather stern expression on her face.
"What time did he say he would return?" she asked
again. The footman answered. Marybeth looked out
at the ice again. "Which way did he go?" Mrs. Wilson
shivered slightly and glanced at her in alarm. "We
will work along the other side." She struck out brisk
pace, Mrs. Wilson hurrying to catch up.

"Lady Marybeth, this is not at all the thing to do,"
the older woman protested halfheartedly, glancing
in the shops in hopes of seeing Catherine. "Perhaps
we should return to Reston House."

Marybeth stopped beside a round barrel filled
with coals. She held out her hands and looked
around carefully. Using a gesture that made Mrs.
Wilson think of her father, the petite girl summoned
a nearby hawker selling hot cider. "Let's have
something to help us keep warm," she suggested,
nodding to him. Her calm manner shattered a few
minutes later when she caught sight of a woman
wearing a cloak the same color as her stepmother's.
"Look! There she is." Marybeth dropped her cup and
started forward. Before she had gone five steps, the
woman turned, her blond curls framing a cold-
reddened face. Marybeth stopped. Her face
crumbled. Her shoulders slumped.

Mrs. Wilson put her arm around the disconsolate
girl. "We'll find her. You'll see," she said soothingly,
hoping that she was right.

"What if we don't? What if she never comes back?"
t' girl cried, brushing away her tears before they
  chance to fall. "What did Papa do to make her
  y?"

The older woman patted her sympathetically, her own eyes filled with anxiety. "Come. Let us get another cup of cider. Then we'll look some more."

The object of their search was in a world all her own. As the man pushing her chair chatted with Graves, Catherine stared at the problem facing her. "How could he?" she moaned half under her breath. She shook her head when Graves responded. The man, worried about her unnatural calm after such stormy tears, looked at her as though he expected her to collapse. She sighed. The sound tore at the groom's heart. For the first time in many years, the man longed to strike his master.

As they passed one of the ships almost buried in the ice, Catherine wondered briefly where it had been, why it was there. Why was she there? she asked herself as she noticed for the first time the hustle and bustle around her.

"Where now, missus?" the man pushing her chair asked. He looked longingly at the bakery shops redolent with the spicy gingerbread and brandy balls.

Graves, seeing his glance, bent his head and asked his mistress. "May I fetch you something hot?"

About to refuse, Catherine looked up. Her groom's face was pinched with the cold. She said quietly, "Dismiss him, Graves. Let us have something hot and then we'll walk back." She sighed again and stood up, her blue skirts swirling against the ice. They walked briskly toward the makeshift tent nearby, cloth folded about the imprisoned mast of a ship.

A short time later Catherine gasped her breath. "What's in this cup?" she choked out.

"A bit of brandy, your ladyship. I thought it would warm you up like," Graves said, the worry in his eyes evident once again. "My old mother recommended it for days like this."

Catherine nodded and smiled weakly. She took another sip. This time she covered her cough by seeming to clear her throat. She looked at the almost full cup and grimaced. "I think I have had enough, Graves." She handed him the cup. For the first time in several hours she was aware of the world, not just as people moving around but as onlookers and participants. "Why, it really is a fair!"

"Watch your step, ma'am," Graves said as she began to look at the crowds around a tent nearby. Curious, she walked toward them, stretching on her toes to see over the crowd of men laughing and pushing to get closer. "Please, your ladyship, come away from there," Graves insisted, holding on to her arm protectively. "It's not the place for you."

Then Catherine saw the women standing at the entrance, their lips and cheeks rouged and their loose wrappers barely covering their bodies. Her face lost its glow. Her eyes were as dark as he had ever seen them. "Oh." The word was so soft that Graves almost did not hear it.

Cursing himself for allowing her to get so close, Graves led her away. She walked silently for a while, her eyes seeing not the gaiety and excitement around her but the stricken look of her husband's face as he had turned and seen her. Once more she almost fell over a patch of rough ice. Once more Graves rescued her.

"Shall I return for the carriage, your ladyship?" Graves asked, not pleased at the thought of leaving her alone.

She shook her head and walked slowly up the area people called the grand mall.

A small boy tugged at her sleeve. "Buy a handbill hot from the press," he begged. Startled, Catherine took the piece of paper he handed her. "Only a penny, miss. A penny for a fairing."

In the midst of shaking her head no, Catherine stopped. Pulling out her reticule, she smiled and handed him a coin. "Lady Marybeth will want something from the fair," she said in a voice only slightly hoarse. She glanced at the city of London, which formed a backdrop for the shops on the frozen river. "How far to go, Graves?"

He looked at the dome of St. Paul's and back up the river toward Blackfriars. "About half."

Catherine sighed. Her feet were cold, and her hands, in spite of the gloves she wore, seemed frozen. She sighed again. Mentally shaking herself, she put her chin in the air and headed off briskly. Ten minutes later she slowed down, the smell of gingerbread tantalizing her. Aware not only of the cold but also of the slight rumbling in her stomach, she turned into a large tent nearby. Graves glanced around, looking for the earl as he had been doing during their walk and then hurried after her.

Catherine lifted her piece of the sweet to her nose and breathed deeply. Its warmth sank through her gloves and into the cold hands below. Savoring every bite, she ate each crumb. No languishing away for me, she thought bitterly. When I am disappointed in love, I eat. She dusted the last crumb from her gloves. "Let's go home, Graves," she said quietly.

As the afternoon had grown later, the crowds had increased. "Tuck your reticule under your cloak," Graves instructed her as his ears picked up the sound, "Pickpocket." Catherine obeyed.

Just as she was certain she would not be able to walk another step, she saw the bridge. Her pace increased. For a moment there was a break in the tent city, and the crowds melted away. One family—the parents and three children—stood apart, laughing as the smallest child, a boy, slid across the ice, intentionally or unintentionally Catherine wasn't sure. Once more she felt like crying. Her shoulders sagged.

Then from the crowd around the swing nearest them a scream rang out. Both Graves and Catherine stopped. They turned. Puzzled, they looked at each other and back at the small crowd that had begun to gather. When they heard Marybeth say loudly, "That is mine; give it to me," they broke into a run, Graves easily out distancing Catherine.

When she arrived a few seconds after the groom did, Catherine stopped short. Graves had a small boy about five years old in his arms. The boy held a lady's reticule in his small blue hands. His feet, wrapped in rags, hung a foot in the air. The child stared at the groom bellligerently. He clamped his jaw shut, refusing to answer the groom's questions.

"That's mine," a soft voice declared. Marybeth reached out and wrenched the bag from the urchin. Then she looked at the man holding him. "Graves, is Catherine here?" He simply nodded. Catching sight of her stepmother, Marybeth rushed to her and threw her arms around her. "Don't leave, Catherine. Please." The tears that were so close to the surface for her stepmother were on Marybeth's face. Catherine put her arms around her and held her tightly. The question of her future seemed even more complex.

"Lady Harwich, Lady Marybeth, you are attracting a crowd," Mrs. Wilson said softly, still rather breathless after scurrying after her charge. They both blushed and stepped back hastily. "What have we here?" she asked as she crossed to where Graves stood.

"He stole my reticule!"

"This child?" Mrs. Wilson asked. She winced as she noticed the child's arms and legs were covered with bruises that were visible through the rents in the boy's pants.

"Probably belongs to a gang. They find them early and train them," Graves explained. He lifted the boy up once more, holding him at eye level. "Where do you live, boy?"

"Perhaps he doesn't hear you?" Catherine suggested.

"Maybe I should drop you on your head," the groom said softly. The boy flinched. "He hears."

"Can he talk?" Mrs. Wilson reached out a hand and brushed a lock of greasy hair out of the boy's face. As soon as she had removed her hand, the boy shook his head, and the lock fell back in place, hiding most of his eyes.

"I heard him scream," Marybeth said. She looked at him. The boy stared back. His brown eyes were as hard as the ice. The crowd around them had grown larger.

"Frow 'im in jail," one man shouted.

The child shivered, whether from the cold or at the statement. Graves wasn't sure.

"Aye. Or give 'im to the nayvee." A sailor laughed.

The adults holding him looked at each other helplessly. "Take him back to the sleigh," Mrs. Wilson said firmly. "We can decide his fate there."

"The sleigh. He's not riding in the sleigh with me," Marybeth said coldly. But as she followed behind with Catherine, she watched the little boy mince across the ice, almost hopping to avoid putting his foot on the cold surface, and she felt ashamed. She moved closer to Catherine, who slipped her arm around her waist.

Striding back to the Frost Fair from his hourly check at the waiting carriage, Harwich saw the small party and stopped. His heart pumped a rhythm that threatened to engulf him. He watched Catherine and Marybeth walk closer, their heads bent in talk, their eyes on the ice in front of them. Caught up in the joy of seeing his wife, Harwich focused on her. Only later did he look at her companion closely. "Marybeth," he shouted, surprising even himself.

The party stopped. Catherine stood as if frozen. The distance she had gained in the last few hours fell away. She heard the words of the agent again and winced again. Pulling away from Marybeth, she half-turned to leave them. Harwich hurried forward. Marybeth grabbed the edge of Catherine's cloak and held on. The boy, seeing Graves' preoccupation, pulled free of his grasp and broke into a run.

"Grab him," the groom shouted.

Harwich reached out a long arm, snagging the child. Slightly off balance on the slippery surface, he fell. Harwich sat there for a moment, a look of surprise on his face, the boy sitting on his legs. The sight of the usually graceful earl sprawled awkwardly on the ice caused Marybeth to giggle and Mrs. Wilson to cover her smile with her hand.

Catherine hurried forward. "Are you all right?" she asked, her eyes not meeting his.

"Here, take this little brat," the earl said, handing the child to the groom. He pulled himself together and stood up. At least he tried to. His right ankle gave way under him.

Catherine sprang forward and put her shoulder under his to hold him up. "Lean on me," she whispered. Between Mrs. Wilson and her, Harwich hobbled to the waiting carriage, his face twisted with pain.

Although he almost had to crawl to get inside the carriage, he refused to release his wife. Breathing heavily, his face gray from pain, he leaned back and closed his eyes for a moment. Then he said, "Graves, leave the boy with us while you see the other ladies to the sleigh." He shook his head wearily. "No arguments, poppet. We'll talk about your being here and about this boy when we reach Berkeley Square." He leaned back and sighed.

The door opened a few minutes later. "They're away, your lordship," Graves said, his face revealing his disapproval as he saw the boy wrapped in a fur lap robe, his hand stroking the dark fur.

"Take him up on the box with you and have the footman hold on to him," Harwich said. He watched under hooded lids as the boy's face puckered when

Graves picked him up. "Take the robe. It's too cold out there for him without a coat." The child's face brightened and one dirty hand grabbed the lap robe tightly.

All this time Catherine had sat stiffly beside Harwich, her face an expressionless mask. The first few minutes of the ride were in silence. Then her husband asked, "Are you ready to hear my explanation, beloved?"

She burst into tears again.

17

Catherine's tears were more than Harwich could bear. He pulled her close to him, his hand stroking her hair and patting her shoulder. Slowly his soft soothing words halted her tears. With effort, she quieted her sobs.

"Beloved?" she asked, her voice still shaky. "Do you love me?"

He looked at her, shocked. He blinked. Then he looked again. She was serious. The thought amazed him. He started to speak. No words came out. He cleared his throat and tried again. "Yes, of course I do." He stopped, trying to find exactly the right words. He was still thinking moments later when the carriage stopped.

"Your lordship! Your lordship?" Thomas sputtered.

"Help me into the small salon," his master said to the footmen who were nearby. With Thomas still fluttering about excitedly, the rest of the party followed the earl and his helpers.

Catherine watched carefully as Harwich lowered himself to the settee, wincing as he lifted his ankle to the table in front of him. She hurried over. "Send for a doctor immediately. Then find me some pillows." Thomas, still sputtering, hurried off. A few minutes later Catherine slipped a pillow under the earl's ankle and another behind him. "Can we take your boot off?"

He shook his head. "Call Edwards. It will need to be cut off."

Catherine looked at Thomas, who was now wringing his hands. "Oh my, oh my," he said, agitated.

"You heard the earl. Call Edwards." Catherine tapped her foot impatiently.

"I can't, your ladyship."

"Why?"

"He's guarding the prisoners."

The room came alive as if someone had just said fire. "What?" Catherine asked.

"Where are they?" Harwich demanded.

"In the pantry, your lordship. Cook and Edwards are guarding them," the butler said, glad that the problem was no longer his. Mrs. Wilson sank back in her chair, her hand pressed to her heart. More intrepid, Marybeth found a stool and put it beside Harwich, her eyes big. She took hold of his sleeve.

The earl glanced around the room quickly, remembering Graves, "Give the child to Thomas, Graves," he said quietly. "Then you relieve Edwards and send him to me. You, Thomas, take the child to your wife and have him bathed and fed. Return as soon as possible to tell me more of this." The room quickly emptied. Harwich looked at his wife. She was standing near Marybeth, her face beginning to show the strains of the day. "Catherine," he said softly, "come, sit down."

She hesitated for a moment and then sighed. She sat beside him, still far enough away so that they were not touching. He smiled ruefully. Just then a loud scream welled up belowstairs. When everyone had settled again, Marybeth said rather pompously, "It's that boy. I told you he screamed."

Her father shook his head, laughing quietly. He glanced at his wife, who was considerably closer to him and whose hand was now in his. "You were right," he said facetiously. Mrs. Wilson moved restlessly in her chair. "Well, what are we going to do with the brat?"

Even the most militant of the lot, Marybeth, agreed when Catherine said in a soft, husky voice, "We cannot turn him over to the authorities."

Mrs. Wilson nodded vehemently.

"These boys are sometimes trained not only as pickpockets but also as picklocks. His master sends him through a small window and then has him unlock the front door so that they can rob the place," Harwich said. He looked around carefully. "With two robberies of our own in the last two months, I don't think we want to chance that."

Catherine nodded.

"Two robberies, Papa? When was the other one? How exciting! I must write Louisa," Marybeth said, her blue eyes sparkling.

"No, poppet. This stays within the family," her father warned sternly.

Marybeth flounced on her stool but finally agreed.

Mrs. Wilson cleared her throat nervously and then asked, "What are we going to do with the child? From his looks he has been treated badly."

"True." Harwich frowned for a moment and looked at Catherine. She was still holding his hand, her eyes fixed on her own visions. "He'll have to leave London." They all nodded. "Then, where?"

"To the orphanage near Reston?" Marybeth asked.

Catherine looked at her quickly.

"I fear he might corrupt the other children," the earl began when Mrs. Wilson interrupted.

"What if I took him with me?" She hurried on. "I planned to leave next week. All but my personal items have been sent. I could leave tomorrow."

"Or the next day. You will need to buy the boy some new things." Catherine looked at her former chaperone closely. "Are you certain you want the responsibility of the boy? He may never change."

"Let me try. It will give me something to occupy my time. I like people more than needlework."

The earl frowned for a moment. "A trial period of a

year, shall we say? I'll provide an allowance for him for his care and schooling. He'll need to be trained for a trade later," he said quietly. It was the first time since he had told the older woman he planned to marry Catherine that he had seen her so happy. In spite of his reservations, he nodded.

Mrs. Wilson smiled happily.

"You'd better watch his hands, Mrs. Wilson," Marybeth suggested. "If I hadn't looked around at that moment, he would have had my purse." She had had visions of being able to supervise his reclamation personally and wasn't happy to see him so far away. "Are you certain he needs to leave London?" Her father nodded, trying to hide a smile. "Then, why can't he go to Reston?"

"Mrs. Wilson's house is in Tunbridge Wells," Catherine reminded her, for the first time thankful that it was not nearby. Keeping Marybeth's high spirits in hand had been hard enough already. If the thief taught her his tricks . . . She closed her eyes quickly. Her stepdaughter's face clouded over, but before she had a chance to speak, Thomas and Edwards entered, the latter carrying his sharpest razor.

The earl's face was gray from pain a few minutes later. Realizing he had Catherine's hand in a grip that was causing her fingers to turn white, Harwich smiled weakly and released the pressure, still retaining her in his possession. "A glass of brandy," he asked quietly. He drank a good swallow and then looked up. "Now, tell me about these robbers."

"There were three."

"And two of them were women," added Edwards. "Your cousin, Mrs. Throckmorton." He nodded to the earl. "And your aunt, Mrs. Hubert, your ladyship."

Catherine sat bolt upright. "My aunt?"

Harwich too had sat up, jarring his leg, and cursed soundly.

Marybeth eased the pillow back under the puffy ankle, now released from its boot. She would have to tell Louisa those words the next time she saw her, she thought smiling to herself.

"And the third?" Harwich asked, a faint premonition sending a frisson up his spine.

"A count, so they say. Two of them had their pockets full of her ladyship's jewels," the butler explained.

"These two were who?"

"The count and Mrs. Hubert." The butler glanced at his mistress, who was staring at him as if he had just announced the end of the world.

"Bring them here," the earl said softly.

When the door had closed behind them, Catherine turned her head into his shoulder. "Oh, Dom." Her face looked stricken.

Mrs. Wilson, realizing how difficult the coming interview would be, made her escape.

"My cousin was with them," Harwich reminded Catherine as the door shut behind Mrs. Wilson. He turned to Marybeth. "I think you should leave, poppet," he suggested. Before she had time to protest, the door opened.

Escorted by Thomas, Graves, and Edwards, the three accused robbers walked in boldly. "Oh, Harwich. I am glad you are home. Tell these bumpkins to let me go," Agnes Throckmorton demanded. She looked at his face and fell silent.

"Marybeth," he said quietly.

Noting the tone of his voice, she rose reluctantly. She paused by the door, looking back at him. Her father merely nodded. Even then she lingered for a moment. He frowned. She pouted and flounced from the room.

"Close the door," Harwich said, noting it was still open about six inches. Before anyone could move, it slammed shut. Catherine hid her smile behind her hand. "Now, Thomas, explain everything. Start from the beginning," the earl commanded.

"When they were replenishing the coal buckets, a maid and a footman found them in your rooms, your ladyship," Thomas began. "We searched the man and found these." Catherine gasped as he held out a basket of gems crowned with her Christmas present. "Davis checked them. When there were some still missing, she and my wife searched the other two. She"—he pointed to Catherine's aunt—"had her reticule full. Davis says nothing else is missing."

"Let me tell you, you pompous idiot, that my niece will have all of your jobs," Mrs. Hubert said, hoping her bluff would work. "You and those women should have kept your paws to yourself. We are quality."

Catherine shrank further behind Harwich.

"Are you?" the earl asked quietly, turning the florid woman to stone. "What were you doing in my wife's bedroom?"

His cousin glared at her two associates and plunged into speech. "We were looking for the treasure she brought from Italy." She pointed at Catherine. "At least they said she did. I know nothing of any jewelry. Tell them, Thomas. There were no stolen jewels on me." She glanced at the other two culprits as the butler nodded.

"Treasure? Tell me, Aunt, just what did you hope to find?" Catherine asked as she got up slowly and walked in front of the woman.

Clarice Hubert's eyes fell. She stammered. "It was the Conte di Perugia. He told me." She tried to pass on the blame.

"And I suppose he told you to fill your purse with jewels too?" Harwich's cousin said sarcastically.

Mrs. Hubert glared at her.

"Do you hate me so much that you would believe the word of a stranger?" Catherine asked softly. Her aunt glared at her, then dropped her eyes.

"And what was the treasure supposed to look like?" Harwich asked, his voice carefully casual.

"He never told us," Mrs. Throckmorton said indignantly. Harwich looked at her, his skepticism evident. Realizing what she had said, his cousin flushed in anger. Already implicated by her own words, she turned on her associates like a caged lion striking out at its trainer. "He said it would be valuable, that we'd be wealthy enough never to have to worry about it again. And she's the one who showed him how to get in." She pointed her finger at Catherine's aunt, who was glaring at her and muttering under her breath.

"You wanted the gold and jewels as much as I did," Mrs. Hubert shouted.

"So there were gold and jewels," Harwich mused. He turned his head and looked at the third person. The count stared back at him angrily. His coat was torn and bruises were beginning to show on his face. Both Graves and Edwards kept a keen eye on him, as though they expected him to break for a window. "Where did you learn of this treasure?" Harwich asked.

The man simply looked at him.

"Who are you?" Catherine asked. She watched him carefully. "Why did you decide to choose us? The only object we brought back to Italy is of no value, except to scholars."

"So there was a treasure." Her aunt's eyes blazed and she took two or three steps toward her niece. Quickly, Catherine retreated to her seat beside Harwich. "Where is it? Not in the house."

"How can you be so certain?" the earl asked. "Perhaps this isn't your first visit?" Suddenly all three of the thieves were silent. "Shall I tell them or do you want the pleasure?" he asked Catherine.

"You," she said in a firm tone. Her hand crept back into his.

Harwich squeezed her hand and then looked at

each of the three before him. "The treasure you were seeking is in the hands of the Royal Society." He laughed to himself as he watched the rage on the faces of the women. The count glared at all of them. "You've gone to a great deal of trouble for a crumbling piece of papyrus. Does a shipping list almost eighteen hundred years old mean so much to you?"

"You lie!" The Conte di Perugia plunged forward, his hands reaching for the earl's neck. He had taken only two quick steps when he was jerked to a halt by Graves and Edwards.

"Attempted murder. Equally serious under the law. I wonder which you would prefer to be charged with. Both are hanging offenses."

The women blanched.

Mrs. Hubert put her shaking hand to her throat. "You can't charge me. Not your own relative, Catherine," she pleaded.

"Did you or did you not steal some of my jewelry?" her niece asked.

"It was he. He lured me into gambling with him. When I lost heavily, he told me I could repay him by helping him reach you. Everything was his idea," Mrs. Hubert babbled. "Your own aunt, Catherine. No, you can't."

Catherine looked at her sadly. She knew her aunt was right. The scandal would destroy them all. She looked at her husband. He too had a similar thought.

"Call the constables," Harwich said. Mrs. Hubert crumpled to the floor in a faint. His cousin was gray about the mouth. The count, however, pretended an indifference he was far from feeling. "Cousin Agnes, see to Mrs. Hubert." She obeyed slowly, but she did obey. "You men take this person." He pointed to the counte. "Put him into a locked area with no windows. The pantry again, if you must. Keep him there until I call for him. Leave a footman outside this door too." Quickly they escorted their prisoner out. "Get some paper, pens, ink, and books, Catherine."

A few minutes later Catherine was back. Her aunt and Harwich's cousin were seated in chairs. She looked at her husband. "Give them both a book and writing material and bring some to me," he said. He waited for a moment. "Now, each of you put today's date, including the year, on the paper. Next write the following statement: 'Today I, your name, robbed the Earl of Harwich's London house.' Then sign your names." He watched them complete their tasks and then wrote his own note. "Catherine, collect them and hand them to me." She nodded, gathered the statements, and sat down beside him again. The earl's face was stern as he presented the women their options. "These will be filed with my lawyer. If you follow my instructions, you will go free." The two shifted forward in their chairs. "You, Mrs. Hubert, will remove to your husband's estate in . . . ?" He looked at Catherine.

"Yorkshire."

"Yorkshire tomorrow. You will not return to London." She gasped, her fingers gripping the arms of the chair. "You may leave." She started to speak and then thought better of it. She hurried from the room. "Now, Cousin Agnes," he said softly. "No, there's no need to talk. 'Actions speak louder than words.' Isn't that what you told Marybeth?" He leaned back. "What was your excuse, I wonder?" He paused to see her reaction. She refused to meet his eyes. He smiled at Catherine and then shifted slightly. "I think the house in Salisbury must be forgotten. It's too close to London. Like Mrs. Hubert, wherever I choose will be your permanent home." She glared at him. "Is there anything you wish to add, Catherine?" he asked quietly. She shook her head. "Then we no longer need your presence. You will stay in your room until I send for you."

Mrs. Throckmorton walked slowly to the door, her

back straight. She turned to look at the two of them, her manner totally unrepentant. She glared at him and walked out proudly.

Harwich closed his eyes tiredly. His hand tightened around Catherine's. Before he could say anything, Thomas came in. "Both the constables and the doctor are here," the butler announced.

After directing Thomas to have his note delivered to Lord Denning of the Home Office, Harwich let the others do their work. While the doctor inspected his ankle, Harwich explained the situation to the constables. Promising the earl that the man would be up before a magistrate within the hour, they went to get their prisoner. Just before they walked out the door, Harwich said quickly, "The man is a vicious liar. He even tried to implicate my wife's aunt and my cousin in the robbery. They are widows who must be protected." The men nodded and hurried on the way.

Catherine, who had been supervising the doctor, looked up quickly. Then she turned her attention back to Harwich's ankle.

The doctor stood up, stretching his back. "It's just a sprain, Lord Harwich. A few days' rest and it will be fine. Do not walk on it. Have someone help you get up to bed. And keep it wrapped. Your man can see to that."

"Thank you, Doctor," Catherine said as she walked him to the door.

"Remember to keep him off that foot. This weather makes unnecessary work for us doctors. This Frost Fair may be entertaining for everyone else, but I wish it were over."

Catherine watched him walk to the front door. "It's no good," Harwich said quietly.

"What?" Catherine asked, shutting the door.

"Trying to evade our discussion. If you try to escape, I'll only come and find you."

She turned slowly and faced him. Her eyes began

to regain a tinge of gold. Once more the door opened. Catherine sighed. Harwich's mouth tensed.

"The doctor suggested that you might like to go to your room, your lordship. Shall I call some footmen to help you?" the butler asked.

About to refuse, Harwich looked at Catherine and changed his mind. "Yes, Thomas, as soon as possible." He waited until the butler bowed himself out. "Catherine, come with me. It's the only place we'll be able to have some quiet."

A short time later Harwich sat against the pillows of his bed, his foot propped on more pillows. He pulled his dressing gown around him. Then he waited. When he had just decided that Catherine had changed her mind and he had swung his legs over the side of the bed, the door opened. Catherine slipped in.

"What are you doing?" she asked. Her face wore a slightly harried look.

"I thought you weren't coming. I was going to look for you."

"Your daughter detained me." She sat in a chair that Edwards had left close to the bed.

"I suppose she wanted all the details?"

"Yes." Catherine smiled briefly at her step-daughter's comments on Mrs. Throckmorton. Marybeth was satisfyingly primitive in her desire for retribution.

"And?" Harwich asked impatiently, pulling himself higher on his pillows.

"She thinks you were too lenient with them."

"Do you?"

Catherine smoothed the muslin wrapper she wore. The room was so silent that Harwich twisted so that he could see better, knocking the pillows under his ankle to the floor. "Stay still," Catherine scolded him as she rearranged the pillows. Before she could retreat again, he grabbed her hand.

"Sit up here with me," he suggested. Catherine

looked at him and did as he said. "Was I too lenient?"

"No." The word was only a ragged breath. "Neither of them enjoys living in the provinces. It is punishment enough."

"Tomorrow we'll get a map and find a suitable place for my cousin," he promised. He reached for her hand, but she pulled it back quietly. "Catherine," he said, and then raced through the next words as if were afraid she would stop him, "what you heard this afternoon didn't mean what you thought it meant."

"I know who lives in St. John's Wood," she said, her eyes flashing.

"I'm certain you do. But none of them are mine. My mistress vacated the house shortly after I left for Vienna. I lent the house to John while I was gone. That's what Smythe wanted to know about." Catherine turned toward him, hope slowly growing in her eyes. Harwich felt the tight band of fear that had been his constant companion since she had run away slowly losing its grip. "Please, please believe me."

"Why haven't you found a new mistress?" she asked, her brow still furrowed.

He looked at her as though she were not quite sane. "When would I have time for one?" he asked dryly. "Have I or have I not spent each night and many days with you, right here? My dear, if you think I could manage that and have a mistress too, you are sadly mistaken." She blushed and acknowledged the honesty of his words. "Why did you run away?"

She shifted nervously. Her hands reached for the tie of her robe and began to roll it nervously. Harwich lifted her chin and forced her to look at him. He frowned a little at the sadness he still saw in her eyes. "Cat, little love, tell me what's wrong?"

The word gave her hope. "Do you really?" Catherine whispered, staring deep into his eyes.

"What?"

"Love me?" She watched as his eyes widened. His arms reached for her and pulled her close. "Catherine Dominique Reston!" he said, almost struck dumb.

"Well, do you?" Her face was serious, as though she were asking the fate of the world.

"Love you?" he tantalized her. He looked deep into her eyes. "I told you in the carriage that I did. I love you, little cat, as I never dreamed I would love anyone. You make my world bright."

Two arms crept around his neck, pulling his head down to her kiss. The soft, warm touch started a fire in both of them. Harwich pulled her into his embrace as if only her total caress could remove forever the fear he had felt. Catherine responded naturally, no longer afraid of her own emotions.

Some time later as they lay there, her head on his shoulder, their bed rumpled, and the pillows supporting his ankle forgotten, he asked again, "Why did you run away?"

This time there was no hesitation. "I was afraid I couldn't face this life if you didn't love me as I love you." Realizing she had never told him, she rolled over on her side so she could look at him. "I do love you," she whispered. She kissed him sweetly.

"Thank you."

"For what?"

"For not making me ask as you had to." She blushed, the red starting under the crisp white sheet she had draped over them and up her throat and face. "I love to watch you do that," he said, his finger following the path in reverse. "But I still don't understand."

Catherine turned over to stare at the canopy above them. "I was afraid. I've lost everyone who loved me." She looked at him, sadness filling her eyes once more. She made her list. "You, when you were too old to enjoy the company of a child; my mother; my father twice; my aunt—my aunt rejected me before she even knew me." The hurt in her voice caused an ache in her heart.

"Catherine," he whispered, and kissed her as though he could make the memories disappear. The fires he started burned through some. When he could breathe again, he added, "You've won all our hearts—mine, Marybeth's, Mrs. Wilson's. Promise me you won't run away again."

"I'm not very brave," she protested.

"But the problems don't go away just because you are no longer there, little coward."

"I know, and I'll try," she promised.

"Just remember that I love you," he whispered.

Catherine snuggled closer. "Your daughter said the same thing."

"Our daughter," he said proudly. "It's a wise daughter that follows her father's lead."

"Well, if you'd told me you loved me before today, I might not have run away," Catherine reminded him.

"But then, little cat, we would have missed the first Frost Fair in two centuries, because I am not going back. Remember the doctor told me to stay off my ankle." He raised up on an elbow and smiled down at her lasciviously. "And what better place to stay off it than in bed?" He reached for her, but she rolled away.

"What about Marybeth and Mrs. Wilson and . . . ?"

He stopped her words with a kiss. "They will keep." And they did.

In later years when Harwich and Catherine entertained their family for Christmas, their children and grandchildren always demanded one story. "Tell us about the Frost Fair and about how you found Paul!"

Then Mrs. Wilson would take the youngest child on her knee and tell the story of the Frost Fair and the little boy who was caught stealing purses. When she smiled up at the blond lawyer who was usually by her side, his own children on his lap, Harwich and Catherine smiled too, their eyes turning to a handsome young man with reddish-brown hair and golden eyes like his mothers.

For them the story always ended with a whispered "I love you, little cat."

Author's Note

Although Lords Andover, Bentiwick, and Castlereagh were involved in a treaty proposed to Joachim Murat, the King of Naples, the situations in this book are fictional, as is Dominic Reston, the fourth Earl of Harwich.

The discoveries at Herculaneum made supposedly by Mr. Durrell were actually made a half-century earlier by amateur archaeologists tunneling through the ruins.

About the Author

A native Texan, Barbara Allister has been in love with the written word all her life. She has a master's degree in English literature and has taught on both the college and high-school levels. She is presently employed as a high-school teacher.